To Glenna,

The true, honest, loving wonderful
constant in my life.

Saintly Death

Saintly Death

Jan A. Sainsbury

Saintly Death
A Book World, Inc. Publication
First Printing: May 1997

This is a work of fiction. The characters, names, incidents, dialogue
and plot are a product of the author's imagination, or are used
fictitiously.

ISBN 1-881542-34-3
Copyright © 1997 by Jan A. Sainsbury
An Original Trade Paperback

Published by:
Book World, Inc.
9666 E Riggs Rd. #194 Sun Lakes AZ 85248
http://www.bkworld.com

Monday: Day One

He was wearing thin cotton gloves, the kind undertakers wear. Once white, they were now pale pink, closely matching the color of his hands. He had soaked several pairs in a weak solution of cranberry juice and water, then carefully dried and soiled them to obtain the precise shade he needed. To a casual passerby the man's hands would not look gloved. There would be nothing to attract attention.

He had been in the room for less than an hour and was confident the setup would work perfectly. He checked the mechanism, installed fresh batteries, adjusted the tension on the gizmo he had made, and sighted through the telescope one last time. He left the window open.

Cracking the door a few inches he placed a *Do Not Disturb* sign on the outside knob, stood quietly, and listened for any sound of trouble. Hearing nothing, he entered the hallway and set an attache case just beyond the door. Removing a tube of *Krazy Glue* from his pocket he squeezed most of it on the door's latch, lock, and jamb. Closing the door behind him he placed the nozzle of the tube directly into the keyhole and squeezed. The rest of the water-thin glue flowed freely into the slot. Capping the empty tube he put it in his pocket. Walking down two flights, he stripped off the pale pink gloves and stuffed them in the same pocket. He pushed the elevator button with the corner of the attache case. No one was in the elevator when it arrived, and, again, he used the corner of the case to push the lobby button. He rode to the ground floor and left the building. No one paid attention to him. He looked as if he belonged; in many ways, he did.

1

Crossing the street, walking west, he carried the attache case past the fifteen-foot high granite wall that surrounds Temple Square, the centerpiece of The Church of Jesus Christ of Latter-day Saints — the Mormons.

Temple Square to a faithful Mormon is not unlike the Vatican to a devout Catholic. It is where the power is. Inside the wall, on ten acres of manicured lawn, stands the Mormon Temple, its spires reaching toward heaven, its holy men transacting the business of God. In its shadow sits the great turtle-backed wooden Tabernacle, famed for its acoustics, its organ, and the Mormon Tabernacle Choir.

The man continued west toward a rental car parked near the Salt Palace, once home for the Utah Jazz basketball team before the team moved to the larger Delta Center in 1991.

Typical, the man thought. Fucking typical! Forever provincial, the local powers-that-be trade in 13,000 seats for 19,000 seats. The Salt Palace had been the smallest NBA arena in the country. It was too small the day they moved in. He didn't like basketball, but he sure could have planned things better than that. He could plan anything better than any of them, he thought. Stupid bastards.

He placed the case in the trunk of the car, snapped open its latches, and removed a small black box the size of a cigarette pack. He picked up a newspaper and folded it around the box. He placed his gloves and the spent tube of glue in the case, closed it, and slammed the trunk shut. He fed the parking meter to capacity. More than enough time, he thought, to kill someone.

Walking back to Temple Square as any tourist might, he thought about the four million tourists who visit this centerpiece of the Mormon empire every year. No one would notice just one more very ordinary looking man gawking at the historical buildings, looking for all the world like one of the faithful.

Standing before a kiosk just inside the temple gates, he studied the posting of the tour schedule for the museum, Tabernacle, and Temple grounds. Sidling up to a group already on tour he listened to a guide recount the story of Joseph Smith Jr., his vision, and his translation of golden tablets, given to him by an angel of God, into the Book of Mormon. The man carefully noted the exact spot at which he had aimed the crosshairs from the window of the Hotel Utah Building half-an-hour earlier.

Holding the folded newspaper carefully, he slightly extended the antenna on the small device he clutched inside. His thumb rested next to a button on the black box, and his eyes moved from one tour group to the next. He stood next to two women and a man holding leather bound copies of the three most precious church books, the *Book of Mormon,* the *Doctrine and Covenants,* and the *Pearl of Great Price;* they paid no attention to him, nor to the newspaper he held. No one noticed the shiny tip of the thin antenna pointed toward a window less than one block away.

Hundreds of tourists — men, women, and children — dressed in every conceivable manner, were milling through Temple Square. Some, on this bright cool day in March, wore sunglasses. So did he. Even in sunglasses, plain and devoid of any style or designer influence, no one would mistake him for an incognito celebrity. He looked and acted like a nobody avoiding the glare of the noonday sun.

Most of the visitors stood in pockets of rapt attention, huddling together in front of overly-neat and remarkably clean-cut tour guides, listening to an oral history of the church. The man knew he would only be in Temple Square for a matter of minutes. The main danger he faced would be from still and video cameras. He constantly scanned the visitors to Temple Square, and deftly avoided the line of sight of anyone raising a camera to take a picture. He also avoided looking at the six church surveillance cameras he knew existed, one near the front gates, one at the main entrance, and four more at the corners of the grounds. Others might exist, but he doubted it. The church, he thought, was very careful not to let the general public see the trappings of its own paranoia.

He made it a point to stand as near as possible to small pockets of people, never isolating himself, never standing alone for more than a few seconds, always moving from group to group.

Soon he would have to leave the Temple grounds before anyone thought to seal them off. From where he was it would be easy. He would move directly toward the gate. Before anyone realized what had happened, he would be outside and on his way. It was only a matter of fifteen or twenty yards.

One guide moved his group toward the statue of Mormon pioneers pulling a handcart across the plains. Soon the group tightened up, twenty or more, right where such groups usually posed for photographs. It was directly in front of the spot the man had selected from the window.

Most of the group listened to the remarks of the tour guide with unashamed reverence; a few, at the edges, were merely curious. The trio next to him moved slightly then stopped again. On the pretext of wandering awe-struck in Mormon mecca, he simply moved with them. They were oblivious to his presence.

Before moving on to the next point of interest, one person in the tour asked the guide to take a group picture. They had listened to well-scrubbed guides recount the saga of Mormon pioneers pulling their handcarts across the Great Plains to the Promised Land — their holy state of Zion in Utah. It was time to record their visit on film. The guide was only too happy to help. Perfect. Just like other days, and other groups, thought the man. Only this day was different. This day was his.

He knew he would get their undivided attention, the leaders of this church. Today was Day One. Day One of a month of hell on earth for thirteen men, men he despised, men who believed themselves to be the direct spiritual descendants of Jesus Christ and the Twelve Apostles, men who called themselves living prophets of God on earth.

"Scrunch together, folks," the guide said.

Taking a quick look around, the man noted that everything was perfect, and thought, briefly, that God must be in His heaven; all was right with the world. Amen. And then he pushed the button.

From the grounds of Temple Square the shot sounded more like the muffled backfire of a distant car than the report of a high-powered rifle. The man knew that in the hallway on the fifth floor of the Hotel Utah Building the shot had shattered the calm air. But from where he stood it was strangely quiet. He started walking toward the main gates the moment he pushed the button. Now, only steps away, he heard the rising wail of a woman's scream, and the telltale sounds of crowd confusion and panic welling up behind him. By the time the scream was full blown, he was past the main gate, turning west toward the Salt Palace. Behind him he heard more shouts and screams, and for the first time since leaving the room he displayed a fleeting grin.

People ran from across the street toward the Temple grounds. As any tourist might, the man looked back to see what all the commotion was about. He shook his head, as if to say, Who knows? and continued walking at a leisurely and constant rate. He reached the car just as the sound of police sirens ripped the air. They were still far away, but the sound was moving closer, and more sirens, seemingly from every direction, joined in the strident medley. He entered the rental car and drove off, carefully. He headed toward his room in the Tri Arc hotel, southwest of the city center, near Interstate 15.

It was going to be a wonderful night, he thought. He would dine at one of Salt Lake City's best restaurants, ravage one of its best looking hookers, and later, in his room, waiting for the news broadcasts on television, he might even read a few pages of the *Book of Mormon*. Like the ubiquitous Gideon Bibles in hotels throughout the rest of the nation, in Utah, hotel rooms were stocked with the Mormon religion's most sacred tract. One to a room. Free, if you wanted to take it with you at check out time. How ironic, he thought.

The man driving toward the Tri Arc was well dressed, but nothing he wore was memorable. His look was that of a modestly turned-out Brooks Brothers' client, conservative, neat, but nondescript. His hair was precisely middle-of-the-road with no discernible style other than common. His one distinctive feature was the unnatural coloring of his right eye. The left eye was hazel and unremarkable. The right eye was also hazel, but most remarkable. It had a slash of blue forming an inverted triangle cutting directly through the iris and extending slightly above and below the pupil. The pupil appeared deformed; its roundness seemed altered by the intrusion of this cobalt blue aberration. Everyone confronting the man failed in their efforts to look at just his left eye, or his forehead, or the bridge of his nose; each, in turn, from the first day of his consciousness, stared into his right eye as if it were a black hole sucking in their attention. He did not like it. It was memorable. He hated being memorable. Today he had worn a single hazel contact lens in his right eye. When it was in place he felt free. It was as if he were invisible. Lens in place, he was the man no one remembered had passed their way.

The man knew what it was *really like*. People do not remember a face-to-face encounter, unless they are allowed to focus. He was sure he could get away with anything, as long as he remained nondescript; as long as he gave others nothing to focus on; as long as the public was so incredibly unobservant.

He was sure he would have made the perfect spy. Even Le Carré's fat and toad-like *George Smiley,* whose wife described him as "breathtakingly ordinary," was too odd not to be remembered in his studiously ill fitting clothes. The man knew his greatest strength was his anonymity. With his contact lens in place, no one ever remembered seeing him. He took great pride in that. Standing five foot eleven, he was neither too tall nor too short. His weight was normal. Not handsome, not ugly, his face was common. More than that, it was boring. There was nothing in its expanse of expressionless flesh to remark upon. No freckles, no broken nose, no discolorations, no high cheekbones, no nothing. If anything was unusual, other than the eye hiding beneath the contact lens, it was that he seldom smiled. And when he did, it was not a real smile, but a self-satisfied and fleetingly cruel grin. He wore no gold chains around his neck, no rings on his fingers, no cuff links, no tie tacks, no lapel pins. Even his voice was forgettable.

When the man worked at his regular job, he did not wear his contact lens. Everyone who met him, remarked then, or later, to him or to someone else, that they had met a man who was unforgettable. His right eye, they would say, was fascinating. Absolutely fascinating.

The man's mind was full of the hurtful memories of hundreds of overheard comments:

"Oh, yes. I know him. The one with the funny eye."

"Of course, bring that nice man along; you know, the one with that odd colored eye."

"Such a nice child. My goodness, look at his eye!"

"You mean old weird eye. Yeah, I met him. Strange."

Yet, when the man put in time at his regular job, he really didn't care. He didn't call that working. That was putting in time, he thought; like doing time in prison. Working was something else altogether. The man considered his plotting and scheming and planning, and finally, his doing of evil, to be his real work. For this he needed anonymity. For this he needed that single contact lens to cover his only flaw. Without it he was putting in time, and was recognized by everyone as the guy with the funny-odd-strange-weird eye. With the lens in place he could go anywhere, and no one would remember he had passed their way. It was like magic. He loved it. God, how he loved it.

Tuesday: Day Two

Thomas Aloysius Terrance Mahoney wasn't a Mormon. He wasn't even a *Jack Mormon*, the kind that belongs to the church but doesn't keep the faith. He was a Catholic who lived in Utah for three very good reasons. There were quite a few Catholics in Utah, which meant more than a few Irish, and, by extension, a goodly number of drinkers; the trout fishing was fantastic, even if he didn't get knee deep in a mountain stream often enough; and his one and only true love, his late wife, had been a Mormon who missed Utah, its mountains, and its open spaces when they had first met in New York City.

The first reason was the least important to Mahoney — he wasn't religious, and he knew how to drink alone; the second reason was quite important — cold, fast streams, and fighting trout kept him sane; the third reason was the most important of the three — his wife had died in an automobile accident two years after moving to Utah. He could not bear to leave the mountains his wife loved so deeply. When he looked at the mountains, when he drove through them, when he fished in their cold streams, he thought of her. He loved thinking of her. How the hell could he ever leave a place so full of memories of this woman who loved him without reservation? As long as the joy of remembering was greater than the pain, he could not leave.

Mahoney sat at his desk in the Salt Lake City police department, thumbing through a well worn book on the art of catching rainbow trout, when Heber Mark Grant called across the day room and told him there had been a shooting in Temple Square.

Mahoney, as everyone called him, was a homicide detective usually assigned to every killing that came along.

8

He wasn't saintly. He wasn't deferential. According to his superiors, he wasn't even very professional at his job. Too much of a loose cannon. He did, however, have an arrest and conviction record that kept the powers-that-be off his back. Mahoney knew, for example, that if he ever stepped in a meadow muffin of bureaucratic horseshit he would find himself cleaning it up alone. There were at least three officers above him who were his intellectual inferiors, and his departmental superiors, just waiting to find him up to his ass in muck. All three were Mormons. There would be no help for the irreverent detective who smoked, boozed, swore, and drank coffee endlessly. And here, thought Grant, was one more chance for Mahoney, to foul up — a homicide smack dab in the middle of Temple Square.

"You comin', Heber?" Mahoney said as he passed Grant's desk.

"Yeah, sure," Grant said as he reached into a drawer for his .38. Clipping the holstered revolver to his belt, Grant made the swing around the desk and was five paces behind Mahoney as the elevator doors opened.

Heber Grant was second in line for departmental kudos on the homicide squad, despite his youth, and first in line for credit from the powers-that-be. He was a Mormon; what else with a name like Heber Mark Grant. He was a militant non-smoker, non-drinker, non-swearer, non-rule-breaker, who, according to Mahoney, "Was so tight assed Mormon-straight he'd puke on his shoes if someone made him drink a cup of coffee in the morning." Weird behavior for a cop in America, but not in Utah, not among the Latter-day Saints. Grant, thought Mahoney, was definitely deeply entrenched among the Latter-day Saints.

"Who gave you the call, Heb?"

Mahoney knew that calling Grant anything but Mark, or Grant, pissed him off. Calling him Heber was bad enough, since every time Mahoney did it, it was in a tone that implied Grant was some throwback to the dark ages of polygamy and the Avenging Angels of Brigham Young. To call Grant "Heb," which Mahoney pronounced with a long "e" rankled, since Grant took it to be some sort of Jewish insult. It never occurred to Grant that "Heb" could be considered an insult to Jews. He just failed to think along those lines. Grant didn't particularly like Jews; but then Grant didn't particularly like Catholics, Protestants, Blacks, Orientals, and a Sunday-Go-to-Meeting shit house full of other groups.

His general animosity was directed toward *gentiles*, a term with a specialized definition unique among Mormons. It simply means everyone other than a Mormon. Mormons call all non-Mormons, including Jews, *gentiles*. If you're not a Mormon, you *are* a gentile. Jews have trouble with this distinction. Mormons don't. Only Mormons are not gentiles.

Grant, to exist in his world, forced himself to get along with gentiles. When he was a young Mormon boy, growing up in Provo, Utah, he thought they were called genitals, until someone explained the difference in spelling, pronunciation, and meaning.

"I told you, Mahoney, not to call me that. Please don't."

"Fuck you," Mahoney said. "Now who gave you the call?"

Grant got red in the face and fumed a bit.

"Willis Hollings. You know, at the church tourism office. Seems a woman screamed as a bullet tore into some guy's chest. Darn near ripped his heart out."

Darn was a word Grant used only when he was riled up, or caught in the intensity of verbal battle with Mahoney.

Mahoney didn't answer, he just looked straight ahead and lifted his head abruptly as if to say get on with the driving, stupid. They continued in silence until they stopped in front of the main gates of Temple Square, the geographical, cultural and spiritual center of Salt Lake City and the Mormon church.

The tourist, John Williamson, a Mormon from St. Paul, Minnesota, had been visiting on a family pilgrimage to this promised land. Accompanied by his wife, his six children, and his brother's family, another six in all, the fourteen Mormons had joined a tour group consisting of a dozen more. They had become instant friends, and wanted their pictures taken at every landmark along the tour. John Williamson now lay dead, a gaping hole, red and black and moist, in his chest. The family and new-found friends were sobbing and gasping, doing their best to control themselves. Young kids crowded around and gawked as if it were an episode of their favorite TV cop show.   One little boy kept saying, "Is he dead,

Mom? Is he really dead? Is he? Is he?! Wow!" He repeated it at least four times that Mahoney heard. Given a different situation Mahoney would have smacked the kid in the mouth and told him to shut up. Mahoney knew he should really smack the mother in the mouth and tell her to teach her son better manners or get him out of there. Mahoney didn't really like kids. Too damn many of them, he thought; they're loud; they're little; they move like ferrets; and you can't trust them. Mahoney sighed at the thought. When his wife was killed she had been six months pregnant with his first child — a son. It would have been a son, Mahoney thought. I could have taught him to fish.

Mahoney stayed drunk for three weeks, and then, one day, simply snapped out of it because he realized he wife would have wanted it that way. Enough is enough, she would have said. Get on with it. After drying out for a few days, Mahoney went back to work almost a month to the day after his wife's death. The night before he returned, he went to what had been their favorite restaurant and sat at their favorite table. He ordered two Bombay martini's straight-up. When they arrived he set one across from him. His wife didn't drink, but he thought she might start now. Mahoney mustered all the strength he could and held his glass up in a toast. Looking across the table he said, "Enough is enough. All you have to promise in return is to stay in my dreams." He drank the martini, then reached across the table and picked up the other one. He clinked it against his empty glass and whispered, "I promise," and drank it quickly. There were tears in his eyes. The waiter thought he had gone nuts, but approached the table and asked Mahoney if he wanted another drink. Mahoney said no. It was hardest thing he had ever done.

Bending over Williamson's body Mahoney could see the entry wound was larger than normal for a gunshot. He lifted the dead man's shoulder and blood spilled out from underneath. Mahoney could see that the exit wound was massive and disturbingly ugly. Jesus and Joseph Smith, thought Mahoney, who the fuck would want to do this? And why?

Mahoney turned the scene over to the lab team as he and Grant began to question those who were standing closest to

Williamson at the time of his death.   The answers were all
the same. Cookie cutter stuff. They heard a pop or backfire,
from over there, pointing east toward the Hotel Utah Building
across the street from Temple Square. They heard
Williamson moan or groan or gurgle or gasp. They heard
someone scream as Williamson hit the ground a second or
two later. They heard the sounds of panic, confusion, yells,
and finally the buzzing of a gathering crowd pushing in to see
the dead body. They heard children cry, laugh, and ask if they
could go now. One man saw a woman vomit near the base of
a tree. Another man stepped in it, then threw-up himself.

Mahoney found himself wondering why some people
could look at the ravaged body of a murder victim with
detached curiosity, yet become ill at the prospect of stepping
in a stranger's vomit.

Police, dispatched immediately to the Hotel Utah
Building, cordoned off the structure from ground to roof. No
one in, no one out. People in the lobby were irate; they had
no idea poor John Williamson, father, husband, picture-
perfect Mormon, lay face up in Temple Square with a hole in
his chest Mahoney could shove his fist in. Some, mostly
tourists, were madder than hell at not being allowed to leave.
Some, stopped dead in their tracks by patrolmen as they were
exiting the front of the building, threatened to sue the city for
this unwarranted delay in their travel and tourism plans. One
man, more obstreperous than most, confronted a cop and
demanded to know why he was being detained. The cop said
that there had been a shooting and a man had been killed.
Looking disgusted, he said, "Well, fuck you, I didn't do it,"
and started to push his way past the cop. He was later
interviewed in handcuffs by Mahoney, who concluded he was
not guilty of the shooting, but was simply, in fact, a certified
asshole. Mahoney hated assholes.

By the time Mahoney and Grant made their way to the
Hotel Utah Building, police spotted eleven open windows on
the Temple Square side. An enterprising patrolman sketched
the side of the building on a note pad and circled the windows
that were open. Each floor was sealed off, and Mahoney,
using a patrolman's radio, relayed instructions to shut down
the elevators, and post a patrolman, gun drawn, on each floor
near the stairs. No one was to leave the floor they were on.

Everyone attempting to leave was to be detained for a statement before more cooperative types were interviewed. "No exceptions," Mahoney said. "Repeat. *No exceptions.*"

The gates to Temple Square, according to one guard, were closed immediately after Williamson was shot. Mahoney shook his head. Immediately, my ass, he thought. Forcing a smile for the two uniformed guards Mahoney pressed the point. One guard admitted they both ran to the fallen man when the screams started. They knelt beside him. They saw he'd been shot. One guard stayed with the body, the other radioed for police and an ambulance, then ran back to the gates and closed them. Mahoney knew in his gut that the sequence had to have taken at least a minute — maybe more. Mahoney could taste his morning coffee rising in the back of his throat. Who knew how many witnesses had been lost through those steel gates?

Visitors caught behind the closed gates were lining up to show their I.D.'s, make their statements, and leave their addresses before exiting the grounds. All those with cameras and video equipment had film and tape confiscated and labeled. They would be copied and returned.

Entering the old Hotel Utah, Mahoney gave the window sketch to the manager of the building and told him he wanted three lists. The first was a list of what function each of the rooms served and whether or not the rooms were occupied with groups, meetings, or individuals. The second was a printout of the event activity list for the building, along with room numbers and the names of event participants. The third list was a full staff printout, with those currently on duty in the building topping the printout. Mahoney gave instructions that he wanted list number one in two minutes or he'd have the manager's ass for lunch.

The original Hotel Utah closed in August of 1987 the victim of a fading reputation. Owned by the Mormon Church the structure underwent a $50-million renovation project and a change in its basic nature. Once a stately hotel it was now just another church building with a fancy lobby harkening back to the glory days of the past, and offering restaurants and gardens and church trappings to tourists baffled by those who still called this non-hotel, *The Hotel Utah*. Officially it was now the *Hotel Utah Building*. It held a branch of the

LDS Church Distribution Center, an extension to the LDS Church's family history library, and rooms converted into a Mormon church for the meeting of two wards, the parish or congregation-like divisions in the Mormon church. Traffic throughout most of the building was unrestricted to clean-cut Mormon-looking types who appeared not to be tourists. Church security guards and programmed elevators prevented access to several highly sensitive floors.

List number one in hand, Mahoney and Grant eliminated the first two floors, for the time being, as not being high enough to sight over the wall surrounding Temple Square and hit a person standing near the Pioneer statue. The roof had been temporarily eliminated since it was the first place the police covered along with church security guards. There were no bullet casings and no sign of anyone or anything on the roof. Police were dispatched to the adjacent buildings to seal them off front and back, but the immediate concern was the Hotel Utah Building.

Reports were rife of a shot coming from the Hotel Utah Building, so the investigation logically centered there. One man had sworn that he heard a shot in the hallway of the fifth floor just as he entered the elevator heading for the lobby. When he got to the lobby he told a guard what he had heard and received a polite response that it would be looked into. The man then went to a newsstand and browsed for a while looking through racks of postcards containing pictures of the Mormon Temple from every conceivable angle. He finally bought a *Time* magazine. When he reentered the lobby two policeman had just burst through the main doors. Not trusting the guard to pass along his description, the man repeated his story to one of the cops.

The fifth floor was first then; Mahoney and Grant checked the rooms following the printout and sketch of the open windows. Only two fifth-floor windows were circled on the sketch: rooms 512 and 528. Room 512 was occupied by a Mr. and Mrs. Daniel Smith. In the old hotel days, Mahoney thought, it would likely be an afternoon tryst; Mr. and Mrs. Smith, indeed. But now the room was one of a few remaining rooms reserved for Mormon VIP guests. Mahoney knocked once, waited a moment, then used the manager's pass key. Opening the door, guns drawn, they found the room empty. The bed had been used, along with one crumpled towel in the bathroom. A condom wrapper was on the nightstand next to the bed. Mahoney smiled. Maybe things hadn't changed so much after all.

"This guy's a fucker, not a killer," said Mahoney.

"You're sick, Mahoney," was Grant's only reply as they both left and headed for 528, a small meeting room.

The same knock, a second or two wait, and Mahoney started to insert the pass key. It wouldn't go in. He couldn't see anything wrong with the lock, but the key just went in a quarter of the way and stopped.

Gesturing Grant aside, Mahoney put a shoulder to the door and let out a massive "oofff" of air as he bounced off and back. The damn door didn't even rattle. Grant grinned. Nodding at each other both Mahoney and Grant put their shoulders into it, but the result was the same. The door was massive, old, solid, and as rigid as a ship's spar.

"Shit," said Mahoney. "Get a fire ax." The patrolman on the floor, gun still drawn, ran toward the exit sign and the stairwell.

Chopping down the door proved no small task. Mahoney realized that he was working up the best sweat he'd had since an athletic encounter with a rather limber young woman a week ago Sunday. Finally, the center of the door gave way, and the wooden panel splintered. At the breakthrough they dropped to the floor. They waited, but there was no sound. Mahoney called out, "Police!" Still no sound. Peering through the wide crack in the door Mahoney saw a tripod, a rifle, and a gadget hanging under the trigger housing with an antenna protruding from its side.

"No one's in here," said Mahoney. "Chop the hell out of it."

As they entered the room, Mahoney called out to the uniformed cop behind them, "Get the lab boys up here, *now*. Tell them to bring everything they've got. Everything! Do it!"

"Good heavens," said Grant, "what's going on here?"

"Heber, you never cease to amaze me." Mahoney said. "In case it has escaped you this is where the deed was done."

"But . . . "

"No, buts, Heb. The son-of-a-bitch used a remote control. We've got some serious shit coming down in this city. I think our dead man was a target of opportunity; he was just some unlucky bastard who stopped to have his picture taken. Mr. Williamson is bait in some madman's game. And we're the fish. Bet your ass on it."

Mahoney picked up an envelope resting on the small conference table in the center of the room. Holding it by its edges, he lifted it up to the light of the window, and turned to Grant.

"I'll bet you a month's pay, Heber, that there isn't a fuckin' fingerprint on anything in this room that has to do with the shooting, including this love note."

Saturday: Three Months Earlier

The man drove his 1984 Chevrolet south on Interstate 25, glad to be out of the traffic surrounding the Denver metropolitan area. With the cruise control set at 55 miles per hour, he was in no hurry. He was, however, being very careful. This was no time to get a ticket. Approaching Colorado Springs, he had made the 600-mile journey from Salt Lake City in less than fifteen hours, stopping only twice, once for gas, and once for a hamburger at a fast food drive-thru window. It was late, near midnight, and he knew precisely where to go. He had been here before, staking out his target.

Driving to a gun shop near the edge of town, he parked across the street and watched the area for over an hour. He had thought about farming the job out to a low-life in some red-neck western bar, but that had its drawbacks. He could be identified, and killing the man after the job entailed too many risks before the fact. He had decided two weeks ago, parked in this same location, to do the job himself.

Prior to leaving the Denver area he had stolen a set of license plates from a car he was sure would be parked overnight without being moved. He would only need them for a few hours. Forty miles out of town, he pulled into a quiet rest stop and placed the stolen plates over his own with the help of four strips of double-sided carpet tape. The tape was hard to handle with cotton gloves on, but it was necessary to be careful. One mistake now would haunt him later.

With no one in sight, the man left his automobile, cracked the trunk slightly so that it still appeared closed, and walked across the deserted street to the side entrance of the gun shop.

17

In his hand was a long, round duffle bag made of black nylon. It was empty. He used a glass cutter to remove a small panel in the door's window. He placed one exposed end of an insulated wire, four feet long, against the metal foil strip and scraped until it contacted the foil under the clear protective coating covering it. He taped it in place. Reaching inside, he did the same to the foil strip on the door jamb, using the other end of the long wire. He repeated the process with the second strip of foil. With the jumper wires in place, he moved to the lock.   A quick grin covered the man's face, and just as quickly disappeared. He had been in this shop that day, two weeks ago. He knew where every- thing was. This is where he had purchased the duffle bag. It was specifically designed to hold three hunting rifles and enough ammunition to keep a survivalist happy for weeks. A nice touch, he thought.

Years before, the man had obtained an automatic lock picking device, looking for all the world like a small gun with metal feelers protruding from its business end. He had ordered it from a company he discovered in a *Soldier of Fortune* magazine ad promoting the sale of lock picks under the guise of offering a lock smithing course. It was sent to a post office box he had rented under a false name in Grand Junction, a town near the Utah-Colorado border. He had used the lock picking device many times over the years. It worked as advertised. The door's lock rattled at the device's vibrations, the pins lined up with the cylinder, and the bolt opened from the turning pressure on the device. Carefully, the man opened the door just enough to squeeze through, while the jumper wires maintained contact between the foil strips on the window and the door jamb. Ducking under the wires, he was in.

He took what he needed — rifles, scopes, handguns, and a war chest of ammunition, including some rather exotic loads. He also took several packages of smokeless black gunpowder, a standard crossbow, and a small pistol-like crossbow that fired six-inch bolts. One of the reasons he had picked this particular gun shop, from the dozens he had looked at, was its inventory of supplies for survivalists. It was also poorly protected by an out-dated alarm system.

He left as he came, leaving the wires connected to maintain the alarm circuit. Waiting until a lone car passed and its lights faded into the distance, he went back to the car, placed the duffle in the trunk, and left.

At a deserted intersection several miles away he stopped long enough to pull off the taped-on license plates and throw them into a creek at the side of the road. With the items he had been collecting over the past three months he now had what he needed. Let the games begin, he thought. Fifteen hours, and a dozen cups of coffee later, he was back home in Salt Lake City.

Wednesday: Day Three, Morning

Mahoney's desk always looked the same at 8:30 in the morning; a messy in-box; a messy out-box; no Mahoney. The desk had a messy stack of papers piled on it higher than both the in-box and the out-box put together; the telephone cord looked like a failed knot-tying test for some Boy Scout merit badge; one crumpled paper towel looked remarkably stiff; three paper coffee containers with chewed edges, two of them empty, both with scum on the bottom. The third container had half-a-cup of coffee still in it, and some fuzzy green mold floating dead center.

When Mahoney entered the office at 9:15 that morning, everyone else had been to work for forty-five minutes. Mahoney walked to his desk, attempted to flatten out the stiff paper towel, reached into a brown bag and placed two powdered sugar donuts directly on his desk. He pulled a fresh container of coffee from the same bottom-wet bag only moments from self-destructing. He pulled off the cap, spilling some of the coffee on his desk, and threw the cap and the bag toward the waste basket. He missed. He carefully shoved the used containers toward the back of his desk. To Mahoney the front of his desk was next to his belly, and the back of his desk was that part furthest away from him as he sat in his chair. To everyone else, those who approached Mahoney, and his toxic waste dump of a desk, the containers were at the front. Mahoney loved such inconsistencies. He often wondered if the phrase "Behind my back," really meant in front of his chest; he reasoned that the front of his back was behind him; and thus, behind his back had to be in front of him. Mahoney liked this kind of woolgathering. No one ever wanted to talk to Mahoney about these things. He noticed

20

things like that.

Everyone did know enough to stay away from Mahoney until he had his coffee and his mouth was ringed with powdered sugar. Contact before this, his most sacred daily ritual, was not recommended.

Candy Martin, Candice to her enemies, walked across the day room floor carrying a glassine envelope containing the killer's "love letter" found the day before. Mahoney had read it — so had Grant — before it was taken to the lab to find out if it held other secrets. Candy assumed it was important enough to be taken to Mahoney immediately. Mahoney could have cared less this early in the morning. He knew they would find nothing. The words he had already read, Mahoney knew, was all he was going to get from that damn note.

Standing in front of Mahoney's desk (in back of it by his way of thinking), looking at the rumpled detective stuff the last arc of a powdered sugar donut in his mouth, Candy knew she wasn't supposed to say a word until the powder disappeared from his mouth, and the new coffee container was empty. Oh, well.

"Mahoney," she said, tentatively, "here are the results of the lab tests on the letter and envelope you found yesterday. Do ya want 'em now?"

Mahoney brushed at his chin with his hand and finished the last gulp of coffee in the container. He leaned over the desk and peered into the old half-empty container with the mold on top.

"Damn," he said. "That's repulsive. Okay Candy, as long as you've shithoused my breakfast put the plastic down and get your beautiful ass outta here. I'm still hungry."

Candy had no sense of humor. Either that or no desire to let on that she understood Mahoney would be delighted to bite her on the ass if she'd just listen to reason. He would start with a nibble, he thought, then some light love bites, and a couple of seriously probing . . .

"Open your eyes Mahoney its past 9:30. Some of us have been up for hours while you, my crude friend, lust after powdered sugar donuts and Candy's backside."

This was the most graphic Grant had ever gotten with Mahoney. Grant was standing directly in front of Mahoney's desk when Mahoney opened his eyes. He knew it had been a mistake to tell Grant that he lusted after Candy's posterior. Somehow, that afternoon several weeks ago in the car, on a routine investigation, Mahoney had let rip with a fantasy of rear-end daydreaming brought on by the sight of Ms. Candice Martin bending over the file cabinet directly across from his desk. She was wearing a mini-skirt and smoke-black pantyhose, the combination of which erased from Mahoney's memory banks everything of importance related to the day's other activities. I should have kept my fuckin' mouth shut, thought Mahoney.

"Heber, why don't you break down and say something clever like *candy ass*, or just a straight forward, 'Fuck you, Mahoney, you're a bag of shit.' Can you do that for me Heber?"

"You're disgusting. And you're old, Mahoney. You're old, and you're disgusting."

This was pretty good for Grant, Mahoney thought. Maybe, given two or three years, he would work up to a healthy damn it. No. Not Heber Mark Grant. Straight-arrow-son-of-a-bitch.

"I like you, Heber, no matter what everybody else says. Pull up a chair and lets go over this shit."

Mahoney could smell his own breath, and peered, one more time, at the mold in the half-empty container. He considered offering it to Grant, but even Grant wasn't that dumb. Besides, Grant would rather get caught masturbating than drinking coffee. And to a Mormon, masturbating was a mortal sin. He could show Grant a biblical reference for masturbation, thought Mahoney, but no where in that good book did it mention Juan Valdez and his damned Columbian beans.

Mahoney and Grant, side by side, read over the lab report. No prints. None. Typed on a non-distinctive typewriter, most likely an old Underwood, it was the commonest of the common. Unless the guy's stupid, thought Mahoney, it was most likely a public typewriter in a library or office. A billion of those floating around. Hell there were thirty of the old clunkers in his own day room. The paper was Hammermill Duplex Copy Paper, found in thousands of copy machines in thousands of offices. The envelope was Mead All Purpose for Home & Office #75050, fifty to a box, sold in nearly every store in America.

The rifle and ammunition would take longer to pinpoint, but preliminary findings were depressing: several unidentified latent prints on the rifle, none on the cartridge. The ammunition was an expanding bullet designed to rip open a fairly big hole on impact, an even bigger one on exit; not too rare, not too exotic; tripod was hand-modified, top-of-the-line, heavy-duty. The tripod showed a few latent prints, unidentified. The scope was high quality but common. There was nothing on the gadget that pulled the trigger. No prints on the batteries inside the gadget. They were Duracell AA's, as common as dirt.

The letter was simple, if not straight forward:

To whom it may concern:
This is Day One of a thirty-day reign of terror over which you have no control. I intend to do the following:
Within the next thirty days I will target for death the President of the Church of Jesus Christ of Latter-day Saints, and some members of the Council of Twelve Apostles, the so-called Living Prophets of God on Earth.
I will not tell you how many I intend to kill, nor when I intend to do it, nor how. You will know when it happens. What I did today was to show you how close I can come to striking at the heart of the church. It was simply to get your attention and to prove I mean to do as I say.
I may kill all of the Council of Twelve Apostles, or just a few. Whatever suits me. But if the church officials pay me $100 million I will let the President live. After all, how much is the Living Prophet of God on Earth worth to the Mormon Church? Surely, mere money doesn't matter to the Church. I will contact you again, in a manner not dissimilar to this, and give you my instructions on how the money is to be paid and delivered.
Just to prove my ability, I will kill one of the twelve apostles very soon. If I am not

*paid exactly as I say, I will, eventually, kill the
President of the Church. Should I decide that
my instructions are not being carried out to
the letter, I will abort my plan to extort money
from the Church, and I will simply kill all of
the Council of Twelve Apostles, and the
President of the Church. The Mormon Christ
and his twelve apostles will die. Your choice.*

*By the way, I may kill a few other select-
ed members of the church leadership just for
the hell of it. Especially, if you don't take this
seriously.*

Moroni Goldblum

"Good God, Heber, it reads worse the second time around.
Has there been any reaction from church officials to the
photocopy we sent over, or to the protection we offered the
church officials?"

"One phone call, from the office of the First Presidency.
They request a meeting of our investigation team and their
people at 3 p.m. today. I guess we're going."

"No shit," Mahoney said as he quietly shook his head.

Mahoney and Grant spent the rest of the morning and
early afternoon sifting through interviews and reports, and
coordinating other aspects of the case. The incident in
Temple Square, as it was being called, was a sniper homicide.
Nothing more. The press had been shut out of the information
contained in the letter. Mahoney knew that wouldn't last
much after 3 p.m. The two detectives made notes and
sketched up an outline of steps to be taken. They compared
ideas, and theories, and decided, in concert with the chief of
police and the mayor's office, that Mahoney and Grant would
present their case to the church officials and watch the shit hit
the Temple. Mahoney's phrase. It disgusted Grant.

After meeting with the top brass at 1 p.m., Mahoney and
Grant put the finishing touches on their plan-of-action and
headed for a small restaurant near the Church Office
Building, close to Temple Square. Mahoney had chili, and
privately hoped it would go to work in the middle of the
afternoon meeting. Grant had lettuce, bacon, and tomato, on
white bread. Mahoney had coffee. Grant had milk. Typical.

Wednesday: Day Three, Afternoon

Entering the twenty-eight-story Church Office Building, the tallest in the city, Mahoney and Grant were all business. The building is the administrative headquarters for the church and for the faithful — the six million members of the Church of Jesus Christ of Latter-day Saints.

Mahoney and Grant were apprehensive when they learned the meeting would be in the Church Office Building. They had hoped it would be held in the smaller Church Administration Building where the real power resides. It is the Church Administration Building that houses the offices of the First Presidency and the Council of Twelve Apostles. The First Presidency is comprised of the President, Prophet, Seer, and Revelator, who is the lineal successor to Joseph Smith Jr., and speaks, according to the faithful, with the direct authority of God. It also houses the First and Second Counselors and the Council of Twelve Apostles, comprised of twelve men, spiritual successors, say the faithful, to the twelve apostles of Jesus Christ.

The rest of the church leadership centers among the Quorum of Seventy, seventy elders in the church, who act in the name of the Lord, under the direction of the Council of Twelve Apostles.

In all, eight-five men watch over the administrative and ecclesiastical duties of the church. Eighty-five men. No women. Perish the thought, ran through Mahoney's mind. The church, he thought, may well be the last truly exclusive American men's club.

In the less rarified atmosphere of the Church Office Building, where the work really got done, Mahoney and Grant, would, most likely, still be shunted off to functionaries. The First Presidency, like the Pope, never sees

anyone unless they have a check for a million or more, and a
faithful record of service to the church. But the Church Office
Building it would be. The second team, thought Mahoney.
Maybe the third.

A tall, well-dressed man, quiet and obsequious, met
Mahoney and Grant as they approached the reception desk.
He seemed to come quietly, out of nowhere, his timing such
that Mahoney couldn't help but wonder how he knew they
had actually arrived in the lobby of the building. Someone
must have been watching, or the man had simply lurked
behind a pillar, anticipating the effect of his precisely timed
arrival. For some reason it almost made the hair on
Mahoney's neck stand up.

"Detectives Mahoney and Grant, I presume," said the
man. "I'm Wilford Howe, assistant to the office of church
security. Would you follow me, please?"

No handshake, no smile, no wasted motion, as he turned
to lead them to the elevator. He said nothing as they smoothly
ascended to the fifteenth floor of Salt Lake City's only
skyscraper. As they walked out of the elevator, Mahoney
marveled at the neatness of the place. Maybe, he thought,
everyone ate the wastepaper as soon as a single piece
surfaced. No dust. No ashtrays. No unkempt stacks of paper.
Most definitely, no containers of coffee cluttering the
desktops.

Mahoney leaned over to Grant and whispered, just low
enough to avoid being heard by their guide, "I couldn't work
in this fuckin' place. It's sterile."

Grant mugged his displeasure at Mahoney's profanity
staining the air in this church building. He was glad Mahoney
whispered. Mahoney usually shouted things out as if he were
back in the Metropolitan Hall of Justice yelling at some
assistant D.A. who had screwed up one of his arrests. Grant
didn't like it, but he found himself thinking how right
Mahoney was. It was sterile. Even the air seemed purer than
what they breathed at headquarters. It was quiet. Very quiet.
He could see the heads of people bobbing up and down, and
walking within partitioned space. But there were no raised
voices, no jokes being told. It was a very serious place. No
one smoking or drinking coffee. That part of the picture was
nice, thought Grant.

Motioning them through a door marked "Security Conference Room," the man disappeared as quickly as he appeared — like the dusty butler in a gothic novel.

A man seated at a solid oak conference table rose and moved forward with his hand outstretched. Mahoney noticed that just before the man rose he pressed a buzzer at the end of the table. No doubt to call the troops, thought Mahoney.

"Good afternoon, I'm Warren Kimball, chief of security operations for the church. Detective Mahoney, Detective Grant," shaking both their hands in turn, "I'm glad to meet you both. I wish the circumstances could be better."

Mahoney was puzzled. How the hell did this Kimball character know he was Mahoney, and Grant was Grant? He never asked, and the gothic butler hadn't uttered a word. Well, the son-of-a-bitch has done his homework, thought Mahoney. Either that or he's one of those Mormons who can spot a non-Mormon a mile away on general principles. Mahoney, himself, could spot a Mormon at least seventy per cent of the time, and given five minutes of conversation the number shot up to about ninety-eight per cent. Why not the other way around?

The moment Grant finished shaking Kimball's hand, a door at the back of the room opened and four men walked in. Kimball didn't introduce them, nor acknowledge their presence. They sat down at the buzzer-end of the table and left a space for Kimball. Kimball turned and walked back to take a seat as he said, "Sit anywhere you'd like, gentlemen."

"Now," he continued, without even the hint of asking if anyone would like a cup of coffee, "tell us what you have."

Mahoney was lusting after a cup of coffee.

The men looked the part of FBI agents. Indeed, Mahoney was familiar with the terms Mormon FBI, Mormon Secret Service, and, particularly, Mormon Mafia, applied to the church's security agents. In Utah, most real FBI agents are Mormons, just as the leader of church security, and his top men, are usually ex-FBI agents. It makes things much easier for both the FBI and the Mormon church to coexist in the church-state of Utah. Telling the difference between "Mormon FBI" agents and real FBI agents is nearly impossible. Hoover's penchant for short haircuts, conservative suits, and a Teutonic bearing, mirror a perfect Latter-day Saint security agent to his polished wing-tips.

Mahoney had read some of the Mormon church's doctrine, but he had also read a great many more of the alternative publications rife in Utah. Many were written by ex-Mormons who documented the publications with footnotes and references from church historical documents not often privy to even the faithful. He had learned, between reading and working in the police department, a fair amount about church security, and the church itself.

The job description of church security is simple. They do anything the leadership of the church tells them to do. Period. It is a truism, long understood by the faithful, and critics alike, that members of the First Presidency are *much* better guarded in public than is the President of the United States.

Kimball, just as his predecessor had been, was an ex-FBI agent. And before each of them the legendary J. Martell Bird had put his mark on the Church's security operation. Mahoney had met Bird, and had followed his impact on church security as it related to the Salt Lake City police department. Bird was one of J. Edgar Hoover's right-hand men in the bureau during its rough and tumble days. Bird, himself, boasted that he was one of only seven agents Hoover ever trusted. Bird was also part of the FBI team that bugged Martin Luther King's hotel room. He was appointed head of church security by Ezra Taft Benson, the thirteenth President, Prophet, Seer, and Revelator of the church. Benson, before becoming church president, while still a member of the Council of Twelve Apostles, was the highly controversial Secretary of Agriculture under the Eisenhower administration.

Under Bird's reign over church security, the offices of the First Presidency became a fortress. It was fully protected from public scrutiny. An apartment for the church leader, in the old Hotel Utah, was outfitted with bulletproof glass, and the walls were layered with massive sheets of steel to protect the prophet against bombs.

During these tumultuous latter-days, the church security office expanded its role as ushers and guards at public gatherings, to a virtual Nixonian secret police, complete with a goon squad, electronics experts, and an intelligence division to track and report on the pure and the unpure.

The church security office was no second class police state. It was filled with militant, well trained, non-smoking, non-drinking, intolerant Mormons who were clones of the Mormon personal police force that Howard Hughes hired to surround him in his last days. If you couldn't trust a Mormon security agent, who could you trust? The need was very real.

Apostle Boyd K. Packer, called "Darth Packer," by some, for his dogmatically right-wing view of church authority, once said publicly, "When you are at war, and we are, security is crucial."

Security is so crucial, in fact, and the threat so real to the leadership of the church, that underground tunnels lead from the Church Administration and Office Buildings directly into the Temple and the Tabernacle. It is a routine joke among the "heretics" in Utah that it is a wonder the First Presidency and the Council of Twelve Apostles ever see the light of day.

Around the massive conference table, Kimball, the painfully eager, and relatively new, head of security, sat with his four-horsemen. Having only recently replaced his successor, Kimball was eager to prove himself worthy of the Bird tradition. Sometimes he tried too hard.

All present had copies of the killer's letter on the table in front of them.

Mahoney started.

"First, I would like to say that I think it is a waste of time and talent, and potentially very dangerous, to have this meeting without the president and the apostles present. This is a serious threat, as evidenced by the death yesterday of Mr. Williamson in Temple Square."

Mahoney could feel Grant tense from head to toe.

"Detective Mahoney," said Kimball, in a monotone that made him sound like a teacher scolding a school kid, "members of the First Presidency and the Council of Twelve Apostles do not ordinarily concern themselves with secular matters, particularly those involving local law enforcement."

He made the words "local law enforcement" sound like a joke.

"I am the one in charge of church security, and as such I

will be the one you will deal with in this matter. We don't have much time, so would you please get on with it."

Grant started to open his mouth to speak, but Mahoney could not be contained.

"Death threats are not secular matters! Death threats are serious crimes, and should be treated as such. I have no doubt that you, the president, and his apostles are busy. But we are talking about their lives here. It is likely that one of more of them will be killed in the very near future if you don't take this threat seriously."

"Please get on with it then," Kimball said. No one else moved a muscle.

"I resent having to go through this more than once, but here it is." Grant could see that Mahoney was obviously pissed off. He realized he was holding his breath. Relax Grant, he thought. Mahoney continued.

"The person threatening the president and the apostles is a professional. He may not be a professional killer, in fact, but he operates like one. He is most likely a Mormon or an ex-Mormon with a real or imagined gripe, and he knows the church, possibly as well as you do. I believe he's a psychopath. He has no compunction at killing, and revels at the possibility of doing it again and again. Money is of no importance at all and a red herring at best. He has set out a 30-day calendar of promises that includes, at least, the killing of the president and one or two of the apostles — at most, the mass murder of the entire hierarchy of this church above the level of the First Quorum of Seventies.

"He is not going to wait long, and if my guess is right, one of your apostles is as good as dead before another forty-eight hours passes. Maybe less.

"It is my recommendation that the church agree to pay the man, immediately, so that we can see how his plan develops to secure the money and escape from the police. That will be our best chance to capture or kill him. It is the only way we have to buy time and protect some lives."

Mahoney leaned back in his chair and crossed his arms. He found himself thinking about coffee, and wondering if there is no coffee, might there possibly be some Canadian Club in the credenza behind these five smug bastards.

The room was dead quiet for fifteen seconds, which

Mahoney took to be a good sign, and Grant took to be a sure sign of the imminent end of the world. Grant's gut was in knots. There might be some church history being made here, but Grant didn't like being in the middle of it — possibly on the wrong side.

Kimball started asking questions, rather than responding to what Mahoney said.

"Why do you say he's acting as a professional?"

"Because there are no prints, no fibers, no eye witnesses, no credit card trail, no panic, no valuable paper, envelope, or typewriter leads, and the rifle and ammo used to kill the first victim can only be traced back to a dead-end theft at a gun shop in Colorado."

Mahoney took a breath.

"The fingerprints found on the rifle, a *Weatherby Mark V Magnum Deluxe*, were put there by the guy who owned the gun shop. The weapon costs nearly $1,500, and he left it for us to find. It is my guess he has the money for the weapon, but an outright theft leaves a weaker trail. He is probably a loner, doesn't trust anyone but himself. On that basis a middleman is out. I am sure of one thing: he is not a typical crazy. He knows what he wants to accomplish, and he has a singular vision of how to get it.

"The ammunition was a large caliber Remington Soft Point Core-Lokt round. Remington calls its their 'No. 1 mushroom,' a dum-dum bullet to you and me. It doubles the size of its caliber upon impact. It's also a dead-end trace to the same gun shop. There wasn't a fingerprint on the spent cartridge. This man was thinking ahead. He bought, or mostly likely made, a complex solenoid device to electro-mechanically pull the trigger. It was made specifically for this weapon and attached with a small thumbscrew below the trigger housing. He shows considerable ingenuity. No prints, even on the batteries used to power it. If prints are overlooked anywhere, it is usually there or on a cartridge. He is not dumb.

"Finally, the aim-point of the rifle was well thought out. It was at low chest level for an average adult male. That means that he had his choice of targets. With that kind of ammunition, one shot was going to rip into something — a man's chest, a woman's upper chest or neck, an arm, or a kid's

head. If it hit you in the shoulder, you would most likely
spin like a top. I don't think he cared whether or not he killed,
only that he did major damage to a person standing in Temple
Square. Fortunately for the killer, and unfortunately for Mr.
Williamson, the round hit him nearly center chest. The killer
got lucky. Mr. Williamson didn't. It was a calling card.
Something to get our attention.

"He sealed the door lock to the jamb with cyanoacrylate
glue, Krazy Glue probably. It wasn't meant to keep the police
out, because he was long gone before the rifle was fired. It
was meant to keep some building custodian or maid from idle
entry to tidy up before he had a chance to remotely fire the
thing. You might be interested to know that an identical
Remington soft point bullet was used to murder Dr. Martin
Luther King Jr., in Memphis. The rifle used was never
identified since the ammunition is manufactured to double its
caliber on impact. It destroys the riflings, as well as the
target. In our case, he wants us to know. He wants us to run
all over the country trying to trace Remington ammunition,
Duracell batteries, and Underwood typewriters for God's
sake. He's playing games, and he's not about to stop.

"Now, I don't know about you, Mr. Kimball, or your
four-horseman sitting next to you, but that stacks up as pretty
damn professional in my book."

Mahoney could feel Grant tense up again, this time he
could actually see it happening as Grant seemed to grow an
inch taller in his seat. To Kimball's credit he didn't flinch. A
pro of sorts, thought Mahoney. Probably that puckered-
asshole starched-collar FBI training. The four-horseman
might as well have been cast in bronze.

"Why do you think he's a member, or ex-member of the
church?" asked Kimball.

"You can see what I see in this letter," said Mahoney.
"He uses the correct theological terminology for the church.
Although he uses the word Mormon, his initial reference is to
The Church of Jesus Christ of Latter-day Saints. He has it
correct down to the hyphen in Latter-day and the lowercase
"d." He capitalizes the 'C' in church, which is something
members do, as a shorthand referring to the LDS church.
When someone in Utah asks me if I belong to the church, I
can *hear* the capital letter. Somehow Mormons can hardly

bring themselves to write down the word church without using a capital 'C' unless they are talking about some other church."

No one was making moves to leave so Mahoney pushed on.

"He says he will kill the members of the First Presidency, which could mean all three of them, the President and his First and Second Counselors. He says he may kill all of the Council of Twelve Apostles. He spelled 'twelve' instead of just using the number. Also, he doesn't just say the Twelve Apostles as a non-member, a gentile, might. He says the Council of Twelve Apostles. He also refers to the president as the Living Prophet of God on Earth. Again the capital letters. Although the correct title is President, Prophet, Seer, and Revelator, most Mormons refer to the church president as the Living Prophet of God on Earth. Gentiles don't. He signed the letter 'Moroni Goldblum.' Moroni is a very big deal to Mormons, but it is an esoteric reference. Most non-Mormons in this country have never heard of the angel Moroni. The only ready reference books his name appears in are Mormon tracts.

"Believe me, Mr. Kimball, the guy is one of your own, or was one of your own. And if I had to bet my life on it I'd say he is still a member of the church in good standing."

Kimball stared at Mahoney, ignored Grant, and after another pause, which lasted long enough to drink a toast to ten dead Irishmen, he finally spoke.

"I'm impressed, Detective Mahoney. You've done your homework. And you may be right. I will take this up with my superiors and get back to you."

"Get back to me!" yelled Mahoney. "There is no time to get back to me! We need to take personal charge of the men we sent over to guard the First Presidency and the Council of Twelve Apostles. We need to have a detailed schedule of the church leaders' activities for the next thirty days. We need to coordinate a defense plan and an attack plan with your men in church security. We need a complete roster of your men, their backgrounds, and how they're posted. We need . . . "

"We will get back to you!" said Kimball, more forcefully than Mahoney expected.

Kimball stood abruptly, a nd the four-horsemen did

likewise as if attached to the same marionette rod.

"Mr. Kimball," Mahoney said, "I would like to stress that we have no time for the theology of what's right and wrong here. And we have very little time to tiptoe around your egos or those of the church leaders. You have a General Conference coming up in less than thirty days. The Tabernacle will be full of the faithful, and, may I add, the First Presidency and the Council of Twelve Apostles. They will be on public display. Out in the open. This man is going to do what he says. We have no leads, and no hope of catching him before he makes good on at least part of his threat. Unless, of course, we can agree to pay him during his first direct contact with us. No one is smart enough to evade police while trying to pick up $100 million in cash and run with it. It's the only card we have to play. Don't try to bluff this man by stalling. Someone will get killed, and the first target, according to the letter, will be one of the Council of Twelve Apostles. I would think they should be included in your talks."

"Detective Mahoney," Kimball said in his most condescending tone, "we will be the judge of who is, and who is not, included in our discussions regarding this matter."

"By the way, Kimball," Mahoney dropped the Mr., "was this meeting taped?"

"Of course," said Kimball, in a hesitating monotone.

"Where is the microphone?" Mahoney asked.

"There are several of them, Detective. Several of them."

"One more thing," Mahoney said, as they all stood facing each other. "There is something we are all missing here. I am sure of it. I have a nagging fear that this madman is going to be one step ahead of us for the next several steps. We would like to be of more assistance than you are allowing us to be. We sent over patrolmen to guard the Church Administration Building and each member of the Council of Twelve Apostles. I've received word back that, so far, you have only allowed them access to the periphery of the building and that no guard was assigned to any of the church leaders. I believe that you should post a uniformed guard at the door of each office in the Church Administration Building, and insist on a patrolman accompanying each member of the First Presidency and the Council of Twelve Apostles everywhere he goes. Including to the bathroom."

"That would be impractical," said Kimball, "and unnecessary, as we have our own private security that is much more in tune with the needs of our leaders than you can possibly imagine."

Smug bastard, thought Mahoney.

That's really neat, thought Grant.

Neat is an overused word in the vocabulary of a great many Mormons. So is scrud, Mahoney thought.

The meeting was over, and the obsequious man appeared as abruptly as he had before to escort them out. Riding down in the elevator not a word was spoken, and when they reached the lobby the obsequious man was no longer obsequious. He simply pointed from the opening elevator toward the entrance doors and nodded an abrupt goodbye. He was now being perfunctory. He was now the perfunctory man, thought Mahoney. How quickly impressions change. The elevator door closed before Mahoney and Grant had taken four steps.

As the two men stepped out onto the street in front of the Church Office Building, Grant, who was nearly mute throughout the meeting, turned to Mahoney and spoke.

"Mahoney, you amaze me. How did you learn so much about the church? I know we went over the thinking about the killer, and the letter, but the details you filled in about the church — it wasn't what I expected."

"Most Catholics who live in Utah," Mahoney explained, without looking at Grant, "know much more about the Mormons, than the Mormons who live in Utah know about the Catholics. Nearly every school principal in Utah is a Mormon, the federal congressmen and senators are Mormon, the state congressmen and senators are over seventy percent Mormon, the local politicians, almost to a person are Mormon. Our police chief is a Mormon, and most of the force is Mormon. You can't take a dump in this town without shitting on a Mormon. Knowing what's what on the journey toward Zion should be a basic survival technique for a gentile detective, don't ya think?"

It was more of a statement than a question, and Grant decided not to answer since all he really wanted was for Mahoney to stop the profanity. The reference to Zion was apt, however, since all Mormons, like Grant, hope, in another life, to reside in Zion where Joseph Smith Jr., the prophet and founder of the church, would build the Zion Temple prior to Christ's return.

Mahoney always thought it was laughable, no matter how seriously Grant and his devout brethren took it, that the Prophet Smith declared Christ's second coming would be in Independence, Missouri. Also Zion to the Mormons.

Mahoney found himself wondering what Christ would actually think of Independence, Missouri.

The Garden of Eden, Mahoney knew from his reading, was, according to Mormon doctrine, located in Davies County, Missouri, about 60 miles north of Kansas City. This holy site is known to all Mormons as Adam-one-Adman, even though it is located in the United States, about 10,000 miles from the Euphrates. Mahoney vaguely remembered that the Bible said four rivers flowed out of Eden, one being the Euphrates and another being the Tigris. Biblical anthropologists have no idea what the other two are. How, in this lifetime, he wondered, did Mormons conclude the Garden of Eden was in Missouri? Mesopotamia, maybe. But Missouri? Who knows? Revelation maybe. The belief is not a minor one. There is a Mormon shrine in Davies County, Missouri, commemorating the remnants of a stone alter that Joseph Smith Jr., pointed to as proof of his revelation. It was, he said, the alter upon which Adam offered a sacrifice to God after he was expelled from the Garden of Eden.

Official Mormon writings by Prophets of the church also claim that the earth is only 7,000 years old, and that Noah built his ark in North Carolina. Having visited North Carolina on several occasions Mahoney had great difficulty with this.

Mahoney found himself chalking up the incredible: Zion isn't Jerusalem, it is Independence, Missouri. Christ's second coming will not be to the Mount of Olives, it will be to the "Show Me State." The Garden of Eden isn't in Asia, it is sixty miles north of Kansas City. Noah built his ark in North Carolina. Jews are gentiles. Catholics are gentiles. Protestants are gentiles. Mormons aren't. The world was created 7,000 years ago. And church security knows best how to protect its leaders.

Mahoney needed a serious drink.

Wednesday: Day Three, Evening

Mahoney wanted to know more about the church's problems with radicals, fundamentalists, and malcontents. And he knew just the man to ask — Maxwell Taylor Jackson.

Sitting in the living room of Maxwell Jackson's rustic home in Little Cottonwood Canyon, he was enjoying the company of his old friend, an excommunicated Mormon who had devoted his post-Mormon life to the documentation of the Mormon church. Mahoney was in heaven. Jackson had offered either coffee or a drink. In over sixty percent of the homes in Salt Lake City, both of these choices were nonexistent.

Since the sun was definitely over the yardarm someplace in the civilized world, Mahoney opted for a drink. Canadian Club on the rocks would do quite nicely, thank you.

"What can I do for you, Mahoney?" Jackson asked. His old friend pointed, and Mahoney settled down into the most comfortable chair he had ever sat in. Jackson sat across from him in matching, well cushioned, splendor. He hadn't visited his old friend for several years, ever since he needed some information on the church regarding Mark Hofmann and the forgery murders in 1985. Since then, things had obviously gotten better for Jackson. The furnishings were richer, more comfortable, and a massive St. Bernard was curled up next to his feet just in front of a fireplace. It was too warm for a fire, but the total feeling was right out of *Field & Stream*. Mahoney could live like this. Easily.

"Want to go fishing sometime Max? Mahoney asked.

"Is the Pope a bear?" was Jackson's response.

Years ago the two men had seen each other often and had fished in the clear streams above Ogden Canyon on more than one occasion. In response to an obvious question, Jackson had once replied, "Is the Pope Catholic?" Mahoney, on another occasion had answered one of Jackson's similarly inane questions with the statement, "Does a bear shit in the woods?" The next time the two men got together, Mahoney had responded to one of those questions with, "Is a bear Catholic?" Later in the same conversation it was Jackson's turn with, "Does the Pope shit in the woods?" During the Hofmann investigation both men had adopted the short cut, "Is the Pope a bear?" It was like telling jokes by numbers. Some people can tell a joke, some can't. It was a bit silly, but it was an inside joke the two men shared. And they always felt good saying it.

The hiatus in their friendship began with the death of Mahoney's wife. It was too much fun being together to allow it to happen at a time when Mahoney seldom felt like laughing. But enough time had passed that Mahoney felt guilty at not having spent more time with Max. Now the memories flooded back, and the old times seemed like hot spiked cider on a cold day. Damn near a necessity.

"Max, I need your help again. We've got a case that is about to blow up in our faces. Someone has threatened to kill the president of the church and his twelve apostles. He has already killed one innocent man just to prove he can do it. I think he's an ex-Mormon who has a grudge against the church, and he wants to take it all the way."

"You know I'll help any way I can. Shoot."

"Listen Max, give me some understanding of why there are so many nuts out there who want to get back at the church. And, specifically, why would anyone want to kill the leadership of the church? Especially now. Is it something I don't know about that has happened recently?"

"Old friend," said Max, "someone has been after this church from the beginning of its time, when the good old founding prophet, Joseph Smith Jr., was martyred at the age of thirty-nine. You know the Mormons were driven from New York to Ohio to Missouri to Illinois, and finally across the Great Plains to this promised land — this Great Salt Lake Valley at the foot of the Wasatch Mountains.

"It prospered. Streets wide enough for a full oxen team to turn around in without backing up. It built its Temple, its Tabernacle, and its empire. It even survived a plague of locusts through the intervention of sea gulls 'sent by God' to save their crop. But locusts are not as tenacious as man. The issues of polygamy, and black skin, and women's rights, continue to haunt the church. The old issues are still the new issues."

"What do you mean, Max?"

"Polygamy was the way of life in the Mormon settlements during the old days. The country viewed the Mormons as less than desirable residents. You know, of course, that pockets of polygamy still exist in Utah and other western states. The police bust an isolated family every now and then on the complaint of some Baptist or Seventh Day Adventist. Complaints are seldom sworn out by practicing Mormons.

"Since its organization on April 6, 1830, the Mormon church has not found peace, even in Utah. In May of 1857 President James Buchanan, who described Mormons as a 'pestiferous disgusting cancer,' sent an army of 2,500 troops to crush the Mormons, and remove Brigham Young as territorial governor. The conflict became known as the Utah War. Lasting slightly over a year, an uneasy peace was restored. There are some who say that war, along with other battles involving similar issues of faith, are not over."

Maxwell Jackson always amazed Mahoney. He was an encyclopedia of Mormon history and lore, and there was nothing he loved to do more than hold forth on Mormons, past and present. It was a labor of love, scholarship, and a tad of pent up theatrics.

"The issue of polygamy grew and festered. The men and women of Salt Lake called it God's law. The people throughout the rest of the country called it legalized prostitution. Brigham Young had twenty-seven wives, and once said, 'I live above the law.' Here's something I'll bet you don't know, Mahoney. Joseph Smith Jr., also had twenty-seven wives. According to a list compiled by Andrew Jenson, a Utah church historian, not only did Smith have twenty-seven wives, but since Jenson published his list researchers have discovered records showing at least another twenty-one wives sealed to Joseph Smith. The guy had at least forty-eight wives. That pissed off a lot of people, Mahoney."

"So what happened?" Max.

"Tired of being ignored, the federal government, in 1887, seized all Mormon property, including the church's beloved Temple Square. Principles were important to the Mormons of Utah, but their property was holy — sacred. So Wilford Woodruff, the fourth president of the church, had a vision."

"You mean when the pressure's on, the president has a vision?"

"Exactly," said Taylor. "It has always been thus. In the final analysis, the critics say, when the Mormon church is under enough pressure, sooner or later God speaks to the president of the church and the rules change.

"Under incredible pressure to repudiate polygamy, which was basically the threat to statehood, Woodruff, who was church president in 1889, wrote that in the early days of this dispensation, the Lord revealed the principle of plural marriage to the Prophet. After Brigham Young led the saints to the Salt Lake Valley plural marriage was openly taught and practiced until 1890. Conditions were such that the Lord by revelation withdrew the command to continue the practice, and Woodruff issued the *Manifesto* directing that it cease. Within six years Utah was a state.

"It is only practiced today by pockets of Mormon fundamentalists. The vision, or revelation, if you will, is referred to still, by the faithful, as 'The Great Accommodation.' That ought to tell you something."

"Could I have another drink, Max? This story is making me thirsty."

No sooner had Mahoney asked for the refill than his glass was full, and Jackson was off again.

"Then came the 1960's. The civil rights movement saw pickets in front of the Temple demanding equal rights for blacks.

"Blacks had always been denied the priesthood in the Mormon church. They could be members, but they couldn't hold the priesthood — they couldn't reach the highest degrees of heaven. Finally, the public ridicule became too much. No one, other than the Mormons, seemed to believe, as they did, that black skin was the mark of Cain."

"I've always known," Mahoney said, "that Mormons believed black skin was the mark of Cain, but what the hell did they base it on? Why did they believe it for so long?"

"The problem," Jackson continued," is that Mormons believe that by direct revelation Joseph Smith `restored' lost truths in the early Mosaic scriptures. In chapter seven, verses eight and twenty-two, of the Pearl of Great Price, one of the big three of Mormon tracts, the Mormons derive their proof that the mark of Cain is black skin.

"One statement in the Pearl of Great Price states '. . . and there was a blackness came upon all the children of Canaan, that they were despised among all people.' And the second source, also in the Pearl of Great Price states '. . . and they were a mixture of all the seed of Adam save it was the seed of Cain, for the seed of Cain were black, and had not place among them.' And that's it. That's what they based it on. And it lasted nearly 150 years because no one put up a big enough stink to make the church leaders change it.

"Remember, Mahoney, the 1980 census showed that Utah was 90 percent white, with Hispanics, Indians, and Asians, making up most of the other ten percent. Less than two-thirds of one percent were Black. If the same percentages hold today, Utah has a population of 1,700,000 and only 10,000 of them are Black. Think about it. In a Utah football stadium holding 50,000 people, only 300 in the audience would be black. In the state of New York that same football stadium would have nearly 8,000 blacks in it.

Mahoney looked into his empty glass. Jackson took the hint and poured them both another drink.

"Finally, the twelfth president of the church, Spencer W. Kimball, announced in 1978 that God had changed his mind. All worthy male members of the church, black or white, since 1978, may be ordained into the Mormon priesthood without regard for race or color."

"Max, you're not trying to tell me that the killer's black?"

"No, that's just it. There are so damn few ex-Mormons or practicing Mormons that are black the odds against it are overwhelming. If you want to know what I'm really getting at, I think your killer is either — a flunky and works for the church — someone who was kicked out on his ass for reasons he finds embarrassing — someone who knows a lot about the church and really does want $100 million, or — some random nut-case who wants to see his name in headlines and on television."

"Great!" said Mahoney. "Four fuckin' choices! But if you had to go with one, which one would it be?"

"Probably a flunky working in the church."

"Why?"

"Simple. The flunky working for the church would allow access to everything from buildings to documents to the schedules of church leaders. Christ, a clerk in the Church Office Building would have enough raw information to raise hell with the church if he or she wanted to. And you have to combine that with our random nut-case, don't you, Mahoney? Anyone who would kill for sport is a nut by definition."

"Ok, Max," said Mahoney, "but why not the others?"

"A person kicked out of the church probably doesn't care enough to kill for vengeance. A person who wants church money, must be a real idiot. There has to be an easier way to steal a few million dollars than this."

"Ok, Max. What about the woman's angle."

"If the polygamy issue was the Great Accommodation," said Max, "and the black issue was the Great Compromise to avoid ridicule in the '70s, then the women's rights issue is the Great Coverup of the '80s and '90s. The church is still playing ostrich, burying its head in the sands of time. The burning issue in the church today, raging like Dante's Inferno, is women's rights.

"Utah was the second territory to vote for suffrage back in 1870, but it was also the state considered to be the major force behind the defeat of the ERA in several western states. Christ, Tom Brokaw even interviewed Apostle Gorden B. Hinckley and J. Willard Marriott, Jr., of the Marriott Corporation, on the Today Show in April of 1980. Brokaw asked if the church was a major force behind the defeat of the ERA in some of the western states, and Hinckley said, 'I don't know that we have done that.' Hell, he lied! Four months earlier they had excommunicated Sonia Johnson, a Virginia housewife, for her work exposing the church's anti-ERA campaign.

"Back in the 1960s, General Authority Boyd K. Packer was asked about the black priesthood ban at a Boston meeting, and sidestepped that issue explaining that he had a black friend who was disturbed by the church's position. At the end of the meeting Packer turned to the gathering of the faithful and said, and I quote him verbatim, 'If you think this is a problem, the greatest problem the church will face in the coming years will be women.' And that from an apostle!

"This question of women is fundamental to the troubles the church is having now. In 1983 Apostle Neal A. Maxwell gave an interview in which he said, rather forcefully, 'There will be no change regarding women and the priesthood.' Shit, they don't even want to talk about it.

"Now if somebody out there is worried about this issue, it just might be the third straw on his back. One way or the other, for or against, he could think the fabric of his church is being ripped apart."

"But you still prefer the publicity angle linked with the flunky who feels he's been ignored or overlooked?"

"Yup. It's simple, clean, and all too probable."

"Me too."

Jackson poured another drink for both of them. When the two had finished their last drink, Mahoney, laden with several hardback books on the church and its history, left his old friend. He was going to be busy for the next few days.

Thursday: Day Four, Morning

Mouth ringed with powdered sugar, tie speckled with sweet white dust, Mahoney looked through the reports from the men he had assigned legwork on the case. Grant often wondered how a man like Mahoney could look messy and somehow maintain all that dignity. It was another of what Grant had labeled Mahoneyisms. The man, as a man, didn't make sense — and yet there was something about him Grant liked despite the rough edges and foul language.

Most of the team were now calling the case, the Saint Killer, as in, "Got anything new on the Saint Killer?" Unfortunately, nobody had.

Interviews with every witness found in Temple Square who saw the Williamson killing. Nothing. Interviews with everyone else who might have seen someone acting strange or unusual. Nothing. Interviews with gate attendants and tourist personnel. Nothing. Interviews with people just outside the gates when the shooting happened. Nothing. Interviews with personnel at the Hotel Utah Building. Nothing. Task force members viewing the scores of video tapes taken from tourists after the incident. Nothing. Snapshots, thousands of them, sorted by harried workers on overtime. Nothing.

"Grant! Come here!" Mahoney yelled across the day room. Since the assignment of Mahoney and Grant as partners a few months back, there had been no pressing reason to have their desks adjacent to each other. Now Grant's desk was too far away from Mahoney's to make for a convenient work situation. This case changed that. The desk was being moved.

"Would you double check the reports on motel registrations the evening before the killing? Look for anyone who arrived the day before and left within twenty-four hours. Also look for anyone who paid with cash. I don't think we'll find anything, but let's get more guys looking into it. All we got here is registration names, and a bunch of desk clerks saying they don't remember anyone unusual, except for a 400-pound-woman who registered with a midget at Little America. I hardly think they did it."

The man stood by the window in the Tri Arc. He was on the eleventh floor of the thirty-story hotel. It was a marvelous view of the Salt Lake Valley, and he could see the Church Office Building, Temple, and domed Tabernacle in the distance. God he loved this. His stomach tightened with the delight of his own personal vision of the commotion that must be racing through the halls of power in the Church Administration Building. He could feel the tension in the posh trappings of the offices of the First Presidency and the Council of Twelve Apostles.

He knew how they would react. He knew how they thought. This was all beneath them. That's why the television reports had said nothing about the letter and the threat on the lives of these holier-than-thou Latter-day Saints. Saints my ass. They were mortal men who politicked their way into ersatz sainthood. They followed the teachings of a bright but uneducated kid named Joseph Smith Jr., who once said he had received a visit from humanoid space travelers from a planet called 'Kolob.'

He'd get them all, the man thought. He'd get them all.

Mahoney marveled a bit. He realized that in this modern era, in Utah at least, he was being forced to learn more and more about what was the only authentic American church to have really made it. And it made it in a big way, out of the turmoil of religious fervor that engulfed the country in the early and mid-1800s.

Joseph Smith Jr. had told his handful of followers in September of 1823 that an angel of the Lord had visited him several times while he toiled in the fields on a farm in upstate New York. The angel Moroni, Smith claimed, had buried the plates near Smith's home 1,400 years before. The plates contained the written history of an ancient civilization thriving in America, which fell on hard times and vanished, but for a

handful who were the ancestors of the American Indians.
Moroni, the angel, appeared to young Smith again and again
over a three year period. Finally, on September 22, 1827, the
angel gave him golden plates to translate. The plates were
buried on the Hill Cumorah, three miles from Smith's log
cabin.

The gold plates which Smith was able to translate by
using two seer stones called Urim and Thummim, became the
Book of Mormon. Unfortunately for the faithful, when Smith
finished translating the reformed Egyptian characters into
English, Moroni took the plates back. Just like an angel,
thought Mahoney.

On March 26, 1830, 5,000 copies of the Book of Mormon
were published in Palmyra, New York. The book was replete
with grammatical errors and was continually revised. From
its origin, until the present, there have been over 4,000
changes in the wording. Mormons, however, believe the
Book of Mormon is the holiest of books, while the Bible, the
King James Version, is also holy, but a lesser document
nonetheless. The Eighth Article of the LDS church reads,
"We believe the Bible to be the Word of God as far as it is
translated correctly." A great out, thought Mahoney.

In October of 1982, at the General Conference of the
Mormon Church, the General Authorities of the church
announced with almost Hollywoodesque fanfare that a
subtitle was added to the Book of Mormon, the cornerstone
of the faith. From now on it would be called the *Book of
Mormon: Another Testament of Jesus Christ.*

Mahoney spent part of the night reading the Book of
Mormon. He finally gave up after two hours of wading
through its Bible-like verse, and began to read scholarly
works about the document. Much easier, he thought.

Many believed Joseph Smith Jr., was nothing more than
a quack and a con man. Mahoney knew from his own
research that the founding prophet of the church, and self-
styled apostle of God, had once declared that the moon was
inhabited by six-foot-tall people who dressed like Quakers
and lived to be a thousand years old. Mahoney liked that.
Brigham Young, who succeeded Joseph Smith Jr., after
Smith was killed in a riot at the Carthage, Illinois, jail,
believed that the sun was also inhabited. Mahoney liked that

even better.

Despite this propensity for odd thinking, even in the 1800's, Smith's church grew as his missionaries found new converts. In 1840 the Illinois legislature allowed him to build a new settlement that he called Nauvoo. Then, in 1842, Smith had a vision of the Celestial Marriage — that nearly everyone else, including many Mormons, termed polygamy. With every Mormon man given the right to marry ten virgins, public opinion turned against Smith; his baptizing for the dead, which happens to this day in all the temples of the church, added fuel to an already out-of-control fire. In 1844 he announced as a candidate for President of the United States to establish a Kingdom of God on earth, led by him, as Prophet, Priest and King.

Mahoney marveled at the rich tapestry of the church's history. Anti-Mormonism flourished and Smith and his brother Hyrum were arrested and jailed at Carthage, Illinois. On June 27, 1844, the jail was mobbed in a riot of religious hate, and the two men were shot to death. Within three years 148 of the faithful arrived in the Great Salt Lake Valley. Three of them were women.

Mahoney shook his head. Today there are six million members around the world, and Utah is literally full of them.

The man inwardly giggled at the glory of it all. He was finally getting revenge for all those years of being stepped on by the best and the brightest of the faithful. Church leaders were full of bullshit and he knew it. And now he was going to get even.

From personal experience he knew, by heart, the sacred testimony every Mormon learns to say by rote: "I testify to you, I know the Book of Mormon is true. I know Joseph Smith was a prophet of God. I know the Church of Jesus Christ of Latter-day Saints is the only true and living church on the face of the earth."

The man grinned, a full and menacing grin, as he looked at the sun illuminating the six main spires of the Mormon Temple, and the great Tabernacle in Temple Square, only yards from where he had pushed the button that ended the life of one devout Mormon from St. Paul, Minnesota. The sun's gleam was diffused by the constant haze caught in the inversion layers that plague the valley at the foot of the Wasatch Mountains.

The man looked at his watch and felt excitement wash over him as he saw the hour approach 11 a.m. Minutes more, he thought. Minutes more in the life of an apostle of God.

In the hallowed and still halls of the Church Administration Building, long, wide corridors stretched from office to office. In one of the offices sat an apostle of God, oblivious to the threat that someone out there wanted him, or one of his kind, dead. It could not happen to him. Not to one of God's chosen.

Sitting in a deeply tufted leather desk chair of enormous proportions, surrounded by mahogany and brass, and resting on the deepest beige carpet money could buy, Apostle G. A. Fielding leaned back and sighed over the work load of saving souls. He had been in his office for a half-hour and had barely made it through an outline of the upcoming General Session of the April General Conference of the church, scheduled for the beginning of next month.

Things looked fine, he thought. After all, he had seen scores of conference ceremonies just like this in his years as a Saint.

Apostle Fielding was third in line to succession as President, Prophet, Seer, and Revelator, the Mormon equivalent of Pope. This meant that he was third in seniority, since succession came not from being a counselor in the First Presidency, but from the presidency of the Council of Twelve Apostles. The death or succession of two more apostles to the presidency would place him as president of the Council, and thus, next in line to hold the Keys to the Kingdom.

He was beloved by the faithful as being the kindly apostle. He was cherubic in his countenance, and endlessly patient with both the faithful and gentiles alike. As apostles of the church went, he was young, at 68, and well positioned to one day head the church. Those in line before him were well advanced in age. The president was eighty-four, and the three before him in line of succession were seventy-nine, eight-one, and eight-three respectively. There would be a time, the faithful claimed, that this liberal, intellectual, and open man would hold the Keys long enough to see the church into the light of a new, bright, and progressive day.

The eighty-five men who ruled the church were known collectively as General Authorities. G. A. Fielding was, behind his back, never called Gordon Arthur Fielding. He was respectfully called General Authority Fielding, always with a slight smile passing between the faithful over the use of his initials in this way. Fielding was loved more than most of the political conservatives who helped to rule the church. When the respected historian Leonard J. Arrington was appointed head of the church historical department, in 1972, during a short lived spate of church liberalism, openness, and historical accuracy, it was G. A. Fielding who led the fight for his appointment. Ten years later, in 1982, Arrington was fired. The times and leadership had changed. Arrington was too much the accurate researcher, and not enough the Mormon dogmatist. General Authority Fielding led the fight against his dismissal. Never the revisionist, he, like Arrington, who was also a devout Mormon, believed the church could thrive in an era of openness and intellectualism. It was Fielding's belief that the church of today would transcend the mistakes of the past, and the continuing revisionism that plagues its historical documents.

Sitting in the tranquil atmosphere of his office, Apostle Fielding thought about the General Conference of the Church of Jesus Christ of Latter-day Saints. It was held twice a year, and attended by a spill-over crowd of the faithful yearning to hear the new revelations and old rhetoric attesting to the religion's boast of being the "only true and living religion on the face of the earth." It was hard work, he thought, a bit irreverently, but someone has to do it. He was smiling, although he didn't realize it.

At that moment he moved his chair back and reached to open the center drawer of his desk to withdraw his notes and suggestions for additions to the president's speech to the multitudes. At that horrible moment G. A. Fielding, one of the twelve apostles, one of those believed to have the authority of the original twelve, was blown to bits in a fraction of a second. This destructive act against a gentle man was to change the life of every member of the church, its Council of Twelve Apostles, and the First Presidency.

One of their own had gone to Zion to join their founding

prophet.

The man in the Tri Arc could have sworn that he heard
the explosion at precisely 11 a.m. He knew he couldn't have,
but he felt it in his heart, in his brain, and in his stomach. He
heard the sound of death descend on the church and destroy
a saint. Good, he thought, that should stir up some action.

All hell broke loose in the Metropolitan Hall of Justice.
When the call came in to the day room of the Salt Lake City
police department, all Mahoney said was, "Fuck! It's
happened!"

Grant, finally at a desk directly across from Mahoney,
turned ashen. They were out of the building in less than thirty
seconds. This time, Mahoney, thought, the meeting would be
in the Church Administration Building, and the chief of
security, and all his men, would not be able to put things back
together again. The explosion would give them access to the
top-most echelon of the Mormon church. They would no
longer have to deal just with Kimball. Now the church
leaders would have to do what Mahoney said. Or so he
thought.

As Mahoney and Grant arrived at the Church Administration Building, ambulances and police cars were already on
the scene, and the forensic van was screaming to a stop
behind them; the ant-hill activity began.

Mahoney spotted Kimball standing at the front door,
undoubtedly waiting for them, trying desperately to get his
scattered ducks in some sort of a row. Reporter's cars and
television vans were arriving. Police were marking the
exterior with bright yellow "Crime Scene - Do Not Cross"
ribbons, reaching from one column to another surrounding
the entrance. Mahoney ignored Kimball, and Grant mumbled
something to him as he tried to keep up with Mahoney who
was leaving Kimball sputtering behind. Both detectives knew
this would be a very grisly scene. They could already smell
the stench of explosives and scorched human flesh. Faces
were long, and voices strident.

Mahoney stood at the scarred, blackened doorway of the
office and looked at the body of this apostle of the church. He
looked all too mortal with the front of his body torn away,
and part of his chin and face missing. Mahoney could see two

fingers to the left of the desk, leaching drops of blood into the beige carpet. There was black and red and gray all over the wall behind the ravaged chair. The desk top was in splinters. No one outside was asking if the man was dead. Everyone knew.

An initial examination of the crime scene revealed the expected — remnants of a C-4 plastic bomb and a switch. Grant, on Mahoney's instructions was trying to keep Kimball from crawling all over them, while at the same time arrange another meeting. This meeting, Grant said, repeating what Mahoney had told him on their way over, had better be meaningful. It had better include someone directly representing the Council of Twelve Apostles and the First Presidency.

Listening to Grant, Kimball knew it was Mahoney talking, and it made him angry. He found himself wondering how best to shift the blame for this incident to Mahoney and the Salt Lake City police department.

Warren Kimball loved his job. I'll be damned, he thought, if I am going to let some glorified, local flatfoot, a gentile to boot, point his finger at me. Kimball was in charge of an office of over a hundred "operatives," his favorite word for every security officer, mercenary, thug, or night watchman. To Kimball they were all investigators, members of what Kimball thought of, privately, as his personal troop of Danites. Mahoney knew about the Danites.

In the early days of the church, there were attacks against Mormons in general, and Joseph Smith in particular. Hundreds of Mormons were killed for their beliefs and practices. Yet there was also great unrest within the ranks of the faithful as the Mormon camp moved west in search of the Promised Land.

Leaving New York, the Prophet Smith led his Saints to Ohio, then Missouri, then Illinois, hoping to find a suitable gathering place for the faithful. The internal strife increased as they moved, and dissidents from inside the ranks fast became the greatest threat to the religion's survival. To quash dissent, a few Saints very close to Joseph Smith formed a most secret society to kill those who challenged the authority of the Prophet. They called themselves the Danites.

A half century later, a young man, still in school, named Arthur Conan Doyle, began a series of detective stories that would become preeminent in the genre. He created a brilliant, but decidedly odd, detective — Sherlock Holmes. In the first of the Holmes stories, *A Study in Scarlet*, Doyle has Holmes meet Dr. Watson, who becomes his chronicler and friend. In their first adventure Dr. Watson relates being confronted by the sinister and murderous Danites. Sir Arthur Conan Doyle writes, as Dr. Watson, "Belated wanderers upon the mountains spoke of gangs of armed men, masked, stealthy, and noiseless, who flitted by them in the darkness. These tales and rumors took substance and shape, and were corroborated and re-corroborated, until they resolved themselves into a definite name. To this day, in the lonely ranches of the West, the name of the Danite Band, or the Avenging Angles, is a sinister and an ill-omened one."

The history of the Mormon's early years is filled with the terror of Danite intimidations, raids, and assassinations of those who spoke against the Prophet Joseph Smith Jr.

Thursday: Day Four, Afternoon

Kimball, being a devout Mormon, had always fancied himself as the leader of the modern Danites, although it was a fantasy he kept to himself. A faithful Mormon did not say the word 'Danite' out loud. Nevertheless, at least half the security force he had assembled and trained were fashioned with that in mind. They were his own personal goon squad. They were the bodyguards and crowd control at the General Conferences of the church; they were the chauffeurs and escorts to the top echelon of the church leadership; they were faithful and loyal to a fault. Kimball had trained them, and disciplined them, and promoted them. They were his.

Now, Kimball stood in the office of the First Presidency's Second Counselor, literally having been called on the rich beige carpet, in a separate section of the Church Administration Building. He had provided guards for the First Presidency, exchanged polite nods and good-days with them in passing, but this was the first time he stood before a member of the First Presidency to answer for a massive breech in security. He could feel sweat running down his side just under his right armpit.

"Brother Kimball," the Second Counselor said without even the hint of an understanding tone, "What in Heaven's name is happening, and just what are you doing about it?"

Somehow, Kimball didn't expect the question to be so blunt, the manner so direct. It was his understanding that these men were above everything secular, and neither asked nor answered direct questions without preambles of faith and eternal salvation. So much for that. Kimball took a breath that was a bit too deep, and answered.

"Sir, I understand there has been a death threat found by the Salt Lake City police department in connection with the shooting of the man in Temple Square on Monday. We were led to believe that the shooting was an isolated case, and that the threat against the church leaders was the raving of an amateur and a madman. My men and I met with the detectives handling the case and were assured that everything was under control. I posted additional guards, unobtrusively, throughout the grounds and at the entrances of all our key buildings and offices. No one entered or left who was suspicious, or not known to us, without being detained and questioned by me. No one could have planted a bomb in this building since the killing in Temple Square. I am at a loss, Sir, as to how this happened. We are, however, redoubling our efforts to provide air-tight security from this point forward. And we will have answers to this tragedy very soon."

The surface of Kimball's upper lip was so wet with sweat that there was little semblance of control left in his otherwise military bearing. Kimball was afraid.

"Brother Kimball," said the Second Counselor, "did you or your men take any notes of the conversation during your meeting with the detectives?"

"No, Sir, no notes," replied Kimball, ramrod stiff, and increasingly uncomfortable, parboiling in his own juices. "The meeting was a preliminary fact-finding session to determine the seriousness of the threat."

"Well, Brother Kimball, it certainly appears to be pretty damn serious doesn't it?" The Second Counselor was almost shouting.

Kimball had never heard a member of the First Presidency swear before. Somehow it pleased him. It seemed appropriate. It seemed human.

"Yes, Sir," Kimball said. "It is serious and we are treating it as a full-fledged emergency attack on the church and its authorities."

"I suggest," said the Second Counselor, "that you take one more look into that bombed out office, and at the dead body of our beloved Brother Fielding, to see just how serious it is. If you cannot stop this carnage immediately, and assure us all of our safety, you will not be the head of church security for very long. Do you understand?"

"Yes." Try as he might Kimball couldn't swallow.

"Then listen to me closely. This is not the kind of trouble

we can pray away, although believe me we shall try. It is the kind of trouble that must stop now! I want you to have those detectives, and your best men, in this office in one hour with a plan of action on how this threat is to be eliminated. We want the killer. We want him now. I will see you all in exactly one hour. Now get out of here."

Kimball now knew exactly what the expression, "With your tail between your legs," meant. He would be walking funny for some time. It actually felt as if his pants were full.

Mahoney was still questioning workers in the Church Administration Building when Grant appeared and told him that Kimball wanted a meeting in the office of the Second Counselor of the First Presidency in less than an hour. Grant seemed impressed and excited, much to Mahoney's chagrin.

"For God's sake, Heber, don't treat this like you're getting an audience with the Pope. That meeting sure and hell wasn't called by Kimball, since his ass is up for grabs in this thing. And speaking of asses, you can bet Kimball is trying to cover his at the expense of ours."

"I just meant that they are finally going to get off the dime and cooperate on this thing."

"Jesus Christ Almighty, Heber," Mahoney was spitting out the words, "you've been on this police force long enough to know how the system works. They're not going to be wrong. We are going to be wrong. They are going to be the good guys. We're going to be the bad guys. Don't you see? We should have prevented this! We had the killing, we had the letter, we had the goddamn plan of attack, we had the target identified within a finite group of a dozen or so, and we had the time frame. Now all we have is one dead apostle, and a blown-to-hell office smack in the middle of the Church Administration Building. Worst of all it happened not fifty yards from the President, Prophet, Seer, and Whatever of this fuckin' church."

As Mahoney and Grant were shown into the office of the Second Counselor, Mahoney was disgusted and Grant was in heaven. He had never been in the close presence of a member of the First Presidency before.

Seated behind a massive desk was a silver-haired man looking for all the world like the CEO of a major automobile company. Seated on chairs to the side of his desk were

Kimball and the four-horsemen. Three more chairs were
directly in front of the desk, but placed so far back that it
seemed to signify an area where only untouchables sat. The
guide gestured toward them, and then disappeared in a way
Mahoney was becoming used to. Mahoney and Grant sat
down leaving the single chair to their right empty. Who is
that for? Mahoney thought. No one was saying anything —
waiting, it appeared, for the silver-haired Second Counselor
to the Prophet to start the meeting. No coffee, no small-talk,
no donuts.

No sooner had Mahoney wondered about who the third
chair was for than he got his answer. The door opened and in
walked the chief of police. Jesus Christ, thought Mahoney,
they summoned him to the hanging.

"Now, gentlemen," said old silver-hair, "I would like to
know how it came to pass that an apostle of this great Church
could be murdered in these offices and you were unable to
stop it even though you had been warned it would happen?"

Mahoney stood bolt upright.

"I'll answer that," he said. "Starting with Mr. Williamson,
we had nothing more than a . . ."

"Who is Mr. Williamson?" asked silver-hair.

Mahoney looked at Grant, Grant looked at Mahoney, both
of them looked at the chief, and the chief didn't look an
anybody.

"My God," said Mahoney, "haven't your security men
told you anything?"

"Now, just a minute," said Kimball, but he was silenced
with a wave of the hand by the Second Counselor.

Mahoney said, "Mr. Williamson was the man killed in
Temple Square on Monday. He was a Mormon on vacation
here with his family."

"He was a Mormon?" the Second Counselor asked of
Kimball.

Kimball nodded in a most sheepish manner.

"Go on," said silver-hair, nodding at Mahoney who's expression dripped with disgust.

"Starting with Mr. Williamson, we had nothing more than
a random killing by someone from a window in the Hotel
Utah Building. We found the room, broke in, and found the
letter."

"What letter?" Silver-hair again.

Mahoney stole a quick glance at Kimball and changed his tactics.

"We would be saving a whole lot of time had you read the transcript of the meeting we had with Mr. Kimball and his men," said Mahoney.

Mahoney was waiting for, "What transcript?" But the room was silent. Silver-hair didn't even glance at Kimball; he didn't take his eyes off Mahoney.

"I see," said Mahoney, pausing long enough to make his point. "We met with church security and informed them of the situation, and our fears that the gunman would strike again, mostly by some other means, and directly at an apostle of the Council of Twelve. We predicted that it would happen within forty-eight hours or less. As it happened, the bombing took place in this building less than twenty hours later. We offered our services and manpower as guards and bodyguards for the First Presidency and Council of Twelve Apostles. Our men, however, were deployed differently than our initial instructions to them, by Mr. Kimball's office. We were relying on your cooperation here since we had nothing to go on in the way of leads from the shooting of Mr. Williamson.

"We also were told by your security office that they didn't want our help or interference. We were told that church security would handle it."

Glances went from silver-hair to Brother Kimball. Kimball was avoiding as much eye contact as possible.

"We requested a meeting with the First Presidency," continued Mahoney, "and expressed our concern for the urgency of the matter. We assured your people that unless an all out effort was made by top church officials nothing could be done to avoid the loss of at least one more life, and that life would undoubtedly be a member of the Council of Twelve Apostles. We were assured that church security was handling the protection of the church leaders. We were told in no uncertain terms that church security would determine the plan of attack and the proper method of informing the leadership of the church. Apparently, that was not done. We were told that the proceedings were taped, and that the leadership of the church would receive copies. We were perfunctorily dismissed and sent on our way."

Oh, shit, thought Grant, surprised that he had mentally uttered that phrase. Oh, well, he thought, it is only my job, my church reputation, my life, and my future.

"What do you have to say about this," said silver-hair, looking directly at Kimball.

"Detectives Mahoney and Grant met with me and my four lieutenants," Mahoney cringed, "and outlined the facts surrounding the killing of the man in — of Brother Williamson — and discussed the letter setting forth the threats to the church leaders. He assured us it was the ramblings of a crank and that it was well under control through their office."

At this point Mahoney was one pissed off policeman, and Grant was sinking into a slump of self-pity.

"Why," said silver-hair, "weren't we apprised of this letter containing the threats?"

Kimball jumped to answer.

"But, Sir, you were. I sent copies to the office of the First Presidency shortly after we received them, along with a memo from me indicating that church security would double efforts at protection and surveillance. As you know, Sir, all threats or crank letters coming to the church are routinely sent to my office. We review them, take action, and send a copy to your office, along with an action memo from me."

Kimball was beginning to sense a reprieve, and began to adopt his former smug attitude.

The Second Counselor rose from his desk and walked out of the room without saying a word. He left the door open. Mahoney looked at Kimball, and Kimball looked at Mahoney just in time to see Mahoney mouth the word, "asshole," directly at him. Grant was dying in his seat.

Two minutes later silver-hair reentered the room with two sheets of paper in his hand; one was the memo from Kimball, and the other was a photocopy of the threatening letter signed Moroni Goldblum. Silver-hair sat and read both documents carefully, then reread parts of both pages.

"Continue," was all he said.

Not knowing who he meant should continue, everyone seemed to sit transfixed. Mahoney jumped in.

"We told Kimball that it was the work of a professional, a Mormon or ex-Mormon, and that the threats were serious. We then told him that . . . "

"Exactly what did you tell Brother Kimball about those things?" the Second Counselor asked.

Mahoney was fuming now and near the end of his patience.

"The first thing I told him, Sir, when we entered the room, was that I didn't want to have to repeat all this again and again as we climbed up the ladder of authority in the church. He assured me he would be the judge of who should know what, and when they should know it."

"Is this true, Brother Kimball?" Silver-hair sounded somewhat miffed.

"In a way, Sir. And as you see I did take steps to inform you of the situation and send you a copy of the letter."

"Continue," said silver-hair. His tone a bit cooler.

"I would like to say something." The impact of that phrase, coming from the chief of police, was hard to describe. The room filled with a new tension neither Mahoney nor Grant had really expected.

"I spoke with Detective Mahoney immediately after his visit to the Church Office Building. He informed me, and several of my key men, of his complete conversation with Mr. Kimball. What he says is true; he did request the cooperation of the highest authorities of the church, and of the security office; he did predict the killing of an apostle of the church within 48-hours of that meeting if such steps were not implemented. What he says is what happened."

God bless the chief, Mahoney thought. He always did have a way of sticking to the point and cutting through the bullshit.

"Chief," said silver-hair, obviously distressed and hovering around angry, "if you are implying that Brother Kimball is lying, I will not stand for that. Brother Kimball is a devout Mormon who has been in our employ some time, and has saved our church untold misery through his devoted service. I believe that you may be trying to save the reputation of the police in a somewhat tardy attempt to contain a situation that is obviously out of control."

Tardy my ass, thought Mahoney.

"You are mistaken," the chief said in the most controlled tone of voice Mahoney and Grant had ever heard him use.

"Detective Mahoney is a Catholic and an honest man to a fault. He has been on the police force for nearly twenty

years, and in all that time I have never known him to lie. He
bends the rules from time to time, has personal habits you and
I might not approve of, and he can be disrespectful and
discourteous. But he cannot be dishonest. It may not be his
Catholic upbringing that assures me of this. It may not be his
track record that fully convinces me. But it is his character
that I respect. It is his character that assures me he is not lying
to you, nor was he lying to me when he briefed me on the
events at the meeting with Mr. Kimball.

"And if you have further doubts," continued the chief,
"and refuse to take his word for it over the word of Mr.
Kimball, I would like to add that I am also a devout Mormon,
as you may well know, and I say he is telling the truth."

Three cheers, Mahoney thought. No wonder this guy gets
the big bucks. And none of this Brother Kimball shit, to boot.

"W-e-l-l," silver-hair sounded for all the world like
Ronald Reagan talking to the press corps, "we seem to have
a Mexican standoff."

Mahoney cringed again. Mormons, he thought, are often
racially intolerant, elitist, and very insensitive in their manner
of speaking about race. And this one is sitting near the top of
the goddamn heap.

"Then let's break the standoff," said the chief.

Everyone's face showed anticipation at that remark. No
one spoke. Everyone waited for the chief to explain himself.
It didn't take long — a few seconds at most. It felt like an
hour.

"You put much stock in Mormon truthfulness, and
although I have assured you, as police chief, and as a devout
Mormon, that I know Mahoney is telling the truth, I wasn't in
that meeting. But another Mormon was. Detective Grant is
as good a Mormon as there is. If you doubt that you might
examine his record with the church and with his own Bishop.
His arrest and conviction record isn't as impressive as
Detective Mahoney's, but he is younger, and in time, may
well become the chief of police. He is that good. And, he is
honest. Also, to a fault.

"Detective Grant, you were in that room. What
happened?"

When the chief started his speech, and at the first mention
of Grant's name, Grant knew exactly where the chief was
going. Visions of his name being crossed off every church

record by a silver-haired member of the First Presidency danced in the back of his brain. He was caught between a religious rock and a departmental hard place. Jump in, he could hear Mahoney thinking, the mud's fine.

"Chief, ah, Sir, I can only say that what Detective Mahoney has told you here is the truth. I was there. What Mr. Kimball has said is not true. And upon leaving the meeting, Detective Mahoney specifically asked if the meeting had been recorded, and Mr. Kimball said yes. Detective Mahoney asked where the microphone was, and Mr. Kimball said there were several of them. And that was the end of the meeting. I suggest you ask Mr. Kimball to produce the tape of the meeting if you need further proof of Detective Mahoney's statements."

Good God, thought Mahoney, the kid's all right. He's got balls, and they're golden. He had played Mahoney's trump card before Mahoney could.

Silver-hair didn't move. He just reread the documents and sat thinking, eyes closed, eyes open, eyes closed. Finally he spoke again. Tellingly, he never even glanced at Kimball. Kimball was looking at the carpet.

"Detective Mahoney, could you please take the time to restate why you think the man is a professional type killer, and why you think he is an ex-Mormon? I will not entertain the idea that he may be a Mormon. That would be impossible considering what happened here earlier today. No Mormon would kill an apostle of the church."

Kimball was at least three inches shorter in his chair than he was when the chief had started the ball rolling directly at him.

"Well, Sir, what I told Kimball and the four, ah — the other four gentlemen — the man who shot Mr. Williamson planned it meticulously, and left no evidence as to whom he might be. He is ruthless, as evidenced by the fact that he killed a stranger for no reason other than to get our undivided attention. There are no leads of any value from the paper he used, the typewriter he used, or the envelope in which the letter was found. No prints on those. None on the weapon or the ammunition casing. I believe he is a Mormon or ex-Mormon because of the correct usage of all of the terminology referring to the church, including capitalization and punctuation. His primary task seems to center on disrupting and destroying as much of the church as he can by killing members of the First Presidency and the Council of Twelve Apostles. I think the money is a distant motive, or entirely irrelevant to him. It is just part of the game he is playing with you and the church. I don't think he wants money. I do think he wants publicity. However, I think he wants to kill the Mormon leadership even more. The fact that he signed the letter Moroni Goldblum indicates that he is playing a game, and that by using the angel Moroni's name in conjunction with an obvious Jewish surname he is poking fun at the church and its continuing rift with Jews over the terms *Zion* and *gentile*. After all most Jews find it rather funny that Mormons call Utah the land of Zion."

Silver-hair didn't find it funny.

Mahoney didn't think he would.

"The name Moroni Goldblum might be his way of saying he is a Mormon. Though he may be saying that traditionally, Moroni, or Goldblum, would not be the name of a Gentile in either the Mormon culture or the Jewish culture. Therefore, he's not a gentile. If he is not a gentile, by Mormon usage, he is a Mormon. There might also be some backhanded pun in the word *Gold* as part of Goldblum, that has something to do with ridiculing the golden plates Joseph Smith is said to have translated."

As Mahoney said that last sentence everyone could see old silver-hair squirm in his chair. Even Grant felt the stress of saying, directly in front of a member of the First Presidency, that the translation of the golden plates might be less than fact.

At that moment, Mahoney wished he could have taken back that last sentence and excluded the "said to have" phrase. Damn.

Kimball held out a glimmer of hope at Mahoney's gaff in the presence of a member of the First Presidency. But the glimmer faded fast when the Second Counselor spoke again.

"Detective Mahoney," said silver-hair, "I appreciate your candor and your concern over this matter. It is possible that we have underestimated our ability to cope with this matter internally. Of course, we would like your help as long as you understand that we must serve God before man. Exactly what do you want us to do?"

Brother Kimball heard the gates of heaven slam shut.

Friday: Day Five, Morning

"Mahoney," said the chief, "exactly where the hell are we? And what kind of arrangements have you made with the church security office and the church leaders?"

Mahoney was picking at his fingernails mulling over what he had to tell the chief. There wasn't much new to add. Grant sat by Mahoney's side trying not to look into the chief's eyes any more than necessary.

On the chief's desk, in stepped formation to reveal their headlines, lay copies of both the *Salt Lake Tribute* and the *Deseret News*, both special editions that hit the street not three hours after the bombing. Although the *Tribune* was a morning paper, and the *News* an evening paper, both had managed special editions by virtue of extensive files of pre-written obituaries and feature stories on every member of the General Authorities of the Mormon church. There were primary obituaries, past feature stories, and sidebars of every kind, including ones on G. A. Fielding's family history and the impact of his life on Mormon doctrine and the growth of the church.

The headline in the *Tribune* read: "Mormon Apostle Killed by Bomb." A sub-head read, "G. A. Fielding Victim of Unknown Bomber in Church Administration Building."

The headline in the *News* read: "Apostle G. A. Fielding Dead at Age 78." A sub-head read, "Beloved Apostle Dies in Explosion."

The State of Utah, and the lives of six million faithful throughout the world, were shaken to the core.

"Well?" asked the chief, making no effort to cover up his irritation. Grant squirmed.

"Look, Chief," said Mahoney, "you have everything we have.

No one has been able to identify anybody in the pictures as standing out from the crowd. In other words, everyone looks like a fuckin' tourist. The snapshots are useless since most pictures on every roll are not of Temple Square. They are full of Aunt Marthas and snot-nosed kids, and were taken with cheap cameras by amateur photographers in front of the fountains in the ZCMI mall. The videos we have are so full of zooming-in and zooming-out that you get motion sickness watching them. Our people initially screened the stuff looking for a loner, standing apart from groups, looking odd, or crazed, or fanatical. Nothing doing. The three or four solitary types we traced through the film can't be identified even by the person owning the film. The only persons they can identify are people in their own group. Makes sense. They have no idea who anyone else in the area is. But we're still working on it. I've got them trying to ask the owners of the film to point out someone near them who doesn't belong to the group, just in case this guy was smart enough to puppy up, pretending to be part of them.

"One other thing, Chief, there is no reason why this guy would actually have to be in Temple Square when the rifle went off. It is just as logical, maybe more logical, to assume he was in some other building looking out a window when he pushed that remote button. That's the safe way to do something like this."

As he said that, Mahoney looked puzzled, and his brow wrinkled.

"What?", asked the chief, a bit more loudly than necessary in the small office. The chief wasn't known for being soft-spoken on his own turf.

"Well," answered Mahoney, "I really don't think he was anywhere other than Temple Square. I think he wanted a personal view of the victim. I think he wanted to see the victim's face. I think he wanted to be close enough to feel what he did. To savor it. To make sure.

"We'll keep looking, Chief, but I wouldn't expect any miracles from the Kodak boys."

"Okay, then," said the chief, "where do you expect the miracles to come from? We've got a building full of prophets of God. We ought to be able to come up with one small miracle. Ah . . . don't tell anyone I said that."

There was a pause, and the three laughed. It was the first time for quite a while. It would be the last time for even longer.

The chief continued:

"Are we getting any significant help yet from the church and the First Presidency, or for that matter from that idiot Kimball?"

Mahoney looked at Grant and nodded almost imperceptibly. For a moment Grant was dumbstruck. He had no idea what Mahoney wanted — and then it hit him. Mahoney picked this, of all times, to let Grant get his feet wet as the heretofore non-speaking member of this team. Better in front of the chief, he thought, than looking like an idiot before the living apostles of his own church. Hardly missing a beat, Grant jumped in with both feet, trying desperately to keep them out of his mouth.

"Chief," said Grant, his voice a hair away from cracking, "we know we're not wanted in the church security office, by Kimball, or by his staff. Yet we have the reluctant cooperation of his boss, the Second Counselor. The boys on the task force have started calling him 'Number Two,' by the way. It saves time and confusion."

Grant's voice showed some strain at this last remark, but the chief looked sympathetic. The boy's all right, thought the chief. A bit young. A little stiff. But for a cop he shows promise. Mahoney, his face a deadpan blank, just looked at the two men and slightly shook his head. Mormons, he thought, I'm sur- rounded by Mormons.

Grant continued his non-voluntary report to the chief.

"Kimball has been a bit more cooperative since Number Two," again, a slight pause, "offered his cooperation to the police. Just before we left his office, Number Two reached into his desk file drawer and gave us a printout several pages long. He said it was a list of all security personnel working for the church. He wouldn't let us take the printout, but said we could take notes. I made a lotta notes. When he gave us the printout Kimball nearly had a stroke. Kimball sputtered something about 'clearances' before Number Two silenced him with a wave of his hand.

"There are a score, or more, of uniformed security guards floating around the Temple, the Temple Grounds, and various church buildings. They are readily identifiable. But, in addition, and much more important, the report indicated that there are over a hundred armed security agents, all plain clothes we believe, assigned to the First Presidency and the General Authority. Half these are assigned to the Church Administration Building and the specific protection of the president, two counselors, and the Council of Twelve Apostles. We don't have names, only 'agent designations,' that is to say the printout lists Agent 1, Agent 2, and so on. There are some rather cryptic remarks after each agents name, undoubtedly code, that the security office won't comment on."

"Grant," said the chief, "this is all well and good. I'm glad you got some degree of cooperation started with this man. But for the life of me, I can't see where you're going with this. Just what difference does it make whether or not you have a list of the security personnel. You both might be better off trying to catch this killer, rather than play who's who with the church personnel records. Don't you think?"

This was hard for Grant, but he was into it, and Mahoney was looking at him as if this were a test. He pushed ahead:

"Sir, I think getting to the bottom of what this list is all about might just help us find the killer. Both Detective Mahoney and I have gone over this a lot, and we keep coming back to the same conclusion: we think the killer may be a member of the church security force."

"Explain." The chief was, as usual, to the point.

"Well . . . the killing in Temple Square could have been done by anyone. But the killing of the apostle in his own office, smack in the middle of the Church Administration Building, had to be done by an insider. Unless, of course, we are dealing with an international hit man who also happens to know a great deal about the church, looks like a Mormon, acts like a Mormon, and can convince almost anyone he contacts that he is a Mormon. And that isn't likely. We think the killer is a Mormon, or an ex-Mormon with a gripe. But we don't think he is a professional, in the terrorist sense of the word. He is highly motivated, very intelligent, and obsessed with the church.

"He could have killed Mr. Williamson in Temple Square without any fear of church security, or of being caught. The bombing, however, is a different story. Detective Mahoney believes, and I agree, that the bomb in the apostle's office had been planted there before the killing in Temple Square took place. It is the only answer that makes any sense. And if it's the only answer, it is an inside job."

"Give me your reasons," said the chief.

"Well . . . church security doubled their guard only minutes after the shooting took place. I give them this; from what Kimball did say, he wasted no time in sealing off the offices and effectively shutting down all access to the First Presidency and the Council of Twelve Apostles. We know that these security guys are pretty right-wing, and all have some background in either the FBI, military police, or Army Special Forces. Only the uniformed security cops seem to be drawn from the ranks of traditional police forces. So, they may be rigid, but they are not dumb. They do their job, sometimes too well."

Mahoney interrupted:

"If the perimeter of the Church Administration Building was shut down tight immediately after the shooting, and we know it was because our own men couldn't get in at first, we don't think an ex-Mormon or anti-Mormon zealot could have either. We know from the Mormon bombings in the Mark Hofmann murder and forgery case in 1985, that church security began to sweep their facilities almost daily for electronic devices and bombs of all sorts. The church leaders were terrified after Steve Christensen and Kathy Sheets were killed with pipe bombs, and Mark Hofmann, himself, was severely wounded, all within two days, that the church was the ultimate target.

"You may remember that when Hofmann was accidentally injured by one of his own bombs, everyone started to put two and two together. The church had bought, or received, several controversial Mormon historical documents from both Christensen and Hofmann. Hofmann had been selling scores of documents to Hugh Pinnock, a General Authority of the church, bypassing the church historian's office. Several people thought Hugh Pinnock was the next target of the bomber. And after that, who knows, maybe even the president himself."

This time it was Grant who interrupted. He was getting

bolder by the moment, Mahoney thought.

"We know," said Grant, "that the electronic sweepings and the sniffing dogs did not last long after Hofmann was con victed and the case ended. But they did not stop the process altogether. We know from informants that the facilities are still checked once a week for bugs, other electronic devices, and, we presume, bombs. That's why we have paid so much attention to this list of names. We think the codes behind the agent's designations may tell us something about who these men are, who has the best access, and, maybe, who's background would fit our killer. It is obvious that the church isn't going to give us this information voluntary. And I think I have discovered what the code means."

"What makes you think so," said the chief.

"It's complicated, but let me give you just one example," Grant said referring to his notes, "Agents 1 through 9 have the following code words after their designation: TRIAD ALPHA-OMEGA GARMENT ATONEMENT. Agents 1 through 3 have the additional phrase 'NEPHI I' added; Agents 4 through 6 have the additional phrase 'NEPHI II' added; and Agents 7 through 9 have the additional word 'JACOB' added. May I continue?" asked Grant.

"Please do," said the chief, "but I don't know what the hell good this is doing us."

Mahoney interrupted again.

"Chief," he said, "this is not only interesting, but I think it is critical to our understanding of how the church security force is organized. Grant spent nearly all night on this and I think he's made some important progress. I'd like you to hear this."

"Shoot," said the chief.

Grant didn't smile, but inside he felt like shouting hooray. For the first time since he and Mahoney were teamed up, Mahoney actually paid him a compliment. And directly to the chief, to boot.

"To continue," Grant said, a bit formally for Mahoney's taste, "Agents 10 through 33 have the following code words, some different from the preceding nine, after their designation: QUORUM DUPLEX GARMENT ATONEMENT FAITHFUL. These twenty-four agents do not have any additional code words behind the initial set.

"And finally," Grant continued, "Agents 34 through 50 have the following code words after their designations: ISRAEL ASSIGN-REQUEST GARMENT AGENCY. There are no additional words behind these. The remaining Agents 51 through 108 have routine designations behind their code, such as TEMPLE, or TABERNACLE, or GROUNDS 1, GROUNDS 2, or GROUNDS 3, for example, and are most likely the ones assigned to patrol, in plain clothes, sections of the Temple Grounds, the Tabernacle, and so forth. The last group is a straightforward list of some twenty-three uniformed security guards posted at entrances, and in lobbies, for example. They are simply designated GUARD 1, GUARD 2, and so on, with POST 3, or POST 6, for example, listed next to them."

"Okay, I've listened, Grant," said the chief, "but all I've heard is gobbledegook about AGENT this and ISRAEL that. What does it mean?"

Mahoney nodded at Grant once again, not unlike a father giving his eight-year-old-son a barely noticed sign of approval that he could speak at the table.

"Sir, all we ever see are the uniformed security guards here and there on the Temple Grounds or when the General Conference is in session. Actually, they have a small army and I believe the church is prepared to defend the lives of its prophets and apostles with deadly force."

Grant was cooking now.

"I have gone through a lot of variations to get to this point, and I rejected most of them. The interpretation that stuck is, I believe, very close to the truth.

Mahoney couldn't help but think, again, of the Mormon church's Eighth Article of Faith, "We believe the Bible to be the word of God as far as it is translated correctly." He found himself hoping that Grant had found the right translation of the cryptic printout. He thought he had.

"I actually worked from the bottom up, but I'll give this to you from the top down. The first nine agents all have the designation TRIAD ALPHA-OMEGA GARMENT ATONE-MENT.

"TRIAD means the First Presidency. That's obviously code for the President and the First and Second Counselors

Thus, the first nine agents are assigned to them to provide protection.

"ALPHA-OMEGA," continued Grant, "as we all know, are the first and last letters of the Greek alphabet, meaning from beginning to the end, or from start to finish. It designates total protection around the clock. One full time guard for each member of the three members of the First Presidency, twenty-four hours a day. Three guards, three shifts. Nine guards in all.

"GARMENT, I believe, is a reference to the protective quality inherent in the Mormon Temple garments worn by the faithful."

"I wear Temple garments Grant, I know what they are," said the chief. "But, I can't take any more of this on an empty stomach. I have a command performance with the mayor over chicken-pot-pie at his favorite restaurant, and the damn place is forty minutes away from here. You think he could eat across the street like the rest of us. Let's pick this up again after lunch. And Grant, I trust you will get right to the point when we meet again."

"Yes, Sir!" said Grant, a bit too eagerly. Mahoney, nevertheless, was proud of what Grant had done, especially since Grant probably did it without a drink all night.

Friday: Day Five, Afternoon

Mahoney and Grant sat in the chief's office waiting for him to return. They had gone across the street to a greasy spoon and had meat loaf. The meat loaf was gray. Mahoney noticed that Grant kept covering each piece he ate with a coating of dark brown gravy. Smart move.

When the men returned they checked with other members of the task force and to their disappointment discovered that they were all in the same leaky boat. Nobody had shit.

When the chief arrived he had a round dark spot on his beige tie that looked suspiciously like a crusted over stain from a chicken-pot-pie. Mahoney wondered if he should mention it.

As the chief sat down he said, "I pushed my fork into that damned chicken-pot-pie and the thing spit at me. Landed on my tie. Either of you guys got any cleaning fluid?"

Grant nodded, said something unintelligible, and rushed out of the room. Mahoney closed his eyes to keep from rolling them in front of the chief. A minute later Grant came back with some stuff in a spray can. He aimed it at the chief's grease-spot and pushed the button. A massive wet spot spread over the chief's tie from side to side, reaching the proportions of a silver dollar. The stuff started to dry immediately and began to turn chalk white.

"Geeze, what the hell's that?" asked the chief, staring down his nose at his tie.

"It's good stuff, Chief. It'll get the spot right out. It just has to dry and then we'll brush it off and the spot will be gone."

"I should hope so. You ever used this stuff before?"

Grant looked pale. "Well, no. But they tell me it works, so I bought a can about six months ago and put it in my desk just in case."

71

"You mean you haven't spilled anything on yourself in six months?"

Grant appeared to slink back to his seat in front of the chief's desk, and nodded. The chief just kept looking down at his tie. Mahoney found himself thinking that the tie was one of the ugliest ties he had ever seen. It actually looked better with Grant's big white fuzzy dot drying in the center.

"Garments!"

Grant almost jumped. "What?"

"Garments, you were talking garments."

"Right."

Mahoney recalled from an underground tract he had read on the 'secret' Temple ceremonies of the Mormon church, that Temple patrons, as they are called by the church, are "washed" and "anointed" with oil in preparation for the "Garment of the Holy Priesthood." Fashioned like long-johns, with shorter sleeves and legs, they are dotted with secret markings taken from ritual Masonic robes and sewn into the cloth. Joseph Smith had been a Mason. Part of the Temple ceremony's instructions state that the garments are to be worn twenty-four-hours a day for the rest of the saint's mortal life. A Temple worker, during the anointing and washing period, states, "Inasmuch as you do not defile it, but are true and faithful to your covenants, it will be a shield and a protection to you against the power of the destroyer until you have finished your work here on earth."

Grant continued:

"I had explained that the first nine agents all had TRIAD ALPHA-OMEGA GARMENT ATONEMENT behind their designations. We had finished with TRIAD and . . ."

"Yeah, yeah," said the chief, "get on with the garment stuff. I remember."

"Well, GARMENT is simply code for protection from a destroyer," Grant continued. "They are to receive protection.

"ATONEMENT would be the code word for deadly force to protect these men. From the use of that particular code word I think they are grimly seriously about this. I don't think this is a defensive posture by these security men. I think they may be extremely faithful *Dirty Harrys* willing to blow someone away who gets too close to one of these three men."

The doctrine of Blood Atonement was something

Mahoney knew Mormon leaders did not like talking about. The doctrine held that some sins, such as murder, were so reprehensible that only the spilling of the sinner's blood could atone for his or her sins and enable them to join Joseph Smith Jr., in the Celestial Kingdom. Most of them denied it had ever happened, but the history books were full of references to it, and its practice was widespread in the early years of the church. Some knew that among fundamentalists the doctrine was very much alive in Utah.

Blood Atonement was a doctrine taught by Brigham Young and other church leaders in the nineteenth-century. Brigham Young's Danites and Avenging Angels were part of the Blood Atonement practice. Utah is still studded with fundamentalist groups whose members occasionally murder under the guise of the doctrine. Even Joseph Smith, Jr., the founding prophet, at one point declared that the punishment for dissent in his church was death.

Blood Atonement didn't just require that a dissenter be killed. It required that blood be spilled. The doctrine in its original form required that the victim's throat be cut from ear to ear, the tongue be torn out by its roots, the breast cut open and the heart and vitals torn from the body, for birds and animals to eat, and that the body be cut "asunder" and the bowels allowed to gush out. Murder, adultery, theft, miscegenation, breaking covenants, lying, counterfeiting, leaving the church, or condemning Joseph Smith, his church, or any of the church's leaders all required that a man be killed in this manner in order to be saved.

In the early days of Salt Lake City's construction boom, builders and contractors were often digging up skeletons. They were not in cemeteries. They had no coffins. They had been buried in a few feet of dirt in open fields. Skeletons dismembered, skulls crushed, the signs of Blood Atonement were often recognized.

Grant was really into it now. Mahoney could see the sparkle in his eyes. Mahoney knew that Grant was a devout Mormon, and hard put to criticize his leaders. But, he was also a detective, and had seen his share of street killing. He was a fan of two kinds of books: church history, and thrillers. He loved talking about hit men and scoundrels, but somehow never made the connection between them and an organization that might hire them. They existed in a fictional never-never-land. Mahoney, on the other hand, believed in the peas-in-a-pod theory. You are what you hire. To Thomas A. T. Mahoney, it was as simple, and as complex, as that.

"What about this NEPHI stuff added onto this code of yours," said the chief.

"Oh, that's simple," was Grant's enthusiastic response, forgetting for a moment that the chief might infer from his remark that he, the chief, was stupid if he couldn't figure it out on his own.

"NEPHI I is the first book of the Book of Mormon, NEPHI II is the second book, and JACOB is the third book of the Book of Mormon. NEPHI I, covers the president, NEPHI II covers Number One, and JACOB covers Number Two."

The chief smiled and nodded. "Number One" had been added to "Number Two." Grant was loosening up.

"The next twenty-four agents are assigned to cover the Council of Twelve Apostles. The code words here are QUORUM DUPLEX GARMENT ATONEMENT FAITHFUL. The Council of Twelve Apostles is more officially known as the Quorum of the Twelve Apostles, but is often just referred to as the Council of Twelve, probably to avoid confusion with the First Quorum of Seventy.

"QUORUM in this case, because it follows TRIAD, means the apostles.

"DUPLEX, probably means two shift coverage as opposed to the twenty-four-hour coverage for the First Presidency. The apostles most likely have coverage from morning through early evening, but once safely in their homes, are left to local security systems hooked to police headquarters. We know most of them have that.

"GARMENT, again, means protection from the destroyer.

"ATONEMENT, the same as before.

"FAITHFUL most likely means that the agents should be more discretionary than with UNITY, the First Presidency. Apparently, with the First Presidency, the agents have no restrictions, and could shoot first and ask questions later. With the Council of Twelve Apostles, the agents may have instructions to be a bit more tactful, since . . . "

"Ok! Ok!" said the Chief, "don't beat me to death with it.

Just follow your hunch and make me a miracle."

"That's it, then, Chief."

The chief looked at Mahoney, then back at Grant.

"Detective Grant," the chief said, "you ought to have been a detective."

Grant tensed, but then the chief smiled warmly, and both Grant and Mahoney joined him.

"That was an excellent job," said the chief. "Now what in the world are you going to do with it."

Grant looked at the chief, then at Mahoney. Mahoney looked at Grant, then at the chief. The chief stared back.

Caught in a bind, Grant blurted out: "Simple, Chief. We're going to blackmail the church with it."

Mahoney damn near choked.

Saturday: Day Six, Morning

Church-owned KSL-TV was on the story like gnats on a rotten banana. Toni Dannly was the hottest reporter in the Salt Lake Valley. She had won four local Emmys, which she considered nice. She had also won one national Emmy, which she considered a multiple orgasm. The national Emmy was for field reporting in 1985-86 on what had become known as the Mormon bombings. The story was a twisted tale of document forgery, death, greed, and deceit, wrapped in the trappings of the Mormon church. It had made Dannly's reputation. She knew in her gut that she was only one major story away from going the route of a Jane Pauley — local anchor to national celebrity — Salt Lake City to New York City — Beehive State to the Big Apple. God she wanted it. And all it was going to take was an inside track on just what the hell was going on behind the gray walls of Temple Square. She knew there was more than met her television camera's inquiring eye.

Leaning directly over Mahoney's powdered sugar donuts, Dannly inspected his choice of breakfast food. Mahoney wasn't sure if he could wipe his face and look at Toni's chest at the same time. God they were beautiful. What a waste, Mahoney thought. The breakfast of champions staring him directly in the face and he had to settle for donuts.

"What do you want, Dannly?" asked Mahoney.

"What do *you* want, Mahoney? As if I didn't know."

Toni Dannly and Mahoney had a playful love-hate relationship. He loved Dannly's body, almost as much as she did. Insult on top of insult, he had yet to make a serious pass at her, and she hated his control. He never gave up shit. It was a blow to her rather substantial ego.

"What's new on the killer, Mahoney?" Dannly asked, knowing full well she would get nothing, especially at this time in the morning. There was still one whole donut and a half container of coffee to go before anyone would get a civil word out of Mahoney. She knew it and he knew it, but she loved the game. Oddly, Mahoney fascinated her.

"Why don't you wipe your mouth off and give me the latest dope on what you *haven't* got on this guy?"

"Why don't you kiss my donut, Dannly? What is it, Emmy time again?"

"At least I have some professional honors to show for my work. All you have is a cheap little pension, if you don't blow it, and a few press clippings to show the grandchildren you won't have. Can I have some of that donut?"

"No!"

"Just as well, considering where it may have been. Tell me, Mahoney, do you sleep in a bed, or just in that suit?"

"Try me sometime and find out."

"Fat chance."

Dannly knew this kind of banter was meaningless. The open bravado Mahoney exhibited with sexual innuendo was nothing more than armor plating. Without an audience he was always the perfect gentlemen. She was sure that underneath the armor plating there was a Mahoney who wanted to whisper sweet-somethings in her ear. Dannly was a bit frustrated that nearly every member of the police department in Salt Lake City, and the surrounding counties, had made serious passes at her from time to time. She had the reputation of turning most of them down. Most of them, that is, unless there was a great story in it for her.

"You would be in my bed," said Mahoney, "in a New York minute if you thought it would get you an exclusive."

"No one needs an exclusive that much."

"Tell me, Dannly, do you ever do it, or do you just talk about it?"

"I suppose you know all there is to know about women and what they want, eh Mahoney?"

"I know you, babe."

"That's a song title."

"Fuck you."

Toni Dannly wouldn't get her exclusive this morning.

Mahoney wouldn't get her chest for breakfast.

As Dannly walked away from Mahoney's desk toward the chief's office, she felt her hips swinging a bit more than usual for this time of the morning. Damn, she thought, there is something about this guy that tells me he would be sensational in bed. He's older than I am; he's a bit rumpled; he's obviously horny; he's no fashion plate; but, he wants me. Jesus — the thought turned over in her head — do I really want him? As she pushed open the chief's door she looked back over her shoulder and her eyes caught Mahoney's. He smiled. She smiled. Damn it, she just wasn't sure.

"Morning, Chief."

"Good morning, Ms. Dannly. I see you've been busting Mahoney's balls for a story. Get anything?"

"No," said Dannly, "but I will. I most definitely will."

Grant had been away from his desk during the Mahoney/Dannly encounter, but he knew almost word for word what had been said. He had heard it all before. The sexual innuendo, the mock insults, and the professional jibes. Grant couldn't help but wonder if they had ever been in bed together. Nah. Impossible. In Mahoney's dreams.

Back at his desk, looking at copies of the reports from the Kodak boys, he shared them with Mahoney who was putting the last bite of donut in his mouth. Glancing at the reports, Mahoney's eyes scanned the top sheet until they came to rest on one line that read "Exceptions." Next to the word were two names "John Doe I," and "John Doe II." In another column next to John Doe I, it said, "Appeared in five discernable groups, no match yet." Next to John Doe II, it said, "Appeared in three discernable groups, no match yet."

"What's this John Doe stuff?" asked Mahoney.

"The Kodak boys," said Grant, "have found a picture of two men, John Doe I, and John Doe II, who seem to appear in several different groups, implying that they belonged to no single group, but may have moved from group to group to keep from standing out as a loner. So far most of the groups have been contacted from the addresses linked to their film, and copies of the pictures were Federal Expressed to them.

These five groups have no knowledge of either man. They were not a part of any of the groups they were standing with or near. What now?"

"Have blowups made of the two men, 8-by-10's isolating just their upper-body and head. Have them make about twenty shots of each man in every group they were in. Get them done today."

"Will do," said Grant. He picked up the phone and relayed the information to the Kodak boys, along with thanks for a good job, and was back in Mahoney's face before he had his last sip of coffee downed.

"Now what?" Grant said.

"Jesus H. Christ," Heber, "don't you know any other song. Can't you let a man have his breakfast in peace?"

"How come I bother you more than Dannly does?"

"You're married, and you're ugly," said Mahoney. "Now, have you let the church security office know we're on our way over? If you don't we may find ourselves walking around in the lobby with our thumbs up our asses."

"Already done," said Grant. The two of them would be meeting in the Church Office Building conference room where they had first met Kimball and the four-horsemen.

"Shit," thought Mahoney, "the Church Office Building again."

Saturday: Day 6, Afternoon

The man hadn't slept much. He had been busy.

He had used a public telephone to call his apartment and pick up messages from his answering machine. He listened to his own voice state his telephone number followed only by, "Leave a message after the tone." He punched in his code number. There were no messages.

Earlier in the day he had driven from his apartment, in the avenues northeast of the Utah State Capitol building, to Emigration Canyon. This was his second trip to the canyon in the past week. He had found what he was looking for on the first trip. This time was just for fun. To anticipate. To fine tune. He had located the residence of an apostle of the church.

He was overly careful. There would be additional security guards posted to every church official, either now, or soon, he thought. He was careful only to make one pass by the home, returning again thirty minutes later, following a leisurely drive up the canyon. He could see no unusual activity.

It wouldn't be long, he knew, before every member of the First Presidency and the Council of Twelve Apostles would find himself under virtual house arrest. He wondered if they would hole up in their homes, surrounded by guards. Or would they take the more practical solution of remaining in the Temple, and creeping through the underground tunnels to the Hotel Utah Building's sealed church floor in order to sleep at night. The problem, of course, was family. Most of the apostles were very old men, and were either widowers, or had only their elderly wives to consider. One or two of the younger ones, however, had a child still living at home. The apostles were prolific, and having a large family was considered a duty to the church and to God. Some had as many as a dozen children. A large family was a badge of honor among Mormons in Utah.

He wanted more sleep, and was thankful he did not have to report to his job immediately. His schedule was ideal. It allowed time for work. It also allowed time for play. Just one more thing to do before sleeping.

He searched through the compartments of the fanny-pack, and stocked it with what he would need; gloves, handgun, extra clips of ammunition, knife, handball, lock picks, jumper wire. He took the items from a massive suitcase fitted with secure keyed locks, as well as a combination lock.

The suitcase held a variety of materials, including five 9mm Springfield 1911-A1 automatic pistols, ten boxes of Hornady 147-grain Boat Tail Hollow Point XTP ammunition, eight Ek-Warrior combat knives, one Barnett Demon crossbow and a dozen bolts, the metal arrow-like projectiles used as crossbow ammunition. There was also a smaller crossbow the size of a large pistol, with six shorter bolts. The case also contained C-4 explosive, detonators, fuses, timers, two break-down high-powered rifles, one telescopic sight, and a single Beretta 92F with a 20-round magazine protruding from the weapon's butt. Attached to the Beretta was a Sure-Fire 600 series xenon tactical light for sighting in the dark. Alongside were six plastic CS grenades, tear gas.

Sooner or later, the man thought, I'm going to use all of this shit.

He hung a "Do Not Disturb" sign on the outside of his door. Inside, he wedged a device under the lip of the door. It was a metal door-stop-like unit the man had bought in a catalog catering to travelers. Opening the door would force the wedge tighter between it and the floor, preventing the door from opening; it would also trip a battery powered screech-alarm contained in the wedge. The alarm would awaken the man instantly. It would also scare the shit out of any nocturnal visitor.

It was only a precaution. He was a very light sleeper. Being a light sleeper was wise, he thought, especially when you sleep with a 9mm automatic, safety off.

Soon he would change hotels. He had used this as his base long enough. Maybe after the next killing. Maybe then.

The man showered, but didn't dry off. Instead he lay

naked in the middle of the king sized bed and masturbated to
the thoughts of women and killing, intermixed, as if there
were no difference. Reaching orgasm, the man slept for
eleven hours.

This time no one "appeared" in the lobby of the Church
Office Building. Mahoney and Grant just wrote their names
in the log book, and wrote "Kimball" in the column headed
"Visiting." The person behind the desk politely said, "I
believe you know the way, gentlemen. Brother Kimball is
expecting you," and she gestured toward the elevator bank.

"That's a change," said Grant.

"You're right," said Mahoney, "and it disappoints me that
we won't have the company of Mr. Personality in the
elevator. And another thing disappoints me. You know that
log book at the front desk?"

"Yeah."

"Well, did you ever think that it might be a wonderful
book to read through to find out who has been in and out of
here since the threats were received?"

Grant nodded and started to answer when Mahoney put
up his hand and stopped him cold.

"So did I, at first. But now I realize it would be worthless.
You and I have been in here twice since the killing and the
threats, including this visit. Yet a person going through that
book would only find us entered once. Today. The other visit
wasn't logged by us because that "ghost" materialized and
scooted us over to the elevators before we could sign it. I
think that's maybe a way for security to control the record as
to who comes and goes, and when."

"You mean," said Grant, "that if security has a visitor and
doesn't want a record of it, they just send down a phantom
greeter to intercept them before they log in?"

"We may have considerable difficulty," said Mahoney,
"ever finding out what we need to know from the church's
own records. We should view them as highly suspect, if you
get my meaning."

Grant did, and as they left the elevator and moved toward
the conference room, he vowed not to be tricked by his own
church. After all, he was a detective just doing his job. And
he loved his job. Right now, he thought, it was time to black-

mail the church.

Mahoney and Grant had worked out the plan, but it was Grant's idea. Mahoney was delighted and found himself thinking that this young Mormon punk might not be such a stiff of a partner after all. He might just get to like the kid. Maybe real affection rather than professional tolerance. Grant had already proved to be no shrinking violet. He stayed up all night working on the list and its codes; he stood up well in the face-off with the chief when he explained his conclusions; and best of all, he did some on-the-spot original thinking and blurted out his blackmail ploy in front of the chief. He seemed to have the courage of his convictions. Mahoney liked the idea that Grant hadn't asked his permission to run with the concept. He just announced he was going to do it. He was going to blackmail the church. Balls. Golden balls. So the two of them stayed up late that night eating pizza and figuring out the best way to lead off with Kimball. By the time they finished the last slice, Kimball was dead meat. He was all theirs.

Mahoney saw that the door to the conference room was open. Several men sitting around the table. Kimball was at the end, where he was before. The four-horsemen were there, but scattered around a bit more, and there were two other men neither Mahoney nor Grant had seen before. As they entered the conference room Kimball rose and said:

"Detectives Mahoney and Grant, won't you be seated. Now, shall we get started, we only have a short time?"

Mahoney stood up and in a voice much louder and authoritarian than the dimensions of the room required, said, "As far as we're concerned this meeting is over right now; let's go Detective Grant, we're outta here."

Mahoney started to walk and Grant pushed back and stood to the open-mouthed gawking of Kimball and the other six men in the conference room. As they turned to walk out Kimball sputtered something with "No" and "Please" in it, and Mahoney and Grant stopped and looked at him.

"We will stay in this meeting on three conditions. Our conditions. They are not negotiable.

"Number One: you will introduce us to each person here, giving us their full name and their complete job title.

"Number Two: you will agree to send a transcript of this

meeting, within twelve hours, to my office, and an exact copy
of that transcript to the offices of the First Presidency.

"Number Three: you will stop being so blasted
insufferable and start acting like a human being.

"That's it. Take it or leave it. Now."

It was silent except for the soft whoosh of air being
circulated from ducts in the ceiling. Mahoney made a
palms-up gesture with his hands that, coupled with a slight tip
of his head, effectively asked, "Well, yes or no?"

"I want you to know one thing, Detective Mahoney," said
Kimball. "I am not insufferable, I am just under a lot of
pressure right now, and we have a big job to do and very little
time in which to do it."

Just like Kimball, thought Mahoney, to zero right in on
the only throwaway part in the list of demands. The
insufferable bastard.

When Mahoney didn't answer, Kimball gestured to the
chairs at the end of the table, and Mahoney and Grant sat
down, slowly. Mahoney had seen Kimball make eye contact
with one of the men he hadn't seen before. He seemed to be
seeking approval.

"Detectives Mahoney and Grant — starting at your near
left and working around the table I would like to introduce
you to Brother Chad Davis, director of internal security;
Brother Heber Lakewood . . . "

Mahoney kicked Grant under the table. Heber Mark
Grant didn't think it was funny.

" . . . director of external security; Brother Spencer
Blaylock, director of intelligence; Brother Lyle Hinkley,
director of public information; Brother Benson Bradley,
deputy director of church security; and Brother Hyrum Smith,
assistant to the Second Counselor of the First Presidency."

Bingo, thought Mahoney. The four-horsemen who
flanked Kimball at the last meeting were Bradley, Kimball's
number two in security, Davis of internal security, Lakewood
of external security, and Blaylock of intelligence. Two new
faces were Hinkley, director of public information, which
meant old silver-hair, Number Two, forced the church's PR
flak on Kimball; and Hyrum Smith, Number Two's very own
personal assistant, which meant that Number Two wanted his
own spoon in the pudding. Either that or he was scared shit-

less himself and no longer trusted Kimball and his grim faced bunch to protect him without divine direction from the First Presidency itself. Never get involved in secular matters, my ass, thought Mahoney.

Kimball, Mahoney was sure, was burning up inside, but to his credit, he wasn't sweating. Yet.

Kimball spoke again.

"Now that you've met everyone, may I add that we will, of course, send a transcript of this meeting to your office."

"One requirement on our part, Detective Mahoney," said Hyrum Smith, Number Two's assistant, "we must be assured of absolute secrecy regarding the transcript. If it gets out, particularly to the press, it could prove embarrassing, if not harmful. No convenient leaks from police headquarters."

Lyle Hinkley's head, as director of public information, was nodding up and down like the spring attached noggin of one of those suction-cup toys in the back window of a '50's automobile. He looked like a toady to Hyrum Smith. Obviously, thought Mahoney, Hyrum Smith was the power in this room. One word to Number Two, and any of these other men could be out of work by morning. And they all seemed to know it.

It was blackmail time.

Mahoney began, as he and Grant had discussed. Grant would finish twisting the knife Mahoney had inserted.

"Actually, Mr. Smith, regarding the transcript, my concern is that the First Presidency knows of our plans and has exactly the same information we do. But now I would like to get to the point. My partner and I have worked out some bottom line requests for information we must have from the security office immediately."

"What do you mean — bottom line?" asked Number Two's assistant. Mahoney had been waiting for this.

"I mean the minimum amount of information we can accept without securing a court order to get it."

Hyrum Smith's eyes seemed to dilate at the mention of a court order. Lyle Hinkley blanched. Court order is a phrase Mahoney knew from experience that the church leadership despised. Court orders meant going public with the press, and short of a well crafted and divinely inspired press release, pre-approved by a battery of saints and the church's legal department, public scrutiny was Lucifer's doing.

"Exactly what is this bottom line list," said Hyrum Smith, with obvious disdain.

It was good cop, bad cop time. Grant was the good cop. He was Mormon, and infinitely more likeable than Mahoney. Grant interrupted:

"I do hope you understand, Sir, that we have no desire to interfere with church business, and we will respect the confidentiality of all information we receive. As an officer of the Salt Lake City police department, and as a member of the church, you have my word on that." Grant smiled warmly.

"We require the following items," said Mahoney. "First, a printout of the actual names and assignments of everyone, all 100-plus, on the list the Second Counselor handed me in his office yesterday. We want names, addresses, telephone numbers, working shifts, working locations, the date and nature of their last promotion, and their specific assignments. As part of this we need the same information on the staff, from associates and assistants, to secretaries and file clerks, who work for, and with, the people on the list."

Number Two's assistant, the director of public information, and Kimball, were noticeably distressed.

"Next, we want a detailed outline of your actual plan of defense to thwart the threats against the church," said Mahoney. "Also, we want a telephone number and access code that will assure Detective Grant, and me, that we can reach someone in authority at any time, day or night, without bureaucratic delay. Inherent in that request is that the access be to a person who can make decisions without having to ask someone else."

The tension in the room, as far as Grant was concerned, was suffocating.

"Finally," Mahoney concluded, "two follow-up items. Once that information is in our hands, we will want instant access to the personnel records of anyone on this list we choose to question. We also want a printout, with all of the same information as the main list, of everyone who has quit, been fired, laid-off, transferred, or demoted in the last twelve months. And we also want the reason for that action. That's it."

"You are requesting information that is restricted from

anyone other than the General Authorities, and the church security office," said Number Two's assistant.

"We assumed that," said Mahoney, "but it is necessary."

"Our own security force," continued Hyrum Smith, "is perfectly capable of handling internal security, if that's what you're getting at, Detective Mahoney."

"I'm not getting at anything," said Mahoney. "I am simply asking you for the tools to do our job. We are aware that your internal security does a good, routine job. We know that you have handled bomb threats and death threats many times before. You had considerable experience with bomb threats in the 1960's because of the church's racial policies. We know there was a bomb planted at the front door of the Temple. We know about the threats in the 70's by members of a polygamous cult to kill your president and prophet. You handle crowds well.

"You have considerable experience with pickets, from American Indians, to blacks, to women, and ERA activists. But our man has already killed one person in Temple Square. He was an apostle of your church, in his office, in the Church Administration Building. These are no longer just bomb threats and pickets. These are ugly murders, realities that are not going to stop because of the prayers of the First Presidency."

Mahoney knew that Church security in the 1970's was mostly interested in recruiting student spies from Brigham Young University to ferret out masturbators and gays, and to monitor the BYU faculty. The last experience in dealing with a bomb threat was in the Hofmann forgery case. A friend of George Bush's, who had CIA connections, offered 'special security' to the church in October of 1985, just in case the police couldn't handle it. What Mahoney believed George Bush actually offered was support "just in case church security couldn't handle it." As it turned out the church was never really the target in that case.

"What we want from you," said Mahoney, "is necessary, because in all likelihood, the killer of Mr. Williamson and Apostle Fielding works for church security."

Number Two's assistant nearly jumped to his feet.

"That's preposterous!" he screamed. "That's not even a possibility. Our men have been screened, and are loyal, faithful Mormons who believe that this church is the one true church on earth."

"Surely," Mahoney continued, "your own security people have discussed this. If they haven't they ought to be fired."

Kimball's eyes squinted with hatred for Mahoney.

"For your own information," said Mahoney, "the killing in Temple Square could have been done by anybody. But it wasn't. It was done by the same guy who left the note on that table in the Hotel Utah Building. The note threatened the First Presidency, and the next day the Second Counselor was dead. From a bomb, for God's sake! Just when do you think that bomb was planted? And who could have planted it? Not some fundamental polygamist from Bountiful who wears a full beard and black clothing, who waltzed into the Church Administration Building with some plastic explosive under his arm? I suppose he just taped it under the Second Counselor's desk, and said 'thank you' to the receptionist on his way out? Give me a break.

"This was set up in advance of the killing in Temple Square, and our bomb squad was refused access to the building because church security was in charge. Well, Mr. Smith? Have you looked under your desk today?"

Hyrum Smith paused rather dramatically, puffed his chest up a bit, befitting his position as assistant to the Second Counselor, scanned the faces of everyone in the room, and ignoring nearly everything Mahoney had outlined, said:

"And what if we refuse to give you this information?"

Jesus Christ, what hath God wrought? Mahoney thought. But they had been waiting for this. They had agreed, even though the idea had been Grant's, that Mahoney would continue to be the bad cop, so that Grant could remain relatively untouched by the hate those in the room now felt for Mahoney. Mahoney continued.

"Simple. We have asked for the information necessary to do our job. No more, no less. We have offered our personnel to assist in the protection of church facilities and church leaders. We have had several meetings, more than we should have allowed, in order to accommodate the wishes of this church in this matter. We have done all we can without your cooperation, and in spite of your refusal to allow this city's police force the access necessary to do its job.

"If we don't get the information and cooperation we have requested, we will have no other choice than to hold a press conference, immediately, and lay out the facts before the media and the public. After all, gentlemen, the Salt Lake City police department cannot sit idly by and watch while your church apostles are picked off one by one. We will have to begin by telling the public that the Mormon church wants it this way."

Mahoney pushed on without allowing any interruptions.

"The first item we will present in the press conference will be that we have been forced to secure a court order seeking access to basic information denied us by the church.

"The second item will be a list of over a hundred armed security agents, broken down by shifts and assignments. It will include the nine agents assigned to twenty-four hour protection of the First Presidency, and the twenty-four agents assigned to sixteen-hour protection of the Council of Twelve Apostles.

"The third item will be a detailed account of this meeting.

"This, gentlemen, is known to policemen around the world, as CYA."

Mahoney stopped. Hyrum Smith looked at Kimball and showed not the slightest bit of recognition on his face.

"That means," said Mahoney, in his most official policeman-like voice, "Covering — Your — Ass!"

The blood had either drained from Hyrum Smith's face, or the ceiling lights had changed hue, since Number Two's assistant now looked somewhat green. Mahoney had to give him credit though; the bastard was generally unflappable.

"We will take this under advisement and get back to you," said Number Two's assistant.

"Before we leave here," said Mahoney, in a slow and steady voice, "you should understand that this meeting was called for 1 p.m., and it is now 2 p.m. We took the liberty yesterday of calling a general press conference on the progress of this case for 5 p.m. in the Municipal Building. That's three hours from now. If we have your personal word of honor, before that hour is up, that you will supply exactly what we asked for, and that the church, or anyone in the church's employ, will not hold its own press conference in the meantime, we will hold our 'routine' press conference updating the case. We will give you until 4:30 p.m. to supply Detective Grant with all of the requested information and assurances, by messenger, to police headquarters. If we do not have your word of honor to that effect within one hour from now, we will hold a 'special' press conference on the content of this meeting, and all other meetings we have had up to this point."

"Are you finished?" asked Hyrum Smith, with a great deal of emphasis on 'finished.'

Mahoney stood, then Grant. No one else moved.

"Yes," said Grant. "Except for one thing. Detective Mahoney told you that a transcript of this meeting was necessary. It isn't. For your information, Detective Mahoney wore a wire here today. These proceedings have been recorded by the Salt Lake City Police Department."

Mahoney looked at the stunned group of men in their immaculate blue suits and pristine white shirts, and said:

"C-Y-A, gentlemen."

Mahoney and Grant were out of there.

At ten minutes before 3 p.m., Grant's telephone rang. It was Kimball. He told Grant that they would provide the information by messenger before 4:30 p.m. Grant told Kimball that he could not accept Kimball's word for that, on orders from his superiors. If they wanted the deal, he had about nine minutes left to have Hyrum Smith call Detective Mahoney directly and give him his word of honor that this would be done. Kimball didn't say goodbye.

One minute later Mahoney's telephone rang. He let it ring three times and then answered it.

"Mahoney, here."

Grant listened intently, but nothing seemed to be happening. Mahoney was just listening. He had a tape recorder on the line and the red record light was on. Finally, Mahoney said, "Thank you very much, Mr. Smith," and hung up.

"Well?" asked Grant.

"He's pissed," said Mahoney. "But you can expect a package to be delivered by 4:30."

They both smiled.

The game was afoot, thought Mahoney.

I'm in trouble, thought Grant.

"Mahoney! Grant!" yelled the chief. "Get in here!"

The chief spent the next fifteen minutes going over what

the reaction had been to the 'routine' press conference. It was anything but routine. The press was off the wall, as they had been since five minutes after Apostle Fielding found out if what Joseph Smith believed about heaven, had been right all along.

The print journalists were the roughest, the men agreed, probably because there was nothing for the television cameras to shoot. No one was allowed in the Church Administration Building by orders of the church. No exceptions. And in this case even the press understood. After all, according to the church, an apostle of God had been blown up in his office, and there were eleven others who didn't know why. But that fiction was destroyed quickly when a *Deseret News* reporter, asked if it was true that a letter threatening the lives of all of the Council of Twelve Apostles and the First Presidency existed.

Mahoney went against the chief's advice to deny everything, and danced around the subject by saying that they had in their possession a letter making some threats, but that because of the ongoing investigation, and the safety of all concerned, the contents of the letter could not yet be revealed. There were scores of questions, all on the same theme: Who was doing this? Were the bombing and the killing in Temple Square connected? Would there be more bombings? How soon would there be a break in the case?

Same questions, same answers. Duck and cover, thought Mahoney. Duck and cover.

The reporter from the *Deseret News* whose question was about the letter, walked up to Mahoney after the news conference and asked if he could talk off the record.

"Sure," said Mahoney, "but I might not answer, even off the record."

"I only asked the question about the letter to get some confirmation that one existed," said the reporter. "You see, I have a Xerox copy of the letter and I intend to run it in tomorrow's special edition. Do you have any comment, Detective?"

"Nope."

That was then, and this is now, thought Mahoney. It was now after 6 p.m. Grant and he were going over the material in the fat manila envelope a church messenger had personally delivered to Grant's desk prior to the press conference.

Saturday: Day Six, Evening

The evening edition of the *Deseret News* sat next to the manila envelope. Mahoney looked through the paper for new information. He had seen the morning *Tribune* earlier in the day. There wasn't anything new in it. Tomorrow would be another story. Whoever had leaked the photocopy of the letter, either from the police station, or from church headquarters, had probably gotten it from his own police department. Bastards. His only hope was that the *News* reporter would not be successful in trying to convince his editor to run it. Mahoney knew the editor would call the church press office. The press office would call a member of the First Presidency, and the word would come down. No copy of the letter in the *News* if, and until, it first appeared in the *Tribune*. After all, thought Mahoney, the church owned the *Deseret News*, its locks, stocks, and barrels of ink. The *Deseret News* seldom hid the truth or suppressed the news. It just avoided breaking stories embarrassing to the church in the hope that if the eggs were left unbroken, no one could make an omelette. Maybe the letter wouldn't appear in the special edition of the *News* after all. Maybe the timidity of the *News* in handling items not favorable to the church would buy time. Maybe one more day.

In truth, mused Mahoney, the *News* had, like the church itself, its own Eighth Article of Faith. Mahoney had actually created it, but he was sure the church newspaper subscribed to it: "We believe the Truth to be the word of God as far as it is translated correctly." It was the paper's job to translate truth correctly on behalf of the Church of Jesus Christ of Latter-day Saints. They were good newspapermen-and-women when reporting most things, but when reporting on the church, they were good Mormon newspaper men and women. Mahoney sighed and went back to concentrating on the pile of papers from the bulky manila envelope.

He was hoping the church would see it his way.

The years were taking their toll on Mahoney. Even the press had a way of forgetting that he was more often helpful than not. It was their job to be skeptical, but he couldn't help thinking that he had been a better friend to the press than it had been to him, despite a few good headlines and some honest praise every now and then.

As a returned missionary for his church, Grant was twenty-four-years old, a model family man and a church treasure, with three children, and a wife who was a leader in her Stake Relief Society. He had been married in the secret Temple Celestial Marriage that "seals" couples to each other for "time and eternity." Grant paid a full tithing of ten percent of his before-tax income to the church, a must if one is to remain in good standing as a saintly Mormon. Adhering to the Mormon's "Word of Wisdom," Grant didn't drink, smoke, or swear.

Mahoney, by contrast, swore like a longshoreman, drank like a disgraced politician, paid no tithing, and even less homage, to the Mormon church. He seldom entered a Catholic church. He smoked expensive cigars at home, and watched an occasional cop show on television. Since the death of his wife he lived only for his job.

The man was well rested, and he liked Saturdays. They reminded him of a restful day to come. He didn't believe in working on Sunday. It was the Lord's day. But on Monday he would kill someone. No use pissing off the Lord on Sunday, he thought.

Sunday: Day Seven, Morning

For Mahoney and Grant it was not a day of rest.

They now had a complete printout of names, addresses, assignments. Grant was right about most of the codes. Mahoney whistled a high-pitched sound of utter amazement when he counted up the people working for church security. Over 100 agents; but what do 100 agents need with 200 associates, assistants, and secretaries? That made them nearly as large as the entire 350 member Salt Lake City police force. In-fucking-credible.

They also got their magic phone number. Again he was amazed at the power of the Utah church. Within six hours of the meeting and the delivery of the manila envelope to Grant's desk, the telephone company had installed a new line to the desk of the Second Counselor. And Number Two wasn't going to give out his unlisted private number to some lowly policeman. He had a brand new temporary line put in which would be removed when this was over. Goodbye, Mahoney. No calling up Number Two for a quick lunch.

The phone line would be call-forwarded to his home, and his limousine cellular, in that order. The cover letter said the number would reach him 24-hours a day until this "horror" was over. It restricted the use of the line to calls from "Detectives Grant, Mahoney, and the Chief of Police — No other call will be taken."

Pretty good, thought Mahoney. I'm a reprobate Catholic, living in Utah, with a private line to the First Presidency of the Mormon church. I'll drink to that.

Mahoney was taken aback by two other items included with the packet. He had asked that additional information be provided of employees fired, laid off, transferred, or demoted over the past year. Mahoney assumed that would take longer than accessing current records. But not so. The secondary

94

list of ex-employees and demotions for the past year totaled
ninety-six. Computers are great, Mahoney thought. The
second item to please Mahoney was the access to the
personnel records:

Church Office Building — Personnel Office
To: *Detectives Mahoney & Grant*
From: *Computer Operations — Personnel*
Subject: Limited Access to Select Personnel Files

*Access has been approved by the Office of the First
Presidency by modem to the personnel records of selected
staff and past employees. (Allowed records have been
designated and coded as SLCPD LIST ONE and SLCPD
LIST TWO.) Access is on a twenty-four hour basis for a two-
week period commencing immediately.*
*Password: Modem settings should be E/7/1 and access
should be through Tyment Network at 801-555-0724. Press
enter twice upon connection to access personnel program.
Upon obtaining a prompt, type in the password TEMP-
SLCPD and press (ENTER). A menu will direct you through
accessing the two lists. All searching parameters are in effect.
Help is available through on-line menu by typing at any
prompt /HELP. Interactive online live operator help can be
accessed by typing at any prompt /HELPME. A land line
operator, in case of difficulty may be accessed by calling 801-
555-1849.*

Mahoney marveled at what a ten percent tithe of the pre-
tax earnings of six million people can create. Even if half of
them don't pay and lose their Temple recommendation
because of it, it's not chopped liver. The last estimates
Mahoney had heard stated that over forty percent of
Mormons paid their full tithing. Most money men estimate
the church's income from tithing alone to be $1 billion a year.
Then, Mahoney thought, there's the income provided by
thirteen radio and TV stations, innumerable church book
stores, four giant insurance companies, several mammoth
shopping malls, and the church newspaper. The real mega-
bucks, however, came from the real estate holdings through-

out the country, all owned outright by the Mormon church.

Mahoney couldn't remember a tenth of them, but he did remember that the church owned giant farms in Florida, Georgia, and California. In Florida, one prime holding totaled 300,000 acres adjacent to Disney World. Land holdings in Los Angeles County were worth $84 million the last time Mahoney remembered reading about church wealth. And that was a decade ago. Who knew what it might be now? He remembered that number only because, coincidentally, it was also eighty-four percent tax exempt. They owned another $36 million worth of real estate in Orange County, and $14 million in Alameda County.

Sunday, Day Seven, Afternoon

After working all morning on paper-this and paper-that, Mahoney was ready to shit paper. He hated the paperwork side of police procedure, yet he knew there was no substitute for information. Unfortunately, most of it came on paper. He swore to himself that after today he would get the hell out of the office and do some fishing. He was beginning to feel like an overstuffed file cabinet.

Mahoney and Grant finally had what they wanted. First things first. Grant began to pore over the main list of names, over 300 in all, which had been entered into the NCIC computer during the night. The National Crime Information Center's computers could be accessed by all recognized law enforcement agencies in the country. Mahoney didn't know whether he hated it or loved it.

The secondary list of ninety-six names had also been entered. Mahoney and Grant wanted arrests and warrants on everybody, including Kimball, and those at the meeting. The reports from the NCIC were just about what Mahoney expected. Of the first 300 names in, only thirty-eight were NCIC hits. Of the next ninety-six names there were eighteen hits. Utah had a lot of "clean sheet" people in it, and the Mormon church, by percentage, had even more. Crime in Utah was disproportionally white collar. Of the thirty-eight, Mahoney and Grant had set priorities on a stack of "agents," and a stack of "support staff." Thirty were agents, and only eight were support staff. Mahoney smiled.

"What are you smiling for?" asked Grant.

"Well, it doesn't surprise me that thirty of the agents are dirty, in one way or another."

"Well, it does me," said Grant. "I would have thought that they'd be squeaky clean going through the church's own screening system. I've heard it's pretty rough getting into church security."

"Not really," Mahoney said. "It just takes a particular type. Have you ever wondered why it was so easy to take an instant dislike to Kimball and the four horseman?"

"Well, I really didn't . . . "

"Well, I did," interrupted Mahoney. That little pimple Kimball is the perfect type for the job. He's on our hit list as well," Mahoney said as he pulled out the NCIC sheet on Kimball.

"Kimball," so it seems, "never did any hard time but was in one scrape after another as a demonstrator against peace groups and liberal causes. It says here he once threw paint bombs at the headquarters of the ACLU during a demonstration protesting their defense of an abortionist. He has spent more than a few nights in lock-up. He was active in the John Birch Society, and was suspected of being an 'enforcer' for their meetings. He had been an FBI agent, but that didn't last long. It was most likely his arch-conservative leanings that caught the eye of his boss, who trained under J. Martell Bird, the security chief appointed by Ezra Taft Benson. It was Kimball who followed suit and continued spying, opening interoffice mail, and surveillance as general practices. Kimball is a little J. Martell Bird twice removed."

"But what," asked Grant, "do you mean by the perfect type?"

"I guess you're too young to remember, or maybe you weren't interested at the time, but Ezra Taft Benson's son, Reed, was part of a group called the Bensonites, who were influential on campus at BYU. All of this right-wing authoritarianism in the shadow of Ezra being first in succession for the presidency of the Mormon church, gave him considerable power. In the mid 1960's BYU students, returned missionaries, and any employee of the church who fell under Apostle Benson's growing influence, were encouraged to spy on the behavior and beliefs of BYU faculty, employees, and fellow students. It's common knowledge that both the FBI and the CIA have continually recruited Mormons, especially returned missionaries and BYU students, as agents. They had excellent role models in the church itself. Apostle Boyd K. Packer, one of the most conservative of the General Authorities, continually warned against leaks of information, and maintained steadfastly that it was the duty of church employees to tell on others. He also warned them to stay away from apostates, and those who have been excommunicated, who have a perverse interest in what's going on at church headquarters.

"You know, Mahoney," Grant said, "I am a returned missionary. Doesn't that worry you just a bit?"

"Not at all," Mahoney said, without even an inflection of doubt, "you are a devout Mormon, but you are not a zealot. It's the zealots we have to look out for. And Kimball's a zealot — with a capital Z. Every church has them."

Mahoney and Grant went over the eighteen names from the secondary list of ninety-six with intense interest. Of the eighteen, however, no one had a felony conviction, with the exception of a grand theft auto on the sheet of one thirty-six-year old man. And that had happened when he was nineteen years old. Forget it.

The paper work seemed endless, Mahoney thought. A cop's lot at best. The details and cross checking were starting to get to him. His head was swimming with possibilities and the horrible "ifs" began to mount. This was the stage of any investigation that he hated. They had enough to start, but not enough to run at full tilt. And when, dear God, he mumbled to himself, is the bastard going to call?

Monday: Day Eight, Early Morning

The man was aware of the increased security on the Temple grounds and in the Church Office Building. He knew, although he hadn't been in the Church Administration Building since planting the bomb that killed Apostle Fielding, that access there would be next to impossible. It would be a long day, much of it spent just waiting, but that couldn't be helped. It was the only way to do it. It was only 3 a.m. He hated this part of the job.

He approached the house located in an exclusive section of Emigration Canyon. The canyon was a rough corridor nature had carved out of the mountains above Salt Lake City through which Brigham Young had brought his faithful in 1847. He whispered aloud, "This is the right place."

Those were the actual words Brigham Young had spoken when he viewed the Great Salt Lake Valley spread before him. The man liked the sound of those words. He knew that the monument in Emigration Canyon was called the "This Is The Place Monument." Like other mangled history in the church, the man knew that Brigham Young, according to church publications, had actually said, "It is enough. This is the right place. Drive on." But the errant quote of "This is the place," continues to pass the lips of nearly everyone, including Mormons, familiar with the story of Brigham Young's band entering the valley. The monument is officially the "This Is The Place Monument." Too bad, he thought. They should have got it right.

As the man reached the secluded and exclusive section of Pinecrest Canyon, an offshoot of Emigration Canyon, he pulled the car onto a side road parking behind an outcropping of brush licking out from the dense forested area. For two or three minutes he had driven with his lights off, creeping along at ten miles per hour, partially from memory, since he had driven the road three times in the daylight.

Leaving the car he began the trek through the brush to the secluded house sitting on the rise in front of him. He was looking for security guards. He knew there should be one guarding this man from morning till evening, but, generally, not through the night. And, especially, not here. Yet, these were not usual circumstances. Had the church, he wondered, which is notoriously slow to change or adapt to any stimulus, increased the guard on this man?

Moving toward the back of the house, lit only by a yard light and the dim glow of a lamp left on in the front of the house, the man quietly disabled the electronic alarm. He was pleased with himself, since he knew exactly what kind of alarm protected the house. He knew the model number, the location, and even the code numbers for activation and deactivation. He had seen the bill, wiring diagrams, and instructions on the preset code, all delivered dutifully by the alarm company. The papers had passed over his desk on their way to the files of the General Authorities. The church, he thought, paid well for the security of their living saints. But like so many other things, apostles of God simply refused to concern themselves with mundane, secular aspects of life more suitably delegated to underlings. At least thirty-five people had seen the papers, the wiring diagrams, and the alarm codes. He was one of those thirty-five souls. Change the alarm codes? Of course not. Don't be silly. An apostle had no time for such foolishness. He was above such earthly matters. He was only to be informed once the installation was made. He was to be told what the code numbers were, for the protection of his life on earth. Hardly necessary, the apostle had said. He was an apostle of God. It was a bother only to be tolerated for the peace of mind of other, more temporal men.

He wore his cotton gloves and a large sized fanny-pack, popular with kids and skiers who don't want to carry anything in their hands. This one, however, extended nearly from hip to hip. It was pulled around to the front of his body, and the center of the pouch was directly over his belt buckle. From it he removed a manual lockpick and a flat piece of spring steel, bent at each end, with which to apply pressure and turn the cylinder as tumblers were lifted into place.

He had rejected using his prized lockpicking device for fear that it would make too much noise rattling in the keyhole. As the pins aligned from the deft manipulation of the lockpick, and the cylinder turned from the pressure of the spring steel shim, the lock opened. He knew he had only thirty seconds to tap in the code numbers on the keyplate inside the door. Using a small penlight held between his teeth, he punched in the numbers and watched as the red light went out and a green light flashed on.

He used his left hand to tap in the code. His right hand held a 9mm automatic pistol. At the end of the pistol, stretched over the muzzle was the heavy rubber nipple of a baby's bottle. It was a crude silencer, he knew, but it was nearly as effective as any other kind. Most of them didn't work anyway. Technically, they were called noise suppressors. They suppressed some muzzle noise, but nothing "silenced" the sound of a 9mm gun blast.

Moving into the house he was alert to the possibility of finding a security guard around any corner. As he moved his head slightly past the edge of the molding on the doorway connecting the kitchen to the living room, he could see a glow coming from the right. It was the telltale, sometimes flickering, multicolored light of a television set. He could barely hear the sound, turned down so low that those sleeping would not be disturbed. How foolish, he thought. Either the security guard was breaking regulations by watching television, or he was simply stupid. Even the minor distraction of watching television, and listening to its sound, negated the guard's presence in the house. What did he think, the man wondered, that an intruder would knock and announce his intention to kill the apostle?

Moving toward the light, and what the man guessed to be the den, he held the gun directly in front of him in a two-hand stance. As he turned the corner of the wide entrance he saw the guard sitting on a couch with his feet crossed in front of him, resting on the coffee table. The man wondered, fleetingly, what one called a coffee table in the home of an apostle of the church.

The guard turned with a start. Sensing the presence of someone entering the room, his hand started moving to the revolver in the holster on his belt, but in his relaxed position, the gesture was nothing more than that — a gesture. The 9mm bullet entered the guard's head two inches under his right eye, and slightly right of his nose. The sound of the gunshot was loud, yet not nearly the full report of an unsuppressed weapon being fired.

With no time to waste, the man hurried from the room and moved up the staircase. The expensive hardwood floors, covered with plush, deep carpet, absorbed all sound of the man's footsteps. There was an open door at the top of the stairs. He could see a made-up bed through the doorway. Turning, he saw another door just beyond, and from it the warm glow of a night light. He approached it carefully. The bathroom.

The last door was open, but his line of sight into the room was blocked by a wall, undoubtedly the side wall of a closet. He paused. Listening. He had not cut the telephone lines for fear that doing so would trip an unknown alarm. He had thought about taking the telephone off the hook in the kitchen, but passed on the idea when he noted that it was a five-button phone. Punching up one line after another to put them on hold would take too much time. Besides, someone awake in the house might see the lights come to life on an extension. He left the phone untouched.

He heard no sound from the bedroom. He waited for two very long minutes. Still no sound. Not even the sliding of an end-table drawer, or the squeak of bedsprings. He then moved quietly and confidently into the room. A soft glow from the yard light entered the bedroom windows, and the man could make out the shapes of two people sleeping side by side in the bed. He could see the gray hair of a man next to the long, gray hair of a woman. Walking to the woman's side of the bed, nearest him, the man placed the muzzle of the automatic directly against the front temple of the woman and pulled the trigger.

The gray haired man was awakened instantly by the

gunshot that killed his wife of forty-two years. Neighbors were too far away to hear the shot, muffled somewhat by the proximity of the muzzle to the woman's head. The man was visibly shaken, frightened from the report of the gunshot, not yet knowing what had actually happened.

"I would appreciate it, old man," said the gunman, "if you would come with me." And he leaned over and struck the man a glancing blow on the head. Not enough to put him out. Just enough to draw blood and hurt him badly.

The old man was muttering a prayer to God as he looked at his wife and the pool of blood which flowed onto the pillow beneath her head. Blood from the gash on his forehead was partly obscuring his vision. The pain was staggering. Fear immobilized him. The gunman walked around to the other side of the bed, and when he arrived he hit the gray haired man again with another glancing blow. While the old man was moaning, the intruder took a rubber handball out of the fanny-pack and shoved it into the old man's mouth. It was a tight fit. Once in, the old man could neither spit it out nor yell above a muffled sob. The intruder yanked the old man to his feet and began to drag him, stumbling along down the stairs, into the kitchen, to the back door, and out of the house.

The intruder had no reason not to kill the old man immediately, except for laziness. He simply did not want to be forced to carry his body to, or from, the car.

The man shoved the apostle into the back seat, and onto the floor of a car that he had stolen from the streets of Salt Lake City only minutes before driving it to Emigration Canyon. Again a blow to the head. This time, harder.

Driving carefully, the man was aware that the canyon was patrolled by private police. Aware that he might be stopped by a sheriff's car or a private patrolmen, he had placed a new nipple on the muzzle of the automatic, and was prepared to kill anyone who tried to stop him. He still had thirteen rounds of soft-nosed ammunition in the standard fifteen-round clip of the automatic.

Action, the man thought. That's what it takes. No hesitation. Momentum. If an officer stopped him and walked to his car, or asked him to get out, the officer would be dead before he knew anything was wrong. The man would fire at the patrol car, repeatedly, pinning down the second officer, if there was one. He would approach the car and fire down and into the officer cowering on the seat, or trying desperately to call for help, fumbling for his gun, or disengaging the shotgun from its clamp by the radio. No hesitation. That was his edge, he thought. And he was prepared to use it to the fullest.

As the man drove to the "This Is The Place Monument" in Emigration Canyon, he was happy. Things were working out well. Nothing had gone wrong. No one tried to stop him.

With little wasted motion, the man parked next to the monument, opened the back door of the car, pulled the apostle out, to his feet. He pushed him a few steps and then forced him to the ground at the base of the monument. Time was passing quickly, he thought. It was probably near 4:30 a.m. He needed to hurry.

Pulling a knife from a sheath inside the fanny-pack, he held the blade and adjusted his hand on the walnut grip. The knife was an Ek-Warrior honed to a razor's edge. It was his favorite. Its tang ran the full twelve-and-a-half inches from heel to tip. At the heel end of the knife was an extended pommel known as a "skull crusher." Protruding about an inch from the butt end of the handle, it was nothing more than a rounded piece of the extended tang used in mercenary fighting to cave in a portion of the skull in close combat. He brought his fist down in a full swinging arc directly onto the head of the apostle. The sound told him it was all over for this saint among men.

The man proceeded with his grisly business. It took him only two minutes. Wiping the splattered blood from his face with a torn off piece of the saint's sacred protective garments, he tossed the cloth away. He left the knife next to the man, removed the black coveralls he was wearing, along with the gloves and a pair of Totes half-boots. He placed all the clothing in a pile on top of the knife and put on a new pair of pink cotton gloves. He got in the car, and drove, carefully, and slowly, out of the canyon, and into the calm early morning traffic of an awakening Salt Lake City. The gun, by his side on the car seat, was ready, just in case.

He stopped at a pay telephone and dialed the home telephone number of Detective T. Mahoney. Mahoney answered on the fourth ring.

"What?" he spit out in a half-asleep rasp of a voice.

The voice on the other end was strange, and, in a way, metallic.

"You have fifteen minutes," the man said, "to place a black duffle bag containing $100,000,000 in unmarked, randomly numbered, twenty-dollar bills in the waste basket at the corner next to Temple Square, across from the Hotel Utah Building. If it is not there do not blame me for what happens."

The man laughed as he hung up, not waiting for a reply.

Mahoney looked at the phone. His head thumping in the aftermath of being awakened abruptly, and from the residual effects of a pint of Canadian Club. This wasn't happening. This sure as hell wasn't happening, he thought. Not to me. Not at 5:15 in the morning on a fuckin' Monday. Fifteen minutes, my ass, you shithead, Mahoney mumbled into the mouthpiece of a dead phone.

Monday: Day Eight, Morning

Mahoney arrived at the station at 6:07 a.m., just over three-quarters-of-an-hour from when he received the call. During that time he had made two telephone calls — one to the chief — the other to Grant. He had dressed, then broken every law in the driver's manual getting to headquarters. No shower, no shave, no coffee, no donuts, no nothing. Fuck! Fuck! Fuck! Grant was already there, and so was the chief. Mahoney felt like his head was in a vise.

The three men agreed that the call was a part of a cruel game, designed to suggest that Mahoney and Grant should keep $100,000,000 on hand for delivery at a moment's notice. They also knew it was impossible. Where would they keep $100,000,000 in cash? Where would they get it, unless the church was willing to provide it? And, noted Mahoney, $100,000,000 in twenty-dollar bills would probably require a duffle bag the size of the Goodyear Blimp.

All hell broke loose in the City of Saints shortly after 7 a.m. A man, driving into the city from his home in Emigration Canyon, passed the "This Is The Place Monument," and thought for a moment that he had seen the body of a dead animal, probably the victim of an automobile collision, lying bloodied near the side of the monument. He stopped his car as others passed by, then backed up, and got out to see what it was.

The motorist hadn't taken two steps toward the grisly scene when he fell to his knees and began to retch. Vomit splattered on his trousers.

The call came into the police almost immediately. Once recovered from his spasms of sickness, the motorist had used his car phone, a luxury most residents of Emigration Canyon affect ed, to call the police.

107

Mahoney, Grant, and the chief of police, arrived at the scene just after the police ambulance and a solitary patrol car. The forensic van had followed them. Pylons were already being set to keep the light early morning traffic from getting too near the scene. Yellow police tape was being strung from the monument to a post near the side of the road. A police photographer who arrived with the forensic team prepared to take crime scene photographs as Mahoney, Grant, and the chief stepped over the tape and moved toward the mass of red flesh gutted near a neat stack of clothing piled like a rumpled pyramid on the ground.

The victim's throat had been cut from ear to ear, his face was slashed beyond recognition, and his tongue was cut from his mouth and rested, like a wet, unraveled baseball, next to the nearly severed head of the victim. The man had been ripped open with an autopsy-like incision made from sternum to groin. The chest cavity and abdominal area had been opened and the man's heart, stomach, liver, and bowels were cut out and spilled onto the ground beside him.

Odd, Mahoney thought. Next to the mutilated body, in a small natural hollow in the ground, was a single black handball.

The chief, looking at the remains longer than he wanted to, simply said, "Jesus, the poor devil."

"Blood atonement," said Mahoney. Disgust saturated his voice.

Dressed only in Mormon garments, ripped open from neck to crotch to accommodate the butchery, the man had no identification, and was, to say the least, unrecognizable.

"Who is it?" asked the chief, fighting the taste of stomach acid rising in his throat.

Grant was leaning against the monument, looking at the remains on the ground in front of him. Tears rimmed both eyes.

Mahoney had looked carefully at the thinning wisps of white hair matted with blood and dirt and sand, and the pallor and aged look of the skin that was visible.

"It is one of the Council of Twelve Apostles," Mahoney said. "Which one will have to wait until we find out the names of the eleven who are, I hope, still alive."

* * *

The man abandoned the car before 5:30 a.m. at a twenty-four-hour Denny's. He pulled into the lot, parked near a group of cars by the side entrance, placed the fanny-pack and gun in a brown paper bag, and covertly removed his gloves. These, too, he placed in the fanny-pack. Closing the car door, he entered the restaurant and had a cup of coffee. When he left, brown paper bag in hand, he passed the car and continued walking. Twenty-five-minutes later he was at the Tri Arc. He entered a side door and took an elevator to his room. He passed no one on the way. He showered and scrubbed and put on new clothes. He bundled the old clothes with the 9mm gun in the brown paper bag.

The man ordered room service, a rather large and showy western-style breakfast, at 6:15 a.m., making much of having just awakened and of needing a carafe of coffee, fast. Later he would dispose of the bag and its contents while on his way to Wendover, Nevada, by car. He would gamble, visit a whorehouse a couple of times a day, for two days, then return to Salt Lake City.

This was really beginning to be fun, the man thought. I wonder if anything is on the news about my little adventure.

By 6:45 a.m. the breakfast had arrived, and the man had tipped the room service girl well, in cash. He had charged the order to his room. As the girl left, the man flicked on the television. There was nothing on about the killing, but he continued to watch. It seemed forever.

At 7:35 a.m., on KSL-TV, the church owned television station, one of the most watched stations in Utah, a slide came up on screen announcing a "Special Bulletin" from the KSL-TV Newsroom. Toni Dannly was at the anchor desk.

"KSL-TV has just learned that a man, as yet unidentified, has been brutally murdered at the base of the 'This Is The Place Monument' in Salt Lake City's Emigration Canyon. Although police are refusing immediate comment, this reporter has learned that Detective Thomas Mahoney believes that, when identified, the victim will turn out to have been a member of the Council of Twelve Apostles of the Mormon Church.

"Detective Mahoney believes this brutal slaying is directly connected to the bombing death of Apostle Gordon Arthur Fielding, in his office, Thursday morning, only four days ago.

"One week ago, today, a Mormon tourist, Mr. John Williamson, of St. Paul, Minnesota, was the victim of a rifle bullet while he stood with his family at the statue of Mormon pioneers in Temple Square. Although police have admitted the existence of a letter threatening the General Authorities of the church, they have not made the details of the letter public.

"With the death of a Mormon tourist, and the brutal slaying of two men, one known to be a member of the Council of Twelve Apostles, city officials and the public are in a virtual uproar. They are demanding to know the content of the letter, and exactly what police are doing to protect the leadership of the Mormon church, and find the person responsible.

"This has been a special report of KSL-TV News. Further details will be broadcast as they become available. This is Toni Dannly, KSL-TV, reporting."

The man liked the report, all except for the part about the person "responsible for these cowardly acts." He knew she was wrong. He knew it took nerves of steel and the bravery of a true soldier to do what he had done. *That bitch had better change her tune*, he thought, *or she'll answer to me.*

The man had written "Toni Dannly" on a small pad of Tri Arc notepaper and was busy drawing in a small dagger after the name as an exclamation point.

Work proceeded in the task force offices of the Salt Lake City police department. The Kodak boys had finally identified one of the two John Doe types culled from the thousands of photographs taken from the film collected in Temple Square. John Doe I was identified by a woman from Michigan as a widower who had been on their tour bus earlier. He checked out. John Doe II remained the only unidentified "loner."

As Mahoney and Grant looked at the picture, again and again, nothing new jumped out and grabbed them by the throat. In the photograph, the man looked so damn normal. There was virtually nothing specific to identify him. No stooped posture, no unusual clothing, no Nikon around his neck, no nothing.

He is carrying a newspaper and wearing shades, thought Mahoney. Big deal. As Mahoney sat staring at the 8-by-10 glossy, he kept hoping he had missed something. He didn't think so, but what the hell. Reaching into his desk drawer he pulled out a small black pouch measuring about two-inches by two-inches, and a quarter-of-an-inch deep. He fumbled with the flap on the pouch as Grant watched with increasing interest. Grant had never seen the pouch before. From inside Mahoney pulled out a metal contraption that unfolded into a lithographer's loupe. At least that's what the printer who gave it to him had called it. Mahoney was in the back shop of the *Tribune* one day, questioning people involving the murder of a printer in an underground parking lot near the newspaper's offices. An engraver pulled it out and inspected an engraving plate with it. Mahoney asked about it. Mahoney liked toys. He was fascinated by it. The man, something of a police buff, gave it to him. He said he had an extra, anyway. Go ahead and take it. You can play Sherlock Holmes, he said. Maybe you'll find a clue.

Unfolded, it looked like a three-sided metal frame supporting a small magnifying lens. The lens was fixed in the frame just over an inch above the base when it rested on the table. Grant kept looking, one eyebrow raising slightly. Mahoney placed the photograph directly in front of him, flat on the desk. He picked up the loupe and set it on the photograph and then leaned over and peered directly into the magnifying lens, his eyebrow nearly touching it. He ran the box-like affair from one side to the other, then back again. Then down an inch or so, and repeating the process, he scanned the entire face and upper torso of the man. He hesitated over one spot near the center of the picture. He sat back with a satisfied smirk on his face and looked at Grant.

"This is our killer. John Doe II. The son of a bitch!"

Grant jumped up and went around the two desks in an attempt to see what Mahoney had seen. He scanned the picture but came up with nothing. Finally Mahoney said, "Look at the top of the newspaper, just where the fold is."

Grant looked.

"Well, I'll be darned. Is that an antenna?"

"It's not a hard-on."

"So you were right all along. The guy was in Temple

Square. He wanted to see that guy get killed. And, he's probably working alone."

"You can bet on it, Heber; this guy wouldn't trust his own grandmother to butter his banana bread. The trouble is, he looks like everyone else. Even this blowup is relatively worthless."

Mahoney snatched the picture from the desk and held it to his chest, face in.

"All right, Heber, describe the bastard to me. From the picture. What does he look like? Come on, you're a trained detective. Describe him."

"Ah . . . he's average build, average weight, ah . . . brownish hair . . . ah . . . "

"That's what I'm getting at." said Mahoney. "If we can't describe him to each other, how in hell are we going to put out a bulletin to pick him up. What? Be on the lookout for a normal guy, average everything, arrest him on sight? Goddamn it and piss on me!"

Monday: Day Eight, Afternoon

The rest of the day went precisely as Mahoney expected. Every fan in the place was covered with shit.

Even with the church's vast resources, it was noon and they hadn't tracked down the identity of what was left at the base of the monument in Emigration Canyon. Everyone involved, from church security to the cops, was swarming all over the place. Eight of the apostles had been located, and were safe. Two others didn't answer or were thought to be in transit. Two more out of town officiating at the opening of a temple in South America.

With two out of town, and eight accounted for by telephone, only two were left: Apostle Mark Banner, and Apostle Preston Taylor. Both were indispensable to the church's faithful. Succession, like that of the United States Government, assured that a President, Prophet, Seer, and Revelator was always, and immediately, in place at the top of the church. Unlike the government, there wasn't even the traditional swearing-in ceremony to go through. If the president of the church died, the senior member of the Council of Twelve Apostles was *the* president of the church. No ifs, ands, or buts; and no delays. So, they were not indispensable to the church's continuation; but these two men, in particular, these two men, were indispensable in the hearts of the faithful.

Apostle Preston Taylor was next in line to the president. It was thought he was in transit. It was hoped that the telephone in his limousine was just somehow not working. His death, many church leaders thought, would bring the Mormon empire to its knees in the wake of the death of G. A. Fielding. Some prayed it wasn't Apostle Taylor; others couldn't bring themselves to do even that, for that would

113

mean an unacceptable alternative — Apostle Banner.

Apostle Mark Banner was sixth in line to succeed the president, but, more importantly, Apostle Banner was revered as the great mediator, second only in his belovedness to General Authority Fielding. His death, immediately following that of Apostle Fielding, would bring a wave of depression over the church unlike any since the death of Brigham Young in 1877.

Brigham Young's death was at first thought to be natural and was diagnosed as cholera morbus by his physician. Later theories stated that it resulted from kidney infection brought on by repeated self-catheterization, or arsenic poisoning administered by his enemies. Despite the conspiracy theories, it is now believed Brigham Young died of appendicitis, although appendicitis was unknown as a clinical entity in 1877. Still theories of murder persisted for years. Now, whether the dead brother was Apostle Preston Taylor or Apostle Mark Banner, there was no doubt about the name of what killed him. It was murder. Unpure and cold-blooded murder.

Shortly after 1 p.m., a young policeman assigned to grunt work on the task force, was the first to knock on the front door of Apostle Mark Banner's home. When he received no response, he walked to the back of the house. Seeing the back door ajar, he entered immediately. The television was still on. The security guard was dead. Shot through the head. And in the bedroom, upstairs, lay the body of Edith Mack Banner, resting peacefully, it appeared, except for the deep reddish brown stain of blood which surrounded her head on the crisp white pillowcase.

Two of the most beloved apostles of the Church of Jesus Christ of Latter-day Saints, were dead within four days of each other. And an Apostle's wife, revered above all other women in the church, was gone to her reward.

There were some who said the wailing of the faithful could be heard from any mountaintop on earth.

Tuesday: Day Nine, Morning

Mahoney had called Number Two's office and was told the Second Counselor would get right back to him. Mahoney was pissed.

"What did he say?" asked Grant.

"Direct line my ass."

"He said, 'Direct line my ass?'"

"No, no, no. But I thought the old fart was supposed to answer that line directly. Wasn't it supposed to be a direct line?"

Mahoney didn't wait for Grant to respond.

"Well, some woman answered, a secretary, I suppose. He'll get right back to us. All I can say is that the temple walls must be shaking like hell over there."

"Along with the apostles, I suppose," said Grant.

"I hope so. Maybe they will get off their holy asses and let us do what we're paid to do. You know, Grant, I may be getting too damn old for this shit. What do you think?"

Grant winced.

Mahoney grunted.

Both men started going through the paperwork that had accumulated from the task force overnight, but their hearts weren't in it. It was now 11 a.m. and Mahoney wasn't going to wait another minute. He started to reach for the phone, just as it rang.

Number Two had placed the call directly to Mahoney, and had simply, and effectively, said, "Detective Mahoney — in my office, in one hour."

Mahoney managed a sputtered interjection before Number Two hung up, and Number Two abruptly said, "Yes. What is it?" He sounded like a Sherman tank was resting on his chest.

"Sir, I would appreciate it if you would have someone provide us with one additional piece of information when we meet. I am sure your security people have already thought of it, but, if not, they should be working on it too."

Pause. No response from Number Two. Mahoney plowed on.

"We received all the material we need, except for one printout. I'd call and get it myself, but if you could intervene I know we would get it faster. In addition to the material we received, I would like a printout of all employees who have been hired in the last six months. If you could have that . . ."

"Yes. Make it two hours. Goodbye."

Number Two, it seemed, didn't have a lot of patience on this particular Tuesday morning. It was 11 a.m.; the meeting would be at one o'clock. Another fuckin' day shot to hell, Mahoney thought.

The policemen standing guard outside the Church Administration Building simply nodded as Mahoney and Grant entered the massive, old, pillared structure located within the same square block as the Church Office Building, but on the opposite side. Inside, however, two church security agents insisted on seeing detailed identification before letting them approach the secretary's desk to announce their appointment. Mahoney could see the bulges under their blazers where the men carried shoulder holsters and weapons. Once the secretary announced that they could go in, one of the two security agents said, "This way, gentlemen."

Mahoney and Grant entered Number Two's office and when the tall, and decidedly ugly, security agent gestured, sat in two large leather chairs facing the desk. This time there was only one additional chair placed in front of the large desk. Kimball, maybe, Mahoney thought.

"The Second Counselor will be with you momentarily," the agent said. He turned and left.

Grant looked at Mahoney, waiting for the agent to leave.

"I wouldn't want to meet that guy in a dark alley."

"Ugly as a warthog," said Mahoney.

The man was disgruntled at having been called into work. He had been planning a leisurely few days getting off roughing up whores in Wendover, and blowing some money on the crap tables. But he couldn't take the chance now.

Once the reign of terror had started, church security's priorities had changed, and in some cases, they doubled the guard. Agents who were off were called to duty. Agents on duty had their hours extended. The man had checked his answering machine only to find an order to report to work. The action meant getting rid of the gun and other incriminating items in a more hurried manner. He washed and wiped and stuffed every- thing into a metal tackle box, drove to a river on the north side of Ogden, Utah, thirty miles away, and dumped them in the deepest, calmest stretch of water he could find. He loved the outdoors. He then drove to work. Just another day in the service of the Lord.

He had been on Kimball's ten days on, four days off, shift for a year now, and loved it. It allowed him time to do his own work, his preparation.

Kimball liked the military sense the unusual shifts produced. He insisted that no agent be assigned to guard any one church leader for more than ten days in a row, nor fill any function long enough to become complacent doing the task. He didn't want any outsider becoming comfortable with the routine by watching one security agent for several weeks. He knew there was risk in change, but safety outweighed the negative aspects of the schedule. The fiasco with the television watching security agent at Apostle Banner's home was a breech of regulations he refused to dwell on. The system was perfect. Only the men had more to learn.

On one shift an agent might guard an Apostle in his office, at a speaking engagement, and on his way to and from his home. On the next shift he might be reviewing inter-office correspondence for subversive activity against the church or its leaders. On yet another shift, he may, in fact, become a spy for Kimball, trying to get information from people who aren't supposed to give it out — to anyone. And once in a while, each agent would draw the supreme assignment — ten days of guarding the Prophet himself, or, at least, one of the Apostles.

To make the procedure impossible to predict, the agent's names were randomly linked to assignments by number.

No one man would do any job longer than ten days running, nor repeat that particular job more than once every few years. All agents had to be proficient in weapons, martial arts, and Kimball's own particular brand of Danite loyalty, to him, and to the church. In that order.

What the man knew, and had planned on, was the fact that as long as he stayed on Kimball's good side he would be designated Agent 1 sooner or later. With a hundred agents, each assigned to fourteen-day rotations, ten days on, and four days off, each agent could cover twenty-six assignments in a year. Within four years, each would automatically rotate to guard the president of the church. And each would average at least three turns in a given year at guarding an apostle of the church. Better yet, each had access to nearly every aspect of the grounds, and even to the Church Administration Building scores of times during the year.

Assuming that each agent is loyal, faithful and trustworthy, it was a brilliant plan. Assuming, however, that just one agent is a killer, bent on assassinating the prophet, or the apostles, it was not a viable plan at all; it was nothing short of an apocalyptic nightmare.

Kimball's fatal flaw, the man thought, was in believing that all of his men were devoted Danites, in love with the church, and blindly following Kimball's inept leadership.

Brother Kimball, the man thought, had overlooked me. I think I'll kill him too.

Tuesday: Day Nine, Afternoon

When Mahoney and Grant were shown directly to Number Two's office, it seemed to both of them that they were being treated with a little more respect than during earlier visits. About fuckin' time, thought Mahoney.

When Number Two finally entered the room, Kimball was right behind. Both men looked ashen and spent. Kimball didn't make eye contact. Number Two looked slightly embarrassed.

"Gentlemen, I am ready to concede that although we may know more about routine security matters concerning this church than the police, we know nothing about preventing the kind of slaughter that has been visited upon our dear Brothers over the past few days. You both have my solemn promise that the First Presidency and the Council of Twelve Apostles of this church will do whatever you ask to hasten the day when we can put all of this behind us. Please tell me what we should do."

Mahoney, suppressing even a hint of victory, said, "We do appreciate the position you are in. Detective Grant and I are also in a difficult position. Two of your top leaders, an Apostle's wife, and one member of the church, have been senselessly murdered by one insane man.

"I, for one," said Mahoney, "am not used to having unabated killing taking place around me. Usually, we get a killing, followed by an investigation, and an arrest. Once in a while there is no arrest and the guilty party gets away. Frankly, gentlemen, in this case, we may have to consider ourselves lucky if this man can simply be killed while trying to evade police. We may never know the real reason for what he has done. And maybe the reason doesn't matter. What matters is stopping the murders."

For some reason Grant found himself thinking that

119

Mahoney had just authorized the murder of this killer, rather than his arrest and subsequent trial.

"I think what my partner means, gentlemen, is . . . "

"What I mean, Detective Grant, is what I say I mean. I believe that this killer must be stopped before anyone else is killed. I would like to ask the church to authorize a story to appear in today's *Deseret News*, as well as in the special edition of the Salt Lake *Tribune*, that says Uncle."

"Uncle?" questioned Number Two.

"Yes, basically a story that says the church gives up and agrees to pay the $100,000,000 when and where the man says. Under any circumstances. Without retribution. Without police intervention. Without prejudice. So help you God. Now."

Kimball blanched.

"We can't do that," Kimball said. "Excuse me, Sir, but what the detectives may not understand is that once we do this we would be open to an ever escalating number of church terrorists."

Number Two nodded slowly in agreement with Kimball.

"Sir, you don't understand," said Mahoney. I do not intend that you actually give the money away. I only suggest that you promise to give it away and let's get on with putting this thing to bed."

"Detective Mahoney, the church's position in this matter is clear. We cannot say that the church guarantees the payment of the money, without retribution, and swear to it, without keeping our word in the process. We are prophets and apostles of God. We could not lie in this manner."

"Are you telling me," said Mahoney, "that the church would rather not tell a lie to a butcher, and have more apostles slaughtered, than to tell a lie and end this thing? Surely, when the story finally comes out, not a single one of the brethren of your church could possibly find fault with such a transparent subterfuge?"

"I'm confused," said Number Two.

He's confused, thought Mahoney.

"I'm confused because you have told us he is not after the money. It is low on his list of priorities. And now you call it a transparent subterfuge. What makes you think he would go for this?"

"Follow me here." Mahoney leaned forward. "If you were a fanatical killer bent of wiping out fifteen leaders of the church on the ruse of wanting ransom money, and you had set the ransom so high that it was impossible to meet, wouldn't you think that so far everything was going your way?"

Number Two nodded.

"And then, after you had already killed two of the most beloved apostles of the church, the church suddenly announced in a front page story, aimed directly at you, that it will pay the full $100,000,000 any way you want, no police involved, wouldn't you think twice about it? Maybe you could have your cake and eat it too. Maybe, if the ad appealed, carefully, to your ego, your intelligence, and your cleverness, maybe you'd get greedy. Maybe you'd want to be the killer who was also smart enough to get away with $100,000,000 in addition to the murders.

"And maybe, if you saw through all of this, you might still think that you could show us all. That you could collect all the money, and keep on killing, apostle after apostle. You'd do it all. You'd show us.

"True, I don't think money is the motive. But I do think that power and superiority, especially over the leaders of the church, may well be the motive. Given one additional chance to prove how superior you are, wouldn't you take it? If you were this kind of person, wouldn't you do it?"

"All right," said Number Two, "You're saying we have nothing to lose because he's going to keep killing anyway. If we interject this ploy into the mix he may slow down enough to collect before he takes up killing again. Right?"

"Right," Mahoney said.

"Right," Kimball said.

Grant could have puked in Kimball's face.

"The Salt Lake City police department," said Mahoney, "will assure the church that whether following the ploy is successful or not, we'll go public that a solemn promise to the killer was made over the objections of the church, and was not approved by the General Authorities. We will write the script."

"How in the world," said Number Two, "would he expect to collect all that money without getting caught?"

"As I said, he thinks he is smarter than anyone else."

"What if he is?" asked Number Two.

Mahoney just looked at the Second Counselor. He didn't say a word. What he wanted to say was: "Then we're fucked."

Mahoney and Grant had agreed to give Number Two a few minutes to speak with his associates and get back to them. Time was critical. Mahoney sat in the lobby, near the secretary's desk, and began to write out some preliminary text for the statement in the paper. Occasionally, the two security agents guarding the lobby of the Church Administration Building would glance down at him.

Continuing to write, Mahoney ignored both of them, the tall ugly one, and the one with the weird eye.

Church officials agreed to the new plan to protect the church leaders. It was in writing. It contained five points:

1. The three members of The First Presidency and the Council of Twelve Apostles, totaling thirteen now, following the death of Apostles G. A. Fielding and Mark Banner, will each be assigned two full-time bodyguards round the clock. Each team will be made up of one member of church security, selected by Mark Kimball, and one member of the police department, selected by Detectives Mahoney and Grant. The teams will work twelve hours on, and twelve hours off, for the duration. No days off. Two shifts of twenty-six men each. Each team must have two guards on duty at all times, one from each agency. Under no circumstances are two security agents, or two policemen to be paired together. If the person being guarded has to go to the toilet, one guard will accompany him, remaining directly outside the bathroom door, until he is through. This precaution will remain in effect at all times, including throughout the night. When the person being guarded retires for the evening, one guard will remain directly outside the bedroom door, and the second guard will be stationed as far away from the first guard as possible while keeping him in his direct line-of-sight. *Caution will be used so a diversion cannot be used to separate the guards from each other or from the person they are guarding.* Twenty-six additional policemen will be assigned to the residences of the thirteen persons being guarded, each on a twelve-hour shift. When the bodyguard team arrives at the residence, the policeman assigned to guard the home, will take up his post

outside the house or apartment. He will not remain in a patrol car, but physically patrol the perimeter of the residence throughout the shift. *No one, other than the bodyguard team, will be authorized to enter the home, even if that person has papers authorizing entry, unless personally cleared by Detectives Mahoney or Grant. No exceptions.* The killer may be posing as a policeman, security agent, or some other official. Remember, a bomb was planted in the office of one of the apostles. Don't let this happen to the place you're guarding. Policemen, with weapons drawn, will challenge anyone approaching the post. Detain them, and call for immediate backup. If a person won't stop when asked, don't argue — shoot.

2. When the person being guarded is transported anywhere, his vehicle will be inspected and started by one of the two guards before any occupants approach the car. While this inspection is being done, they will remain at least one hundred feet from the vehicle. When church leaders meet in the Temple itself, policemen, who cannot enter the Temple, will remain posted outside the entry doors. Church security agents will be selected on the basis of their Temple recommend card, allowing them entry to the Temple. The church agents will remain with their charge, or immediately outside the door where any private meeting is held. Mr. Kimball will make the assignments from a roster of twenty-six primary policemen designated to join church security agents in guarding the church leaders, and a list of twenty-six secondary policemen designated to guard their houses or apartments. He will FAX a complete list of assignments to Detectives Mahoney and Grant. *Only Detectives Mahoney and Grant will be authorized to make changes to the assignment lists.* Once sent, Mr. Kimball no longer has any authority to alter the assignments. Mr. Kimball, and Detectives Mahoney and Grant, will immediately communicate any information received about the case. The information will go no further than the three men.

3. Each policeman on duty will report violations, suspicions, or concerns, to either Detective Mahoney or Grant at the end of each shift. A police stenographer will take the reports down verbatim. Any unreported unusual or suspicious action will result in the termination of the offender.

4. The thirteen church leaders will cooperate with the guards for their personal safety and the safety of their families. They will do what the guards say, without question. The same reporting method will be used at the end of each shift.

5. In all cases the policeman assigned to the team will be in complete charge of the activity of the team. The security agent will obey all instructions given to him by the policeman in charge. All policemen will be in plainclothes (business dress) regardless of their normal assignment.

Mahoney was worried. To get the thirteen church leaders who were still alive to follow the directions of a policeman and a security agent, was a tall order. These thirteen men were not used to following instructions from underlings, no matter what their job or duties. They were apostles of God. Mere mortals obeyed them. The fault, Dear Brutus, thought Mahoney, is not in the stars, but in ourselves, that we are underlings. He hoped his Mormon policemen were up to it. Underlings were often intimidated. And religious intimidation is a powerful tool.

Mahoney and Grant sent the two lists to Kimball. There was one temporary change from the procedure. Instead of twenty-six guards from the church and twenty-six from the police, they would need only twenty-four from each group. Two of the apostles were still in South America, not due to return for another week. Mahoney had suggested to Number Two that they find more for them to do in South America. Number Two thought that could be arranged.

The lists included instructions to Kimball that the assignments were to be in place by 5 p.m. Mahoney and Grant had already instructed the men on their list. For the first time in his life, Mahoney had asked members of the police force their religious preference. In every case possible a Mormon was picked to fill the slot. It wasn't hard. Sixty percent of the people in Utah are Mormons. On the police force, those who numbered themselves among the faithful, exceeded seventy-eight percent.

"Grant," said Mahoney, seeming, for a moment, to have gained enough respect for the man that "Heb" or "Heber" didn't seem quite appropriate, "this is going to cost the department, and the taxpayers, one hell of a lot of money."

"What is?"

"The overtime, for Christ's sake, Heber! The fuckin' overtime! And besides that, the local hoods will have a field day. We're going to have fifty-two policemen assigned as bodyguards or house sitters, and not on the streets. How long do you think it's going to be until everything from snatch-and-run crimes to breaking-and-entering goes through the roof?"

"Not long. Not long at all," conceded Grant.

By 6 p.m. each of the teams was in place, guarding its very own saint from the slings and arrows of some truly outrageous fortune. Mahoney hoped he could get some sleep. Usually, he slept like a longshoremen a day after being paid. Lately, since that telephone call in the middle of the night, he had been hovering just below a state of wakefulness throughout most of the early morning hours. He was too old for this shit.

Tuesday: Day Nine, Evening

Mahoney knocked at the door of Maxwell Jackson, somewhat chagrined that he hadn't called before leaving the office. He hadn't really intended to see Max, but as he pulled out of his parking space at 7:30 p.m. he realized that a free drink and an old friend might be just what he needed. Besides, he had a question or two.

The door opened and Jackson's smile told him he was more than welcome.

"I've been expecting you."

"No shit. You think I'm going to run over here every time there are alligators up to my ass, you're crazy."

"Swim faster."

"Swimming as fast as I can."

"Drink?"

"Is the Pope a bear?"

Jackson poured a double on the rocks for each of them, and Mahoney melted into Max's comfortable chair.

"You need sleep, Mahoney."

"I need a miracle, Max. This thing is going to get worse long before it gets better."

"How is it going to get worse — your killer cut the shit out of an apostle of the church at the foot of one of its most historic monuments? What's worse?"

"More of the same."

"I don't think so."

"Why not?"

"Well . . . I thought you might ask that. You're thinking blood atonement, aren't you? A whole rash of blood atonement ritualistic killings coming down on your pointed little head."

"It had occurred to me that the son-of-a-bitch could have

126

waited for a few more years until my pension was assured. Every time one of these apostles gets bumped off my days with the department number less and less. If we don't stop him somebody is going to have to be sacrificed to the press, the people, and the mayor's office. Guess who? Now, Max, exactly what do you mean you don't think more of the same isn't worse?"

"Well, I think you already know the answer; you just want me to confirm it for you."

"Indulge me."

"The first killing was a rifle shot from the window of the Hotel Utah Building, and it wasn't even a selected target. The man the killer shot could just as well have been a gentile. The second killing was a bomb blast that ripped apart an apostle in his office. And now this one — a blood atonement ritual in Emigration Canyon.

"It stands to reason, Mahoney, that if this nut was going to keep killing in the blood atonement style of the early Mormons, he would have started with the first apostle that way. No. He's going to give you a veritable menu of death. Rifle, bomb, blood atonement, and next, who knows. It might just be random, but it might also be connected to the church in some esoteric way. He might even kill someone with a garrote one day, and resort to having them eaten alive by locusts the next, just to keep you hopping."

"Goddamn it, Max, that's what I'm afraid of. If he keeps to a pattern we might have a better chance. It's this anything goes shit that's hard to pin down."

"The only pattern he's given you is sticking to his plan to kill the apostles and the president of the church. That's the pattern, not the way he does it."

The two men sat looking at each other for about thirty seconds, and then Max spoke.

"Do you want another drink? That one's dead."

"No, I just wanted to relax with a friend. I want to go to sleep tonight, not pass out."

"You're welcome to sleep here. The couch is long, comfortable, and well worn."

"Thanks anyway, Max. I've got to go."

"You'll be back."

"Yeah. I know."

* * *

The man approached the house in Holladay, a suburb southeast of Salt Lake City. It looked quiet, and he was sure all was well. No one would expect this, he thought. The church could care less, and the police had their hands full elsewhere. He had seen to that.

He parked his car a block away from the small modern bungalow, and walked along the dimly lit street. He had picked the time carefully. It was 10 p.m. and not entirely unusual to see someone walk short distances in this neighborhood at night. But there was no one else about. Had there been he might have reconsidered and picked another night. Or just killed the onlooker. He was nothing, he thought, if not flexible.

The woman answered the door in a robe and slippers. She had a pint of Haggen-Dazs Swiss Almond Vanilla in her hand and was eating directly from the carton with a teaspoon.

There was no screen, and as the woman opened the door the man moved directly into the room, pushing her roughly ahead of him.

"What the hell are . . . "

She didn't get the rest of the question out before he slammed his gloved palm into her face and broke her nose. She staggered across the room, tumbling over the arm of a leather recliner and tripping on a matching ottoman only feet from the television set. The television was on; the VCR was running. An image of Humphrey Bogart kissing Katharine Hepburn on the African Queen flashed across the screen as he fell on her. He strangled her until she was unconscious. Blood covered her mouth from the broken nose, and the pint of ice cream was rolling by her side leaving a small trail of white cream on the floor.

He got up and walked slowly to the light switch. Glancing outside, seeing nothing, he turned it off. The only light in the room now came from the pictures flickering on the nineteen-inch screen. God he liked Bogart. He was tempted to watch the rest of the movie. He stood watching for a moment, caught up in wondering whether or not the scene with the leeches had passed, or was still to come. He liked the leeches. It was his favorite scene. A slight groan brought him back to the business at hand. More important things to do, he thought. There was fun to be had.

He left the television on and dragged the woman into the bedroom. He placed her on the bed and ripped her robe open. She groaned again, an unconscious groan. He hit her in the neck with his fist. The groaning stopped. Then he stepped back and looked at her. He liked what he saw, very much. He liked the blood on her face. He could feel his erection pressing against the inside of his pants. He took his clothes off. Looking at her lying on the bed, her abdomen rising and falling in the slow and steady manner that often comes with sleep, he began to undress. The telephone rang once during the time spent on the bed with her underneath his body. He had ignored it, but eventually, after the fourth ring, he heard an answering machine pick up. After her cutesy message, something about really wanting to hear from someone other than a bill collector, God he hated that shit, a voice came on saying, "It's just me — Barb. I wanted to see how you were. Hope you're feeling OK. You haven't picked up yet so I guess you're in a hot tub or a warm bed. Talk to you tomorrow, Hon . . . Bye."

When the man was through he tidied up a few things, dressed, and then reached over and felt Dannly's pulse. It was still beating — slightly. He took an Ek-Warrior from its sheath, placed its point directly under her sternum, pointing its tip upward under her breasts, and nearly centered between them. The heart was almost centered in the chest, but about two-thirds of the organ was on the left side. He angled the blade slightly to his right, her left, and plunged it directly into her heart. He left it there while he checked her pulse, and grinned quickly as he finally felt it stop. He twisted the knife from habit, removed slowly, took it into the bathroom, washed it off, and dried it on a pair of Dannly's panties hung to dry over the shower rod. He was still wearing pale pink cotton gloves.

One hour after he had arrived, the man left. Retracing his path to the stolen automobile a block away, he met no one, and no one passed him. There was no sign of life on the block, only the glow of lights from the houses on the quiet suburban street.

Toni Dannly, had called in early that morning. She was

sick with a minor sore throat. The man had heard the announcement on the early evening news that Ms. Dannly was ill and wouldn't be at the anchor desk. How nice, he had thought; something to do. What he didn't know was that this would be her first absence from the anchor desk during her career at KSL-TV. What he did know is that it would be her last. Toni Dannly was dead at the age of thirty-one.

There would be no Big Apple; no fast track to stardom; no more Emmys.

Wednesday: Day Ten, Morning

Mahoney had gotten some sleep.

Grant, Mahoney suspected, was in better condition than he. All that good living, he supposed. It crossed his mind that he should give up drinking. He dismissed it as an aberrant thought brought on by abject stupidity and not enough morning coffee to put him in touch with reality.

Just as he reached for a donut, the phone rang.

"Mahoney."

"Hello, Detective Mahoney," the man said. "Did you get a good night's sleep?"

"Hello, asshole."

Mahoney reached over and pushed the button to activate the tape recorder attached to the phone. At the same time he motioned for Grant to pick up an extension. The look on Mahoney's face told Grant, immediately, who was on the other end of the line.

"Now, now, big guy, don't get testy. I just wanted to check on how you're holding up after the other night. And I also wanted to give you a piece of news."

In the telephone booth, before placing the call to Detective Mahoney, the man had slipped a battery operated voice filter over the mouthpiece. He had used it on his first call. It was designed to change the frequency and timing of his voice. He bought it for $285 from an electronics surveillance store catering to private eyes and nut cases who liked to play head games with pretty women. He probably didn't need it, his voice was quite plain. Still, he thought, if nothing else, it would add to the drama of the telephone call. He liked that.

"What news?"

Mahoney had motioned to Grant to start a trace. It would be useless, thought Mahoney. This guy isn't that dumb. He isn't about to fall for some obvious efforts to keep him talking until a black-and-white rolls up to the phone booth. Undoubtedly, a phone booth. The bastard.

"Oh, you'll read about it later. Or maybe you'll see it on television. If I were you that's where I'd look for it — on television."

"Don't you feel compelled to give me a clue? That's how dumb cops work, you know. With clues."

"Now, Detective Mahoney, you know full well that I don't intend to make this too easy for you. I will only do what I want to do — occasionally what I am compelled to do."

"Why are you doing this? Did some church leader piss all over you? Did they refuse to let you go on a mission? Wouldn't they let you pour the sacrament wine?"

"It's not what the church has done to me, Detective Mahoney, it is what I am doing to the church that should concern you. By the way, Mahoney, don't be so cute. You know the Mormons use water, and Wonder Bread, at their sacrament. Wine's for Catholics, like you."

There was a long pause until the man spoke again. Mahoney didn't say a word.

"And now you're asking yourself, is this killer a Mormon, or isn't he? Is it me, Detective Mahoney, or is it Memorex? The only thing you know for sure, is that you don't know anything for sure. I might be a Mormon. Or maybe I just hate Mormons. I may even be a Catholic, like you. I may be living alone, like you. I may have a penchant for booze, like you. I may even be a heathen bull in a Mormon china shop, like you. What do you think, Detective Mahoney?"

Mahoney didn't answer. He just waited for the prick to continue. The asshole knew too much about him.

"Don't you even want to know what my name is? Don't you care?"

"All right, what's your name?"

"You can call me Moroni. There's a little golden statue of me tooting a horn on top of the Mormon temple."

"I thought that was Gabriel."

"The hell you did. You're nearly as smart as I am, Detective Mahoney. Not quite. But, near enough to make it very enjoyable watching how you and Brother Grant go about your job. Now, about Gabriel. Since you brought him up you might remember that he blew that horn to announce the births of John the Baptist and Jesus Christ. His little horn is also supposed to announce the Day of Judgement. But it won't. I am announcing the Day of Judgement; and it is now. It is upon the First Presidency and the Council of Twelve Apostles. I am their messenger of death."

"You must be able to do better than that." said Mahoney. "I am not going to call you Moroni, or Goldblum, or the messenger of death, for that matter. I am not going to call you anything but the prick you are unless you give me a name I can buy."

There was a long pause. Grant's eyes were showing white all the way around.

"Call me David."

"Why?"

"That's my name."

"Okay, David. Now, what can I do for you — and what will you do for me?"

"Do you have the money ready?"

"David, you know the money isn't important to you. Why do you insist on having the money? Is it the principle of the thing, or are you just playing around?"

"I think I'll call you back," the man said.

The phone went dead.

The leaders of the church, either on the advice of the task force, or because of their own sense of self preservation, Mahoney had no idea which, decided not to hold public ceremonies for their two fallen brethren. That was good. Ordinarily, the death of an apostle of the church results in a massive funeral ceremony in the Tabernacle, open to the faithful, a spill over crowd watching the televised activities on giant screens in the Salt Palace.

The church information office issued a statement that Apostles G. A. Fielding and Mark Banner would receive private ceremonies in the Temple for family and church officials only. A public ceremony would be held at a more appropriate time.

Mahoney took "appropriate" to mean — when the killing

had stopped.

Still another problem faced the leaders of the church.

Conference. The General Conference of the Church of Jesus Christ of Latter-day Saints was always held at the beginning of April and October. Gathered in the Tabernacle at every conference, and seated in front of the Mormon Tabernacle Choir, were the members of the First Presidency, the Council of Twelve Apostles, and the First Quorum of Seventies, in descending levels marking their relative importance in the hierarchy of the church. Eighty-five men, thirty targeted for death, sitting in full view of thousands. It was a policeman's nightmare. In the first few rows would sit Utah's congressional delegation, nearly all Mormons; a handful of national Mormon entertainment celebrities; and a smattering of the top leadership of several of America's most powerful corporations, Mormons all.

The answer to the question of this April's upcoming General Conference, was not whether to hold it, that was ordained. It would be held. No letters, no threats, no killings, would cripple the church to that extent, agreed the General Authorities. The question was simply how to do it without exposing themselves to the malice of a maniac bent on killing them. What better forum than a nationally televised meeting of the church leadership and several thousand of their faithful followers?

A committee had been formed to arrange precautions. Always another committee.

Mahoney got on the phone to Jackson. They talked for about an hour on the history of the church and violent attacks against it. Good old Max had a lot to tell him.

It wasn't the first time such precautions had been put in place. In 1980 the leadership of the women's organizations of the church were seated in their own private section in the balcony of the Tabernacle. In previous sessions of the General Conference women sat where they chose. So did everyone else. But it had become increasingly important to control who sat where, and why.

Ironically, the Mormon women of the Utah Territory were among the first women in modern America to participate in suffrage. Only the Wyoming Territory beat out the Utah Territory in passing the first suffrage bill. It was Brigham Young's niece who cast the first vote by a women in 1870 in a Salt Lake City municipal election. Just over a century later things had changed; the male leaders of the Mormon church sent out orders to their many women's organizations to participate in the defeat of the ERA amendment. They did just that.

Militant factions of the women's movement attacked the church in the aftermath, and the women had to be controlled. No longer could they sit where they wanted. A small plane circled above the Temple during that General Conference in 1980, towing a banner reading: *Mother in Heaven Supports the ERA.* Mormon doctrine states, in fact, that there is a Mother in Heaven. God was a man. Jesus was a man. The Holy Ghost was a man. Three separate beings. The Mormons believe that God, as a resurrected, physical man, is the literal father of Jesus, who was conceived in the same manner as men on earth. Jesus, therefore, was born of heavenly parents, a Father in Heaven, and a Mother in Heaven, the old fashioned way. Virgin birth had nothing to do with it.

In the late 1970's Sonia Johnson, a pillar of Mormon belief and practice, holding three church jobs, and paying full church tithing, eventually began lecturing on behalf of the ERA and in opposition to the church's anti-ERA position. With the blessing of the General Authorities, the local church leadership in her Virginia community excommunicated her. National press coverage brought spotlight attention to the church's position regarding women. Sonia Johnson termed the reaction of the leadership of the church "patriarchal panic." A leader of the Mormon Young Women's organization responded to the loyal sisters, saying, "When the Prophet speaks, sisters, the debate is over."

First, polygamy, the Great Accommodation.

Second, the Negro question, and the revelation of 1978.

Third, the women's issue, and the pot is still boiling.

Amid the continuing need to segregate seating, control hostile crowds, and deny admittance to the unfaithful, the church's General Conference open-door policy rapidly turned into reserved seating only.

When the panic over the possible disruption of the General Conference settled down in the mid-1980's, things returned to a semblance of normalcy. There were still general reserved sections for the priesthood, for church women's organizations, for the rich and famous, and for the press. But the church's paranoia had become relatively under control. Once again open seating was allowed, restricted, patrolled by ushers and church security guards in embarrassing numbers, but open seating nevertheless. The public, Mormon and gentile, could line up for the 10 a.m. session or the 2 p.m. session for the Saturday and Sunday General Conference. Lines formed when the gates opened at 7 a.m., and the crowd was enormous. Those not making it had to make do with the Salt Palace televised feed. The true diehards remained in line for the afternoon session. All those inside were required to leave after the morning session concluded. A new crowd of general seating replaced them for the afternoon session.

Everywhere the General Authorities looked there were lions and tigers and bears. How do we keep it safe for the leadership?

One apostle had asked during the traditional Temple meetings of the Council of Twelve Apostles each Thursday, "How do we keep from getting shot?"

Oh, my!

WEDNESDAY: Day Ten, Afternoon

After getting off the phone with Jackson, Mahoney and Grant had listened to the tape of the killer five times. The chief had heard it twice. First it was paperwork driving him nuts, thought Mahoney. Now it's the telephone.

Mahoney kept wondering about one passage. The killer had stated that Mahoney would find out some news. He then made a point of saying that if he were Mahoney, he would listen to the television to find out. Specifically, television. Why? Why single out television for a news story the killer wanted Mahoney to know about. More games? But it nagged at Mahoney.

Reaching over, Mahoney picked up the telephone and dialed the number of KSL-TV. He asked for Toni Dannly.

"I'm sorry, Ms. Dannly hasn't come in yet."

"When is she expected. It's important."

"Well, she's usually here by now, but she was out sick yesterday, and we haven't heard from her today. Would you like to leave a message?"

"No, just connect me with her producer, or news director. Who does she report to?"

"That would be Mr. Watson. I'll ring his line."

"Watson here."

"Mr. Watson, this is Detective Mahoney of the police department. Could you tell me when you expect to hear from Toni Dannly? I have some questions to ask her."

"Your guess is as good as mine, Detective Mahoney. I talked to her yesterday. She called in sick. Sore throat. Had to put a substitute on the air. Haven't heard from her today, though. We keep calling, but there's no answer. Just that answering machine. Getting close to deadline, though, so I

137

sent a car around to her house. He should be calling in any minute now."

While Mahoney and Watson were talking a call came in to the switchboard on the 911 line. A beat reporter for KSL-TV had discovered the body of Toni Dannly, dead, at her home.

"Just a minute, Detective, my mobile line is ringing. That might be him now. Hang on."

Mahoney sat staring off into space, worried, when he noticed Candy swinging her cute ass his way. She had an ugly look on her face that made him curious about what she knew. She was moving faster than usual. And she was heading directly for him.

"Mahoney," said Candy, "we got a call on dispatch that Toni Dannly is dead. A patrol car is on its way."

Just then Watson came back on the phone and said, "Jesus, Detective, Toni's dead. She . . ."

Mahoney dropped the phone and bolted from his chair.

"Let's hit it, Grant. The son-of-a-bitch has killed Dannly."

As the two men shoved past Candy, Mahoney said, "Candy, get the M.E. out there."

"He's on his way, Mahoney."

"So are we!"

Mahoney and Grant couldn't believe it. Toni Dannly was on the bed, her body completely exposed, looking like an artist's model reclining on the wrinkled linens of a still life bed. Sun washed in from the front door and spilled into the bedroom. There was a glow about her, and the room. The only jarring aspect of the painting was her face and neck. There was blood caked on her nose and mouth, deep discolorations around her throat, and the jarring sight of a single gash between her breasts from which a small stream of blood had spilled down and collected in her navel. The blood was now dry and had turned a rust brown. A single fly buzzed near the body. Mahoney fought to keep tears back. Both eyes were rimmed with moisture. At that moment, he realized with an impact he found startling, that he had cared deeply for this woman.

Back at the day room at police headquarters, Mahoney and Grant went over what they knew. Dannly was raped, but there was no semen. A condom probably. There was no skin or hair under her fingernails. She had probably been sleeping or unconscious, was hit, and passed out. The rape, obvious from the traumatic nature of the vagina and the internal bruising, had most likely occurred when she was unconscious, or dead.

Mahoney felt sick. His voice, a study in forced moderation, said to Grant:

"Get a team out to Dannly's house now. Tell them not to ignore any of the usual places, but to look, carefully, in all of the unusual places for evidence. Tell them to concentrate on looking everyplace they would never think of looking. Tell them, specifically, that I want them to look for a condom and a knife. I have no idea where he would have thrown them, but you can sure as hell bet it wasn't under the bed, or in the garbage can. There won't be any fingerprints on the knife, but he left the last one at the scene, and he apparently took this one. He probably took it and the condom, and dumped them someplace along the way. Assume he drove back toward the city center and Temple Square. Get some extra men and have them walk both sides of the road all the way into the city if they have to. But tell them that the bastard probably put them someplace strange, in a flower pot, or in a bird's nest, or something wacky like that. He isn't normal, and this is his game. Let's play it with him."

Grant didn't answer, he just nodded and left.

Mahoney went over every lead they had, which took him all of three minutes. He listened to the tape again, but realized that the television comment was the only 'message' it contained. Unless, thought Mahoney, he wanted to dwell on how the killer knew so much about his private life. True, most of it was public knowledge that anyone could glean from newspaper stories about him and past cases. David had tried to make Mahoney believe that they were kindred spirits. Both intelligent. Both smarter than the average bear. Why had he done that? Maybe, thought Mahoney, he had actually been in contact with the bastard and didn't know it. Maybe he had even worked with him somehow. Kimball? No. Number Two? Of course not. Watson? Idiotic. One of the security agents? Possibly. But who?

Grant returned and nodded that what Mahoney had asked

for was underway. It was getting harder to find anyone free to do anything, with all those men guarding the apostles. Mahoney was always saying that work gets in the way of work. Grant couldn't agree more.

Late in the afternoon the phone on Mahoney's desk rang. "Mahoney."

"Did you hear the news, Detective Mahoney?"

"You're a sick man, David. You're a creep, you bastard. Why in hell did you do this?"

"I wanted to let you know that you couldn't just concentrate on the church. That would make it too easy for you. I wanted you to know that there would be other things to take up your time. Other things to worry about. I wanted you to know that no one is safe. Not even you, Detective Mahoney. Not even Detective Grant. Not even his all-American goodie-two-shoes Mormon wife and his three fuckin' kids."

"All right, David. What do you want right now?"

"I saw your story in the newspapers about the money. Do you really think I wouldn't have gotten it without some lame promise from the church that they would just hand it over?"

"That was their idea. The church's. They want this stopped. We were against it."

"Bullshit, Detective Mahoney. That's bullshit."

"No it's not. It's department policy not to pay ransom of any sort. We advised against it. If you try to deal directly with us, we will do everything in our power to stop you and capture you. Or kill you. It makes no difference to me. The church made that promise. We didn't."

"Well . . . I don't believe you, Detective Mahoney, but it is nice to watch you work."

"How many more are you going to kill?"

"Do you want to know if you're next?"

"No, I'm not next. You won't kill me. You're having too much fun playing with me. If you kill me who will listen to your sick drivel?"

"See, I told you you were smart. Like me. That should please you. And you're right, I don't intend to kill you. At least not until I've killed everyone else on my list."

"Who else is on your list, besides the First Presidency and the Council of Twelve Apostles?"

"Why so formal, Detective Mahoney? Why not just call them JC and the Boys? That's what I call them."

Mahoney remained silent.

"Did I strike a nerve?   Are you repelled by a little irreverence?

"Fuck you, David. This time I'm hanging up."

Mahoney hung up.

"You hung up?" Grant said.

"I'm tired of this shit. He revels over being in control. Fuck him. There is nothing else he can do but deal with us. He'll call back."

Mahoney wondered about the name. Was David his real name? Was it made up on the spot to mollify Mahoney? Was it his first name, his middle name, or his last name? Or, thought Mahoney, was it the biblical David who slew Goliath?

The next hour found Mahoney and Grant in the chief's office. Grant was upset. Within two minutes of the call Mahoney had played back the tape to both of them. He had warned Grant that the killer had said something about his family. Grant, under the circumstances, took it well. He didn't bolt out of the room. He just looked at the other two men and said, "What do I do now?"

The chief pulled in some old markers and before another ten minutes had passed had a friend from the Federal Building in the office with the three of them. The chief's old buddy was in charge of the Federal Witness Protection Program in Utah, and the chief wanted a favor. Fortunately, when the chief was a lowly detective he had thwarted a murder attempt on the man's life. The scum that made it was still doing time. The Fed was grateful.

"Here is want I need you to do," the chief said. "We have a real threat on Detective Grant's family. His wife is home and his three kids are in school. Two different schools. Detective Grant will give you the information. You have the mechanism set up to relocate people. I don't want a full relocation, just a temporary transfer to a safe house for the duration of this shitty situation. I don't want anyone at the police department or on the church security force to know where she and the kids are. I don't even want Detective Grant, or me, to know where they are. You can arrange occasional telephone calls, but that's all. Just have a couple of your trusted guys stash her and the kids in a secure safe house, provide her with food and a twenty-four-hour guard. If you can't handle the guard, I'll give you one of my own men. Can you do that?"

The man nodded yes. He told the chief that he would have the women and the children out of the area and in a safe location within three hours. Grant was relieved, to say the least.

Thursday: Day Eleven, Morning

Each Thursday the members of the Council of Twelve Apostles meet in a special room on the fourth floor of the Temple to do the business of the church.

The apostles, as always, sit by seniority in twelve oversized oak chairs arranged in a crescent about an upholstered altar. Dressed in temple clothes, ornate robes and hats, not unlike the trappings of a Masonic high ceremony, they open with a hymn as a loyal saint plays music on an organ in the corner of the room. After the hymn the men join hands around the altar in a prayer circle and ask for guidance. Once the prayer is completed, the men change back into street clothes and begin the solemn business of dealing with the church's pressing matters, usually the economic struggle of managing a multi-billion dollar corporation.

The only difference this time was that four chairs were empty, two belonging to apostles out of the country, and two that had belonged to Apostles Fielding and Banner. Also, the agenda was unusual. A special prayer had been said for the souls of Apostles G. A. Fielding and Mark Banner and for their surviving families.

Their souls were not in jeopardy, however. Not even a little bit. Throughout the history of the church, brave and curious rank-and-file members have whispered about the Second Anointing ceremony in the Mormon temples. Most Mormons had never heard of Second Anointing until Mark Hofmann, who was convicted of the 1985 Mormon bombings and murders, attempted to sell, for profit, a forged historical document dealing with the controversial subject. Practiced in the Nauvoo, Illinois period of the church's history, and publicly ignored since then, the practice is still in force for the hierarchy of the church.

Ordinarily, all church faithful who go through the Temple are admonished that their Temple anointings are part of the path to salvation. But they must wait until Judgement Day before learning if their earthly works are sufficient to allow them to become a god. The Second Anointing, however, is a temple ritual administered only by the President, Prophet, Seer, and Revelator, himself, and is limited to senior church leaders, the First Presidency and the Council of Twelve Apostles. It guarantees them exaltation in the Celestial Kingdom. No waiting. Presto. It's done.

Apostles G. A. Fielding and Mark Banner were now gods of their own universe.

The business of the day was what to do about the General Conference in April, specifically Saturday and Easter Sunday. One suggestion was to pray. Another was to close the General Conference to all but those with the plastic Temple recommend card that was read like a Visa or MasterCard upon entering one of the church's nearly fifty temples, worldwide. The temple recommend card could be electronically revoked for any of a lengthy list of violations. The violations included non-payment of tithe, non-attendance of most church meetings, sexual indiscretions, and even the harboring of a single book in a Mormon's home that might be critical of the Church of Jesus Christ of Latter-day Saints. Surely, one apostle said, the killer couldn't possibly have a valid Temple recommend card.

The final decision made on this particular Thursday, was to 'paper the house' as one apostle, with a penchant for reading about the Broadway theater, had suggested. He explained that the expression came from a producer's need to fill an audience with non-paying customers to give the appearance of a successful opening. Another apostle took exception to the illustration, but generally approved of the idea. The Council of Twelve Apostles would recommend to the First Presidency that word be sent out, quietly, that this conference was to be attended by the faithful who would stand in line from 4 a.m., if necessary, to assure that the entire audience was made up only of loyal and loving members enamored of the General Authorities. A reserved section thirty rows deep, in back of the normal VIP section, would also be used exclusively for seating a special delegation of recently returned missionaries. They would be sent special invitations.

The Thursday meeting was over. The problem had been solved. And for some of the apostles, a new, and colorful, phrase had been added to their vocabulary. Paper the house. One of the apostles wondered privately what all the fuss was about; they had been doing just that for years — only now he knew what to call it.

Mahoney and Grant had shared the tapes with Number Two and Kimball in yet another meeting. Mahoney felt "meetinged" to death. Number Two sat uneasily through the tapes, squirming as he heard: prick, bullshit, fuck you, J.C. and the Boys, and Mahoney's statement that he was hanging up. Kimball was obviously embarrassed.

"Do you really think that was wise?" asked Number Two.

"Yes, I do. Our killer has been in control since the beginning of this thing. We have got to worry him a bit. We need to have his sense of control waver. We need some control."

"But he didn't call you back. You apparently didn't get to him with that approach."

"Yes, I think I did. Had he called me back immediately it would have been admitting his anger and frustration. He'll call back all right, but I believe he'll let us twist in the wind for a while before he does."

"Have you been able to trace his calls?"

"We had both numbers almost immediately and traced both of them. They came from phone booths on opposite sides of the city. One was in a mall, and the other on a remote street corner. Our units arrived after he was gone. Lots of prints, but my guess is, his won't show up. There was a typed note on a piece of paper in the booth on the corner. All it said was, 'Hi, guys. You're late.'"

"That's not his real voice, is it?"

"No. He's using a voice filter to disguise it."

"Did he leave a note at the mall."

"No. I don't think he would take that chance. Someone using the phone right after him might see it and remember him. There was no chance of that at the other location."

Finally, Kimball jumped in.

"Do you think he killed Ms. Dannly to get back at us for assigning the bodyguard teams to the apostles and the First Presidency?"

"No, I think he wants us to take every precaution we can, just so he can prove he's smarter than we are. I think he killed Ms. Dannly for the reason he stated, plus one other."

Everyone looked at Mahoney, and Number Two raised his eyebrows and leaned forward. His face said, please explain.

"What I mean is," said Mahoney, "I think he really wanted to confuse us and dilute the effectiveness of our focus on the church to the exclusion of nearly everything else. He's just playing his game of control. He's telling us if he can't get to the church at any given moment, he will just kill someone else."

"What is the other reason?" asked Number Two.

"I think he just likes to kill. Toni Dannly was raped, but not until she was out cold, or dead. Obviously, he gets his kicks killing or through a combination of killing and sex. That's a dangerous mix."

Number Two took over again.

"His reaction to the newspaper story on our promise to give him the $100 million bothered me. He didn't seem to care, and he never told you how he wanted to get the money."

"That will come in good time," said Mahoney. "We whetted his appetite, and I think he bought it. Remember, he was the one that brought up the subject, I didn't. He also asked me if I really thought he couldn't have gotten the money without a lame promise from the church to give it to him. I think that indicates he had already made up his mind, before he called me, that he is going to try for the money. If we're lucky he won't kill again until he gets the money. But," Mahoney paused, "I wouldn't count on it."

Thursday: Day Eleven, Afternoon

Back at police headquarters Mahoney and Grant, along with other members of the task force, were poring over what they knew about the killer when two patrolmen burst into the room, out of breath, and sporting grins from ear to ear.

"Detective Mahoney," yelled the first patrolman, "we found it!"

The patrolman, still wearing a pair of surgical rubber gloves secured earlier from the police lab, reached into an evidence envelope and withdrew an elongated condom. He held it by a knot tied at the opening end, and the reservoir tip hung straight down under the weight of what everyone in the room assumed to be a rather large amount of semen.

"You told us to look in unusual places," the patrolman was nearly out of breath and had trouble talking, "and sure enough we found this impaled on a stop sign post about a mile from Dannly's house."

"Impaled?" Mahoney asked.

"Yeah," the patrolman said, "with this."

He reached into the evidence envelope and pulled out an Ek-Warrior knife, identical to the one found in Emigration Canyon. Drawing out the suspense as long as he could, and loving every minute of it, the patrolman continued:

"The condom was stuck to the top of the post, one of the old wooden kind. The knife point was jabbed through the rubber just above the knot and into the wood at the top of the post. It was just hanging there. We looked all over the sides of the road, but you told us to look in weird places. I don't know why I looked up. But there it was, just hanging there. The killer must have..."

"That's great work, Patrolman . . . ah," looking at the man's nameplate, ". . . Patrolman Kile. Was there anything else in the area?"

"No Sir."

"All right. Would you please take the condom and the knife to the lab and tell them this is top priority from the task force? Tell them we want the results yesterday. Tell them," the second patrolman was taking notes feverishly, "that we want to know everything: blood type, fingerprints, whatever. And tell them to test the *outside* of the condom to see if it has ever been inside Ms. Dannly."

The two patrolmen looked at each other, and the one writing actually shrugged. But they nodded and left.

"Okay, Mahoney," Grant said, "you've got me. Why the questions about the condom being inside the victim."

The rest of the task force tried not to show it, but most of them had no idea what Mahoney was getting at either.

"Well . . . it's like this. I've talked to this guy several times now, and he is one detached, smart, and cool customer. So far he hasn't left us a single clue. He knew we would find out she had been raped. He knew we would find no semen in the victim. He knew we would rip the hell out of the area looking for the condom. Not finding a condom we would be left assuming he ejects no semen, and there are several plausible medical reasons for that, or that he raped her with a dildo of some type. Say, a regular dildo, or something as crude as a Coke bottle or a broom handle."

Grant was a good cop, but he really hated hearing this stuff. It made him think about his own wife. He wondered exactly where she was. He also wondered what the neighbors and the kids' teachers were saying. He'd be glad when this was over. He prayed it wouldn't last the thirty days the killer had predicted. That would mean nineteen more days of this.

"But I'm getting to know a little bit about how he thinks. He's a bit macho, and I don't think he's impotent. He might not be up for a regular screw, but add a little blood or violence, and he's probably raring to go. He likes to play games. He likes to tease us and fool us. He had to know that sooner or later someone would see that knife in the pole. A kid might not report it, but an adult, seeing the condom hanging there, might think it weird enough to call it in. At any rate, whether or not we found it wasn't the point. He put it there so that if we did, we would rejoice in the discovery of some shred of evidence.

"My first guess is that he would expect us to test the semen to see if we could determine blood type from it. He might not have thought about the outside of the condom. But think of this, gentlemen. If the killer did use a condom, and he has, say, O blood type, what have we really gained. About forty-six percent of the population has O blood. Another forty-two percent has A blood. Now if he has B blood, that's a much smaller group, only nine percent. And if he's AB, that's only three percent. So let's all hope this guy's a secretor, and he has AB blood. Only three people in a hundred have that."

Mahoney knew that in 1930 it was discovered that many body fluid stains contain soluble ABO blood group substances. Fortunately, the majority of the population are secretors, and their blood type can be determined from, not only blood, but from tears, sweat, saliva and semen. Many people, however, are not secretors, and their blood type can't be determined from anything but their blood.

"It may have occurred to you," Mahoney added, "that this guy is just devious enough to have obtained the semen of some other poor bastard and put it in the condom. Semen from someone who isn't his blood type. We'd be on a merry chase over that one. That's why I want to know if the condom was ever inside Ms. Dannly. Of course, he could have stuffed it inside her, then pulled it out. But even this guy should make some mistakes. Hell, he can't be perfect."

The report came back later in the day. Blood type B. Nine percent of the population. Nine in every one hundred American citizens. The condom, the report said, had, indeed, been inside Ms. Dannly. Did this guy want to be caught? Did he want to walk a tightrope with the police? Mahoney wondered. Did his death wish for the First Presidency and the Council of Twelve Apostles extend to himself?

Early afternoon the man traveled by car twenty-six miles
north to Ogden Canyon, then east along the Ogden River as
its waters poured down from the high ground near
Huntsville. The canyon was beautiful at this time of year.
He liked it best in the fall. In mid-March it was still second
best. Fresh. New growth. Streams bursting with the crystal
water of runoff from the earlier snows that blanketed the
canyon. He had lived in Ogden before his mission, and
before his fall from grace at BYU. It was a wonder, he
thought, that he ever got past the security check to become
a member of the force that guarded Temple Square and the
General Authorities.

Driving through Huntsville the man reveled in the
memories of his youth. His mother and father would take
him on trips up the canyon from their home in Ogden. They
would have picnics not far from the small, modest home
that would later become a tourist attraction for faithful
Mormons. Huntsville was where David O. McKay, the
ninth President, Prophet, Seer, and Revelator of the church
had been born in 1873. Prophet McKay had been the
president of the church from 1951 to 1970, during the
killer's most formative years. For his entire childhood, the
man had accepted that David O. McKay was a living
prophet of God walking the earth in his lifetime.

Remembering wasn't difficult for the man. He had been
reliving the hurt and hate of the past for a long time. More
a boy than a man, in most senses of the word, he had been
called to a mission in England at age eighteen. He was
paired with a quiet missionary partner and admonished not
to be separated throughout the calling. A homosexual
relationship developed during the long nights in England.
Soon his partner became obsessed with him. Teaching an
abbreviated gospel from six memorized lessons used
throughout the two year calling, proved restrictive and
boring to both young men. The homosexual relationship
was recreation, mental salvation from the tedium of
repetition and nearly constant rejection.

Showing no guilt himself, and enjoying all forms of sex,
he would often leave this homosexual relationship to sleep

with young women from the community's red light district. One weekend his quiet and jealous partner, increasingly racked with guilt, made a serious mistake. In a fit of jealous rage and self pity he had written home making an oblique reference to "personal and unnatural acts" that worried him and ate at his faith. In a life altering mistake the quiet boy kept a copy of the letter and showed it to his missionary partner. Before the shame of his sins could wash over him further, he hanged himself from a beam in the modest room the two missionaries shared, while his young missionary partner slept through the night. Or so it was reported.

Medical investigators had speculated that the dead missionary may have had "help" in achieving his grisly end. One had even insisted that it was possible the boy was dead before he was hanged. But nothing could be proved. There was no hard evidence. So, as in many cases of "a missionary's word" over unprovable suspicions, the allegations were never recorded in anyone's permanent record. The church hated embarrassments.

The young man denied any knowledge of the allusion to unnatural acts, or of ever seeing the letter. He did remember, he said, that his partner would spend considerable time in the bathroom, with the door closed; more times than he personally thought was normal. He told the investigators from the church that he had tried to talk to his partner, but his partner denied any wrongdoing and blamed his lengthy bathroom sessions on bouts of diarrhea. He added that he had urged his partner to seek guidance from God, and from the church authorities.

The young man was so convincing during the investigation that he was immediately assigned another partner and finished his mission without further incident. It was the beginning of his troubles with the church, and with sex, and it formed a pattern which would haunt him. But for now, his record intact, indeed, enhanced, he came home that most coveted of Mormon youth — the returned missionary.

Parking the car on a hill behind Huntsville, the man knew that the vehicle was all but invisible to anyone in the valley below. He had stalked the area weeks before, and the setting was perfect. There was even a back way out. Risky, but possible. It would be a lengthy drive, but time was something the man used to his advantage. Everyone else used it poorly, he thought. He used it well. He had patience. Few others did.

Removing the long satchel from the trunk he walked to a location between a tall stand of trees that revealed a perfect view of the farmhouse below. It was far away. Well over 1,000 yards; more than ten football fields, end to end. It would be a very interesting shot.

He watched the guard below circle the farmhouse repeatedly, and then take up a post near the front door. Stupid cops, the man thought. Who the hell did they think they were dealing with?

After shoving a sighting rod into the ground on which to steady the rifle, he placed his tools next to it, on the ground. He then sat cross-legged and ate a chicken sandwich he had made earlier in the day. He was getting chicken grease on his cotton gloves, but he really didn't care. He drank a can of soda and checked his watch. Another three hours and it would be done.

With binoculars the man watched the house, below, and the road approaching it. Finally, after hours had passed, he could see the car he had been looking for heading round the final curve and up the long straightaway toward the farmhouse. The guard below had made several more trips around the house, but once again, was posted near the front steps leading to a broad porch and the front door. Picking up the rifle from the ground, a strange looking rifle, long, heavy, and awkward looking, he loaded it with a single round of high-powered ammunition. There would only be time for one shot. Hit or miss he would be on his way before his back door could be reached or blocked.

Lifting the long rifle, he placed its thirty-four-inch barrel in the U-shaped support of the sighting rod, to steady its weight. He reached up and adjusted the sporting tang rear sight. He had practiced at this distance many times, and he took care to adjust the sight precisely. There was no wind. Good, the man thought.

As the car approached the driveway he saw the guard wave at the driver of the car. Once stopped, the car doors opened and the driver stepped out. He looked around, nodding to the guard. The guard nodded back. Another man stepped from the back seat. It was another agent, the man knew. It wasn't the apostle. The Apostle was old and gray and bent.

Sighting directly on the back door opposite where the other man had emerged, he rechecked the sights. He saw the apostle of the church step from the car at the signal of one of the other men. Flanking him, the two men began walking toward the door. The man in the middle was relatively frail. The men were providing modest support for his eighty-two-year-old legs. He followed the old man in his sights. Just as the man had anticipated, as they reached the stairs leading to the porch, they paused for a moment as the old man prepared to climb the stairs.

It was precisely then that he pulled the trigger. He aimed slightly high in case the man moved upward as he attempted to take the first step. But there was no need. The men had paused too long. The massive bullet from the long octagonal barrel blew a hole the size of a walnut in the back of the apostle's head. Bone shards imploded into soft gray matter as the bullet ripped its hole through the brain and exploded from his face.

Thursday: Day Eleven, Evening

Unless things went perfectly for him, he knew he was in deep trouble. Ideally, he should have killed the two bodyguards and the man guarding the house as well. But there was not time for that. Not from that distance. Not with this single shot weapon. By the time he had reloaded and sighted on a second man, the others would have taken cover. He'd never get all three. It was inevitable then that the police would be called almost immediately. He was ten miles into a canyon that left him few options. Fortunately, he had prepared his back door carefully.

The second he saw the apostle forced forward from the impact of the .50 caliber round, he moved directly to the car. He left everything else behind, including the remains of the chicken sandwich. It didn't matter. They probably already knew he was a secretor, and that his blood was type B. After all, he needed to let them have a lead or two, now and then, or they might get bored with the game. If they hadn't found the condom, saliva traces from the chicken sandwich would let them know. Having nothing to do but examine one dead body after another can get to be a real drag, the man thought. The fleeting grin passed over the man's face as he drove down the incline toward the paved road below. He floored the accelerator and headed for a spot about nine miles away. This was not the time for caution. He reached down and touched the 9mm automatic tucked firmly under his belt.

The road formed a loop, around the man-made Pine View Reservoir so popular with weekend boating enthusiasts in the Ogden area. Designated Utah 166, the county road took him north for two miles from where he was, and then west again to join up with 162 North heading toward Brigham City, twenty miles away. On his previous journey to the area, he had towed a trail bike behind him. It was a common sight in Utah. He had hidden it in a grove of trees and brush half-way between Huntsville and Brigham City. The man knew he had only ten minutes, or so, before the highway patrol and sheriff's offices throughout the area converged on the roads leading out of Huntsville. Within eight minutes the man had located the trail bike and ditched the car off the nearly deserted road where it would not be spotted.

He had chained the trail bike to the trailer in the remote case that some kid might come across it. It couldn't be budged without moving the entire trailer hitch along with it, and he had flattened both trailer tires. Removing the padlock, he pulled the chain from its serpentine route through both wheels on the bike, the bike's frame, and the frame of the trailer. Within a minute of arriving, he had started the bike and was traveling overland on a trail he knew well, which led directly through the woods to Brigham City. His stopwatch indicated that nine minutes had elapsed from when the shot was fired. He would be in Brigham City in another ten-to-twelve minutes.

Although the man didn't know it, fate was playing into his hands. To begin with, none of the guards dared move following the shot. Each was sure he'd be next. One guard fell by the side of the apostle. Another jumped under the car. The third huddled at the side of the porch. The men yelled at each other. Where is he?! Where did the shot come from?! One pointed, the others looked. They could see nothing. The radio the house guard was yelling into, produced nothing but static. The deep canyon location prevented clear reception with the Salt Lake City police department. Two minutes were wasted cowering and crawling in the dirt for fear of being shot. One agent finally ran to the car. As he did, he yelled to the guard, telling him to use the telephone in the house to call the police. Then he headed off toward the direction he thought the shot had come from. He was wrong. The men could not conceive that the shot might have been fired from over 1,000 yards. They were concentrating on the farm buildings and the houses closer on the road. The agent in the car headed in the wrong direction.

Next, in a bizarre series of delays, the guard trying to use the house phone to call the police department couldn't find it on his first pass through the unfamiliar rooms. He finally located the telephone in the upper right hand drawer of a desk in the living room. Fuck, the man thought, who in their right mind keeps a telephone in a drawer? What the man didn't know was that the apostle's telephone number was unlisted; he seldom received calls at home. The drawer, to this apostle of the church, seemed like a perfect place to keep it. The apostle had been excessively neat. By the time the guard found the phone and got through to the dispatcher, nearly five minutes had passed.

Adding to the delay, confusion reigned at police headquarters in Salt Lake City as the call came in from the telephone in the apostle's home. The guard, who had called the Salt Lake dispatcher, was explicit about having Salt Lake alert police throughout the Huntsville area; still, nearly two minutes were lost in conveying the information to Mahoney and Grant. The dispatcher, first locating the two detectives, had only then contacted the Ogden police and the sheriff's office covering Huntsville. No one had even thought of Brigham City. Nearly eight minutes had passed since the shooting of the apostle.

Bulletins alerting local area law enforcement to the killer's possible presence in their area didn't arrive at the Ogden police department for another minute. The Sheriff's office covering Huntsville received the call a minute later. The Brigham City police department monitored the dispatch, but assumed the car under pursuit would be sealed off in the Huntsville loop. As police, troopers, and sheriff's vehicles began moving toward Huntsville, blocking the roads leading out of the canyon in every direction, the man was on the trail bike and had disappeared onto an off-road trail heading toward Brigham City.

All in all, Brigham City police failed to respond to the incident until they heard radio traffic indicating that the car everyone was pursuing had not actually been spotted. It may never have left the area. Then again, the dispatches indicated, the killer might or might not be in a car. No one knew. If he was, he may have already left the Huntsville area. Still, every police, trooper and sheriff's car in the area headed for the Ogden Canyon and the Huntsville area.

The Brigham City police finally fired up two patrol cars

to assist in the manhunt precisely at the same time the man pulled the trail bike up to the curb near a public parking area in Brigham City. It was a block away from the police station. He parked the bike, fed the meter to capacity, and casually walked into the parking area. Looking around, he could see that no one was paying any attention to him. He could also see two patrol cars pulling out of the police station, their sirens just starting to wail. He got into his own car. Pushing the button on his stopwatch he noted that twenty-seven minutes had elapsed since he had killed the apostle.

The car he used to travel to Huntsville had been rented two days before, using another false I. D. He had rented it in Holladay where he had ditched the stolen car he had been using.

The man picked up Interstate 15 from Brigham City and drove directly south into Salt Lake City. Driving through the early evening traffic the man thought that the day's activities had gone perfectly. Just perfectly. He didn't turn on the radio. He was content to wait another day to hear the news. After all, he thought, he knew what it was. He had made it. Thinking of news, he wondered, who would be promoted now that Dannly was dead. KSL-TV was his favorite news station. They always covered the church news. He liked that. Too bad, he thought, that he couldn't watch it tonight. He had to go on duty for another twelve-hour shift. Maybe I'll be guarding the Prophet, he thought. Oh, well, sooner or later.

The man entered his own apartment, changed into his blue blazer and gray pants, adjusted the shoulder holster so that it didn't show much bulge under the blazer, and headed for Temple Square.

Friday: Day Twelve, Morning

Utah's media were going crazy. So was every law enforcement agency in the area.

"How in hell could we lose the bastard in Ogden Canyon!? For Christ's sake," yelled the chief, "are we just sitting around here with our fat thumbs up our incompetent asses?"

Talk among the task force was depressing at best. They all felt impotent. Now the chief, usually the model of Mormon decorum, was ripping in to them with language usually reserved for one of Mahoney's tirades.

"Mahoney," the chief said, "brief everyone on where we're at — and keep it brief, for God's sake."

"Chief, men — here's what we've got so far, starting with the disaster yesterday.

"First, the guy is a shot-and-a-half. He blew off the top of Apostle Randall's head from over 1,000 yards. Ironically, he used a Shiloh Sharps Long Range Express rifle. The bullet was a .50 caliber black powder metallic cartridge. The rifle is a modern duplicate of the old frontier Sharps, designed by Christian Sharps and used by professional buffalo hunters between 1875 and the early 1880's. He's no superman. Frontiersmen have routinely made kills at a thousand yards a hundred years ago with this rifle. The ammunition wasn't nearly as reliable as it is now. If the phrase 'sharpshooter' rings a bell it's because of Christian Sharps and his 'Big Fifty' rifle."

"Jesus, Mahoney! I said keep it brief."

"Yes, Chief. The point of the Sharps being left for us to find is another example of this killer's set of balls. The rifle was used during the latter years of Brigham Young's time in Utah, throughout the development of the Mormon church.

158

There is no question the killer is a church history buff, and is possibly an expert with several types of firearms and explosives. He is privy to information on where the apostles live, and their routine. Finally, he plans methodically enough to evade capture, even in a place as remote as the Huntsville area.

"Most likely he has B type blood, limiting him to about nine percent of the population. He probably wants us to know that for his own crazy reasons, or he wouldn't have left us his used condom. And it was his. The son-of-a-bitch left us part of a chicken sandwich to test against. The saliva tested type B, too. Since he is a stone-cold expert with firearms, he probably has extensive police, military, or para-military experience. He knows electronics and alarm systems, as evidenced by the break-in at the gun shop in Colorado, and the handmade device used on the trigger housing of the rifle that killed Mr. Williamson in Temple Square.

"He has several sets of false I.D. We determined that from the tracing of several rented cars that have turned up abandoned near the scenes of his crimes. He is a Mormon or an ex-Mormon. He is extremely careful. And," said Mahoney, pausing for effect, "he's one smug prick on the phone.

"There have been no fingerprints of any kind left on any of the knives, rifles, tripod, telephones, or automobiles that he has used. There are prints, occasionally. But when we track them down they belong to the owner of the gun store, or the last person who used the car before our killer. He likes to make work for us. He likes it when we chase our tails. He also says his name is David.

"He isn't going to stop at killing just the church leaders. He will kill others just for the hell of it, or in an effort to dilute our manpower on this case. The evidence of that is Toni Dannly. He will stop at nothing. He has threatened my life and the lives of Detective Grant's wife and family. I don't think he wants to carry out his threat against Grant's family, or me for that matter. He just wants us to have something else to worry about. He seems to be making his wish come true.

"We have all the collated reports on hotels and motels in the area. We have looked at everyone registered at a hotel just before the incidents started. We have looked into everyone checking out on the night, or on the day after, each incident. No luck. We are now looking at everyone who registered at a hotel or motel before the incidents started and who hasn't checked out yet. The list totals over 314, and we're only up to fifty-six as of today. No luck so far.

"We have compiled a list of all the church security agents and guards. We have checked this list against blood type B, which we are sure the killer has. Detective Grant accessed the church personnel computer and searched the lists we are privy to; of the hundred agents on active duty right now, twelve of them have type B blood. Pretty close to the nine percent national average, given such a small control group."

"Mahoney!" bellowed the Chief.

"Okay, okay," said Mahoney, "I'll keep it brief. We are in the process of checking their schedules during every incident to determine which ones were off duty at the times of the killings. We should have that information in a matter of hours."

At the side of the room sat Mark Kimball, the only "outsider" to the task force. He was the only church representative. He raised his hand and motioned to Mahoney.

"You all know Mr. Kimball, head of church security. Yes, what is it?"

"Detective Mahoney, why haven't you done a similar check on the men in the police department? Why just concentrate on the church security personnel?"

There was a palpable hostility that emanated from the audience and seemed to move directly toward Kimball. Policemen didn't like their own under suspicion.

"What makes you think I'm not checking the police force?"

Grant felt the silence. And he felt the mood change.

The men in the task force seemed to tighten up, and it was obvious they had never dreamed Mahoney would have checked on them without their knowing it.

"You mean you are checking them out?" asked Kimball.

"I already have," said Mahoney. "We identified, from the roster of police on active duty, that nineteen have type B blood."

Some of the men in the room were shaking their heads as if Mahoney had joined the ranks of traitor.

"Of the nineteen, no one was off duty, and out-of-sight of his partner, for more than two of the five killings we have had so far. And one thing we do know, for fuckin' sure, is that this ain't no team effort. We are looking for one guy who did it all."

It was inaudible, but, viscerally, Grant could feel the sigh of relief that flooded the room. Mahoney wasn't the bad guy anymore. He was a good cop doing his job. They were off the hook, and swelled-up proud of it.

"I might add that we also went over the roster of retired policeman, and inactive policemen, and police staff, all those with type B blood; everyone had air-tight alibis for at least two or three of the killings.

"May I suggest, Mr. Kimball," Grant noticed the air of formality creep back into Mahoney's speech when he felt it was proper, "that you do the same with all of your own security people, including past agents, and the two hundred assistants, associates, and secretaries employed by your department. And do it now!

"Please remember, people, that we are taking a shortcut here. We are assuming that this bastard hasn't tricked us with this blood type thing. The chicken sandwich seems to verify that. If he has pulled the condom over our heads, the guy is miles beyond us, and we are back to square one. We will have to interview everyone else, those without type B blood, and determine their alibis for the time frame covered by the five killings. But right now I'm going with the odds."

"Thank you," was all Kimball had to say.

After returning from his shift twelve-hours later, the man changed at his apartment, inserted his contact lens, and drove to the Tri Arc. He was angry with himself for not changing his base of operations after the killing in Emigration Canyon. He placed the large suitcase containing his weapons on a portable cart, the kind flight attendants use for their luggage. He wheeled it into the elevator bank nearest the side door of the hotel, adjacent to where he parked his car. No sense in letting some snoopy porter wonder why he was huffing and puffing carrying a suitcase from the elevator to the car.

He placed the suitcase in the trunk and reentered the Tri Arc to check out. Yes, he had a nice stay, thank you. Yes, he would be back, thank you. No, he didn't have time to fill out a customer satisfaction form, thank you. Fucking fools.

He checked in at the Salt Lake Marriott, a sixteen-story hotel opposite the Salt Palace on the corner of West Temple and 1st South. He was only a block away from Temple Square. His view was of the Salt Palace, and beyond it to one of the seediest sections of Salt Lake City. He liked the bad parts of town.

Placing his suitcased arsenal on a luggage stand near the bed, he removed a shaving kit and a few belongings from a nylon shoulder bag and placed them in the bathroom. He checked to make sure he had a Do Not Disturb sign available to him. He did.

Several hours later two tired detectives walked up to the front desk of the Tri Arc hotel. They had already been to a dozen hotels and everything was starting to look the same. They inquired about two people on their list who had checked in prior to the killings. They learned that one had already checked out. The other, apparently, was in his room. The desk clerk had overheard the telephone operator use a name when switching him to room service. His name was David Peterson. At the mention of the name "David" both men tensed slightly and glanced at each other.

The two detectives stood on either side of the door and one knocked. When the door opened the two detectives rushed into the room and slammed the man who opened the door back across the room and up against the wall. They searched him roughly, and yelled questions at him. They were not gentle.

He was an auto parts salesman from Denver. He was a frightened, weak, and wretched little man, whose bed was strewn with Hustler and Club magazines. He was in a robe, and he was sweating. After fifteen minutes of telephone calls, the detectives established his whereabouts during two of the killings. He had been with a highly respected local politician at a private strip joint in the streets west of the Salt Palace. The local politician was too scared to lie, and upon a promise of not letting this thing get into the press, admitted to being with David Peterson discussing the sale of auto parts to the city's motor pool. The evening had been on Mr. Peterson. It was the same time frame as the Toni Dannly murder. Another dead end.

Friday: Day Twelve, Afternoon

The report on Mahoney's desk read:

CHURCH SECURITY AGENTS WITH TYPE B BLOOD NOT ON DUTY AT THE TIME OF THE KILLINGS OF WILLIAMSON, FIELDING, BANNER, DANNLY, AND RANDALL.
(Nine Found)
Alpert, Michael R.
Bancroft, Richard L.
Davies, John D.
Edwards, Charles P.
Edwin, George D.
Goodwin, Heber T.
James, Brad H.
Jackson, Trent P.
Sampleford, John D.
ADDRESSES AVAILABLE ON MAIN PRINTOUT.

Grant, on Mahoney's request, ran the list again to get the middle names. Mahoney was particularly interested in the middle names of John D. Davies, George D. Edwin, and John D. Sampleford. The printout resulted in John Douglas Davies, George Donald Edwin, and John David Sampleford.

"Do you think it could be John David Sampleford?" Grant asked.

"I hope so, but the way this is going that would be too damned easy. Do Sampleford and Davies first."

"Why Davies?" asked Grant.

"I think Davies, or Davis, is the surname version of the given name David. Can't hurt to run them both."

Mahoney looked drained. Grant was wondering about his wife and kids locked up in some safe house, Lord knows where.

Just before Grant could enter the two names, requesting addresses, telephone numbers, and personnel histories, the phone on Mahoney's desk rang.

"Mahoney," the detective said, as he pushed the record button. He had recorded every phone call since the first time the killer had called.

"I am only going to say this once, Detective Mahoney, so I hope you've got this on tape. Do you?"

"Yes." It was the killer. It was David.

"Good. I want the $100 million placed in large . . . "

"Just a minute," interrupted Mahoney. "I told you I am not going to deal with you on this issue. It's a church issue. They promised to pay you, not me. Besides, the promise to pay was contingent upon having the killing stop. I don't think they expected your last little job on Apostle Randall. For all I know they won't give you the money now. At any rate, you are going to have to deal with them yourself."

Mahoney read off the number of the direct line to Number Two and immediately hung up. Grant's mouth was open. He had been listening on the earphone they had installed on Mahoney's line.

"You hung up again!"

"How observant."

"Don't you think that's a bit . . . "

"A bit what?"

"I don't know. Abrupt, maybe."

"Abrupt! Jesus, Heber, how long are you going to keep thinking that we have to play his game. If you want to get a lion's attention you may have to rattle his cage. Whispering 'boo' won't do it. And it wasn't abrupt, it was fuck-you-in-the-face downright rude! Honest to God, Heber, you've got to loosen up a bit. Abrupt my ass!"

The phone rang again. Again Mahoney pushed the button.

"Mahoney."

"Listen, Detective Fucking Mahoney, hang up on me again and I will kill you."

Mahoney hung up.

Grant nearly shit in his chair.

Mahoney was already dialing Number Two's line on another phone next to his.

"Yes," was the only answer, but Mahoney recognized the voice of Number Two.

"Sir, I have just been talking with the killer, who now calls himself David, and I think he will be calling you directly on this line any second now. Please record each call from now on, if you're not already doing it."

"We're doing it."

"Okay. When he calls listen to his instructions and agree to them, no matter how outrageous they are. Then call me on my secondary line and play back the tape for me. I think we have him flustered." Mahoney almost said "pissed."

"Is that good?" asked Number Two.

"I don't know, but it's something. Anything is worth a try. We can't afford to have any more people die. I'm hanging up now. I have a feeling he's dialing as we speak. Goodbye."

Number Two didn't have time to say goodbye.

"So what do you think is happening?" asked Grant.

"I think he's hitting something, a pillow, a table top, a wall, whatever. I think he is really pissed. I have been his only connection and I refused to talk with him twice in a row. I believe he is thinking that he would lose face if he called back. He is going to have to take some direct action that will get my attention. The only thing I fear is that the bastard loves me."

Grant smiled, but his heart wasn't in it. Mahoney continued:

"I think he will call Number Two and make some outrageous demand that he may not have thought out fully. I think we may force him into making a mistake."

The printout of nine names with three possible Davids circled in red, was pushed aside on Grant's desk as he reached for the earphone. As Grant leaned over he pushed one stack of papers on another. Several of the papers were shoved over the list of names. For now, in the excitement of the phone call and Mahoney's hanging up on the killer, Grant forgot all about the papers on his desk.

The special telephone in Number Two's office rang only seconds after Mahoney had hung up.

"Yes," answered Number Two.

"Who is this?" the man asked.

"Who is this?" Number Two countered.

"Don't be cute. This is David. Does that name mean anything to you?"

"Yes it does. It means you are the cowardly killer of several of my close and personal friends."

"Big fucking deal. Who is this?"

"You don't need to know that. All you need to know is that I am the person authorized to pay you. I am the person that placed the story in the paper. I am the person who has guaranteed the payment without police involvement. More than that I won't tell you. If you are half as smart as Detective Mahoney tells me you are, you won't need to know more than that. I will tell you that I am taking this call in the Church Administration Building, and I am a General Authority of the Mormon church."

The man thought about it while the silence on the phone screamed to be broken. Finally, after dwelling on the compliment paid him by Detective Mahoney, the man continued:

"I want $100 million in used twenty-dollar bills, unmarked and not in any sequence, to be put in large suitcases and placed on a corporate jet, a Gulfstream IV. Lease it if you have to. I want it done tomorrow. The plane should lift off at 1 p.m., Saturday, and fly directly toward Denver, Colorado. At the end of this discussion I will give you a frequency I want the pilot to monitor. He must follow my instructions to the letter. Make sure he has a full load of fuel and that no one else in on board. He will not be injured unless he is not alone, or unless he is armed. In either of those cases he will be killed and the plane destroyed along with the money. I will transmit to the pilot only. I will not repeat myself. I will give instructions only once. Be sure to tell him that. Are you ready to write down the radio frequency?"

"I don't know if we can get the money together by noon tomorrow."

"Of course you can. You have had it ready for some time unless you didn't follow my instructions. And if you didn't that's too bad, because the killing will continue. And this time it will include not only the apostles and the First Presidency, but I will destroy a lot of innocent people along with them. And I am not talking about the General Conference. That's too far away. My retaliation for an error on your part will be immediate. Besides, I have other plans for the conference, unless I get my money tomorrow. Write this down."

The man gave Number Two the frequency, and hung up. He hung up abruptly, not unlike Mahoney had done to him. The prick, he thought. I'll show him a thing or two.

Number Two immediately sent a tape of the conversation over to Mahoney and Grant. They had talked on the phone, and listened to the tape. Now it was time to work out a plan. Mahoney thought about sleep, and how little he would get.

Saturday: Day Thirteen, Morning

It was 5 a.m. and everyone on the task force, along with support staff, was back in the day room hovering over an aerial map of the region. Where the hell, Mahoney thought, was this sick son-of-a-bitch going to send that airplane.

After a nearly sleepless night Mahoney went over what they now believed. Kimball stood quietly at the side drinking a pint of orange juice. Mahoney was on his fourth cup of coffee in less than an hour.

"Okay, gang, listen up. This is what we have," Mahoney said. Mahoney wondered if he was talking a bit too fast.

"1. We think this is a version of the car-chase ransom ruse. You send the money in a car and keep it moving all over town. Finally, at one stop someone takes the money. The theory is that no one can tail the car without making some mistakes. When the mistake is made, the switch is pulled. The airplane makes it more difficult. Since a special frequency is being used, with a directional transmitter the bastard could be anywhere signaling the plane. Once the airplane is up, we can track it, but he could have it land anywhere. The consensus is that he will have it land in Utah. But we don't know that. He stole guns from Colorado. Maybe he has friends in Colorado. Or maybe he just likes the place. The plane could also land in Idaho, Arizona, New Mexico, or Nevada in a matter of minutes after takeoff from Salt Lake City. Some of you have opted for Nevada, but for no good reason other than that's where you'd take $100 million dollars if you had it. We can't cover the entire five state region. Besides, with full tanks, and he specified that, the plane could fly to California or Chicago or Canada. We are simply going to have to monitor the frequency and follow that damn plane.

"2. The pilot will be a policeman, John Carpenter, you all
know him. He's qualified on the Gulfstream IV. He also
happens to be one of our helicopter pilots. We're lucky he
also flies fuckin' near everything else. He will be armed. Also
one other armed policemen, Fred Dupree, Dufus to you, will
be in the plane under a tarp next to the pilot's seat. All the
seats have been removed to make room for the suitcases. The
damn plane is going to be wall-to-wall, floor-to-ceiling
suitcases. The person who comes to pick up that money won't
get it. Dufus, as you all know, is our department's best
marksman.

"3. The money won't be money. However, since the asshole might be watching, we will have a team of men lug
eighty-four-goddamn suitcases into the Zion Bank at 9 a.m.
When they come out, an appropriate ninety minutes later,
those suitcases will be filled with a couple of sandbags each
to simulate the weight of the money. Money is heavy, guys.
One suitcase will be filled with money in case we have to
open one as a delaying tactic. We will transfer the 'money'
into armored cars, and take it to the airport at 10:30 a.m.,
arriving at the Gulfstream at 11:15 a.m. It's going to look like
a parade of goddamned armored cars. The transfer will be
made in about an hour. Dufus will be under the tarp in the
plane before the suitcases are loaded and strapped down. He
must not be seen entering the plane so he will get under that
tarp within forty-five minutes of this meeting breaking up,
which should put him in the plane before 6:30 a.m. The plane
will be fueled at noon, and the pilot will board the plane at
12:45 p.m. At 1 p.m. the plane will take off on a heading
toward Denver. We will be in the tower to monitor the
frequency he gave Number Two.

"4. At the first sight of a weapon, Carpenter and Dupree
are instructed to shoot to wound. We would like to keep this
guy alive to make sure we have the main guy, and not some
accomplice — although I don't think that's very likely. Dufus,
who will be under the tarp, will get up and be ready after the
plane is airborne. He is armed with full steel jacketed shells
and a high-powered rifle with a telescopic sight. He will also
be carrying a handgun. He will have an extra rifle for the
pilot, Carpenter, if it comes to that. Carpenter will be
carrying a handgun in his jump suit. They will also carry a

special police band radio so we can communicate with them directly on a separate frequency.

"Anything else?"

"Detective Mahoney," one of the men said, "what happens if this guy is not the loner you think he is? After all, $100 million is a lot of money. What if he has twenty men working with him and all twenty storm the plane when it lands at some prearranged point? Each man would still get five million dollars. You can buy a lot of loyalty for that."

There were a lot of nods around the room. Even Grant was nodding. He wondered what he would do for five million dollars, tax free?

"I wouldn't worry about it, gentlemen," said Mahoney, although he could see the words had a disturbing impact on Carpenter and Dupree who were sitting in the front row.

"You see, this guy could never work with a gang. He just isn't built that way. No one else, in his mind, is smart enough for him. He wants to be the focus of attention. Twenty men sharing is not his idea of fun. One man bringing down a church, and getting a hundred million for it, is.

"Hey, Mahoney," yelled Carpenter, the pilot.

"Yeah?"

"What's to stop old Dufus here from conking me over the head and taking all that loot to Mexico and fuckin' whores two-at-a-time till his little pink prick drops off?"

"Can you fly, Dufus?" Mahoney asked.

"No," said Dufus, "but that's an idea. Maybe I can learn by one o'clock."

Mahoney wasn't upset at the joking. The team needed it. They were at the edge. They were not only having their professionalism trampled on, but the vast majority of them were Mormons, and they were also seeing the men they believed to be their spiritual leaders being killed off one by one. A joke or two might save their asses.

"Dufus," Mahoney said, "if I were you I would worry more about Carpenter conking you over the head and taking the money to Mexico. What does he need you for?"

There were more chuckles around the room at Dufus's expense. No one could remember how he got the nickname Dufus. It just fit. Carpenter finally said:

"Hell, coach, all it is, is sand."

"Are you so sure?" asked Mahoney, and he walked out of the room with Grant following. As Mahoney passed Dufus he patted him on the shoulder and said: "Better get going. Good luck!"

The routine had been followed, and Mahoney, Grant, and the chief, with Kimball tagging along like an unwanted kid brother on a first date, headed for the airport to set up a control point in an old unused tower a mile from the current one. When the airport had been smaller, years before, the old tower served well. Now that Salt Lake City International Airport had come of age, the old tower sat empty except for training classes for apprentice controllers. They left for the airport before the sandbagged suitcases had even been loaded on the armored cars. They all had binoculars. They all had weapons. They all had radios. And Mahoney, in addition, had a thermos of coffee and a family-sized box of powdered sugar donuts. He hated stakeouts without his beloved donuts. Mahoney even carried a pocket handkerchief expressly for the purpose of wiping the powered sugar from his mouth.

Binoculars in place they watched the loading of the plane. Mahoney felt sorry for Dufus. He had been in there since 6:20 a.m. It was now past noon and the loading had barely finished. Trucks were fueling the plane. Just before 1 p.m. Mahoney wondered again about Dufus. The poor bastard had been on the floor for well over six-and-a-half hours. Mahoney knew that if he, himself, had been curled up on the floor of a gutted airplane for nearly seven hours, he might never be able to get up again. Dufus was a good man. He had younger bones, thank God.

Six cups of coffee and seven powdered sugar donuts later the party was about to begin. Mahoney couldn't figure out why no one else wanted a powdered sugar donut. But they didn't. So he ate most of them. The front of his suit looked like it was dusted with snow. Every time he brushed it the snow melted and formed little white streaks on his tie and lapels.

John Carpenter, pilot, policeman, husband, devout Mormon, and father of five beautiful all-American children walked out on the tarmac of an unused runway near the far end of the Salt Lake City International Airport and entered the Gulfstream IV. He wasn't alone, but he looked lonely. He closed the door behind him, entered the cabin, and true to his professional bearing never let on that Dufus was lying on the floor to his right.

Dufus, however, said, "Hi, John." It came out muffled.

Carpenter kicked him.

There was little room in the Gulfstream for anything else. The suitcases were stacked six and seven deep and lined both sides of the plane. The Gulfstream was designed to carry nineteen people, and with the seats removed the suitcases were stacked like cordwood and tied down with flat nylon straps. Suitcases covered nearly all of the windows and made it impossible to see out from the cabin.

Saturday: Day Thirteen, Afternoon

At 1 p.m. the plane taxied to the end of the unused runway. It received a pre-arranged clearance to take off. It would be tracked by the tower controllers on a special transponder that had been installed in the plane to assure it of a distinctive, easy to track, identity. As the Gulfstream rose above the horizon, Mahoney could see the plane begin its turn, vectoring toward Denver.

No sooner had the Gulfstream climbed to a reasonable altitude than the radio frequency assigned by the killer crackled to life. It was David's voice. Mahoney immediately recognized its plain, monotonous style.

"Forget Denver," the voice said, "do a one-eighty, and do it now. Pick up I-80 West and follow it. Stay directly overhead I-80 heading west. I said, do it now!"

Carpenter put the Gulfstream into an easy turn. A tighter turn would have seen eighty-four suitcases pulling away from their nylon straps and shifting all over hell. He didn't want that.

"Good," the voice said.

Ten minutes went by without any communications. Police and sheriff's cars were heading out of the airport onto I-80, traveling at high speed directly toward Wendover, at the Utah-Nevada border.

Wendover, Mahoney remembered, was where Paul Tibbits and the crew of the Enola Gay trained to drop the atomic bomb on Japan. Now, like then, it was a desolate area. Today the only thing to recommend it, Mahoney thought, are a few adjacent casinos and two whorehouses along a mile-long stretch of highway. From the air it looked like a giant truck stop. Carpenter could see it in the distance.

173

The radio again.

"Land on the Bonneville speedway, near the public observation tower. Don't cross into Nevada. Do it now!"

Carpenter could see the shimmering salt flats extending for miles along the highway. It was utilized for race cars seeking world land-speed records, but it would make an ideal landing strip for the Gulfstream. Carpenter could land easily enough. He instinctively looked for a wind sock, but there wasn't one. Still the salt flats were wide and long, and even a novice couldn't miss that runway. No tower, no radio, no airport. Just a strip of salt cutting through the desert and ending a few hundred yards in front of the Utah-Nevada border.

Wendover was 115 miles from the Salt Lake City International Airport. The Gulfstream was there in minutes. The police cars still had more than forty-five minutes of flat-out driving to do before they could arrive on the scene.

Mahoney had arranged for a jet helicopter to follow the Gulfstream at a healthy distance. It could make Wendover in another ten minutes. Two armed marksmen were aboard. He had also radioed the Nevada State Patrol. They were asked to stay in the general area, but out of sight until further notice. Since there were always troopers policing the highways in the vicinity of the gambling houses, Mahoney felt confident no one could sneak out of the area. Utah troopers were also speeding along the highway toward the salt flats. Mahoney was also sure that if David was at the salt flats, his plan was to get on the Gulfstream and fly out of there as quickly as possible. Dufus and Carpenter were the flies in David's ointment. At least that's what Mahoney hoped.

As the airplane landed Carpenter radioed Mahoney.

"We're on the ground. What now?"

"Taxi toward the observation tower but stop about fifty yards before you get to it," Mahoney radioed.

Mahoney asked Carpenter to keep them informed.

"Shit," said Carpenter, off mike and to Dufus, "does he think I'm going to keep what goes down here to myself?"

Dufus had been out from under his tarp as soon as they had reached altitude. He now sat on the floor with his back against the bulkhead, keeping his head down, below the front windows. His rifle was on his lap.

"Mahoney," Carpenter radioed, "there's a man walking from a jeep toward the plane. He's a plain looking guy. I can't see a weapon. He's wearing sunglasses and a trucker's hat. What do you want me to do?"

"Open the door, but do it carefully. Stay out of sight and have Dufus back you up. Remember, our guy's a stone cold killer. If it's him, his only plan will be to kill you immediately and fly the plane out. We have to assume he can fly. So be careful, but let's at least hear what he has to say."

Jesus Christ, thought Carpenter, he's going to kill me, but I'm supposed to hear him out. Carpenter instantly wanted out of this chicken-shit outfit.

The man approached the plane and Carpenter opened the door and stood back out of sight.

"Hey, in there! Anybody home? I'm supposed to get three suitcases from you guys."

"Who sent you," yelled Carpenter.

"Damned if I know. Some guy I met yesterday in Salt Lake City paid me $500 to come out here and get three suitcases. I'm supposed to open them up and dump the contents out on the runway. Weirdest thing I've ever heard of. But $500 is $500. Know what I mean? Shit, you guys aren't drug runners or anything, are you?"

"Wait a minute!" Carpenter yelled out.

Dufus was sitting with his rifle pointed at the door. He didn't like this one damn bit. He wanted to get up and shoot the bastard.

"Mahoney," Carpenter radioed, "this guy seems normal as can be, for Utah. He said some guy paid him $500 to drive out from Salt Lake City, meet the plane, and get three suitcases from us. He says he's supposed to open them and dump the contents on the runway."

"Fuck," said Mahoney. His mike wasn't open. Grant looked pale, and the chief shrugged at Mahoney.

"Chief, I have to assume the bastard has got binoculars on this guy. We did put one dummy suitcase full of money on that plane. But we sure as hell didn't put three. The smart bastard. If we let this guy dump three suitcases he's going to be pounding sand up his ass after the first one. We better get them out of there."

The chief agreed with Mahoney; there was nothing left to

do but bluff their way through. Refuse to give up the suitcases, close the door, and get out. Anything would be better than letting those sandbags hit the dirt.

"Carpenter," Mahoney radioed, "close the door, leave the guy standing there, and take off. Now! Head home. Let's see what our prick David does next."

"Roger."

Carpenter shut the door, went back to his seat, started the engines, and began taxing toward the end of the runway. The man just stood there staring up at the plane in disbelief as it rolled away from him.

"Hey!" he yelled. "Hey! What the hell's going on? Hey! Suitcases! Hey! Goddamn it! Suitcases! Hey! Fuck!"

Mahoney radioed to the Utah and Nevada troopers the only description of David they had. Average, average, average. Look for somebody as plain as vanilla ice cream, with binoculars, maybe a radio. Pick up and hold anyone fitting that description for the Salt Lake City police. Stop every occupant of a car if you have to. Search the car, and detain the driver. Armed and dangerous is an understatement.

Damn, thought Dufus, all that undercover work for nothing. His legs ached like hell.

There was a flurry of activity at the landing strip in Wendover, and at the gambling joints along the one-mile stretch of I-80. Nevada troopers had the guy with the trucker's hat in custody, and had rounded up eleven average looking men carrying cases of one kind or another. Within a half-hour all of them were I.D.'ed, photographed, and released. There were no binoculars, no radios, and nothing to hold them on.

State troopers had, as previously arranged, set up road blocks five miles beyond Wendover, and five miles in front of it, when they finally got the word from Mahoney that the plane had landed. Cars were piling up slowly, the drivers bitching and moaning that they had better things to do but sit on a desert highway watching a bunch of troopers all lined up in a row.

The police helicopter, following instructions, had finally caught up with the Gulfstream, after it was on the ground, but took an extremely wide berth around Wendover. That was hard to do, since there was restricted air space on either side of the road. Ten miles north of I-80, just before hitting Wendover, is the Hill Air Force Range, restricted. Seven miles south of I-80, right up to Wendover's back yard, is the Wendover Range, the Desert Test Center, and Dugway Proving Grounds, also restricted. The helicopter took the northern side and stayed the full ten miles distance from I-80. When it passed Wendover it flew west another twenty miles into Nevada, there was no other route without hovering over the damned Gulfstream. The helicopter circled around waiting to be called in on the chase. Staying out of sight was the shits.

Mahoney radioed Carpenter and Dufus that it was over.

Carpenter was never one to hesitate. He punched the Gulfstream hard and headed for Salt Lake's airport. He seldom got a chance to fly one of these corporate babies, and he wanted to see what it could do. After all, he was off duty when he got back. He and Dufus were nearly at the airport by the time the helicopter got back to Wendover trying to spot any off road vehicles in the area.

As the Gulfstream was about to land at Salt Lake City the man sat in scrub grass at the end of the runway. He knew all general aviation planes would land on this runway, on this day. Salt Lake's airport just isn't that big. David had been monitoring the police bands as well as scanning all airport frequencies on two portable Bearcat units. The idiots thought he was in Wendover. He wasn't. He had never left good old Salt Lake City.

The Gulfstream flew overhead, low and slow on its approach over the markers at the end of the runway. The man aimed his high-powered rifle carefully and began shooting. He got off eighteen rounds. Five missed; three plowed into the underbelly of the cabin; seven hit the fuel tanks in the wings; one cut into the tail assembly; two ripped into the flaps and control surfaces of the right wing. He could see the plane tip to one side and try desperately to correct. They knew they had been hit. Stupid bastards, thought the man.

Carpenter frantically tried to remain airborne. Dufus, to his credit, just held on and occasionally muttered "shit" under his breath. Had Carpenter been higher he might have pulled it off. At landing altitude it was another story. Out of control and too low to recover, the Gulfstream pitched and shuddered

as it lost airspeed fighting the crabbing caused by the
damaged control surfaces. As the plane touched down too fast
on one wheel, the right wing tip hit the ground and the plane
lurched forward, tipping its nose to the ground. The
Gulfstream's right tire blew on impact with the ground. The
sleek craft pitched right and cartwheeled once, bursting into
flames as the jet fuel spilling from the wing ignited in the
shower of sparks.

Mahoney, Grant, and the chief, in their tower control
center, watched in horror as Carpenter and Dufus died near
the middle of the runway. From where they were they had no
idea the plane had suffered damage from the killer's rifle. It
appeared, from their point of view, that Carpenter had lost
control, cartwheeled, and burned. There was no time for
Carpenter to radio his status. He was too busy fighting to hold
on to the few remaining seconds of his life.

The man left the rifle, got in his car, which he had parked
behind a stand of trees at the deserted end of the runway, and
took the back road from the airport, past the oil refinery, into
the town of Bountiful, only a few miles away. He had passed
only one car along the route. It was filled with kids having
too much fun flirting and drinking beer to pay any attention
to a solitary man driving fast, but carefully, along the back
road behind the airport.

Mahoney and Grant spent the rest of the day with Mrs.
Carpenter and the five Carpenter children. Telling them was
harder than anything Grant had ever done. Mahoney,
unfortunately, had done this several times before. It was
nearly as difficult not having anyone to tell about Dufus.
Dupree was single and carefree. His parents were dead and he
was an only child. He lived alone in a rented room. He drove
a paid, restored 1957 Chevy, and still wore bell-bottom Levi's
as a throwback to the '60s. No one knew his girlfriend's name,
or if he even had one. The only thing about Dufus they knew
for sure, was that everyone who knew him, loved him. There
just wasn't anyone to tell. All of his friends were cops. They
already knew.

Mahoney couldn't breath.

Nothing else happened Saturday. Thank God, Mahoney
thought. When would there ever be time again for the fast
streams, the cold water, and the beautiful rainbow trout that

fight so majestically, as if life were made up of nothing but tomorrows?

The man was on duty again. Another interminable twelve-hour shift. After a full day of work, the kind of work he loved, going to his job was repugnant. He couldn't do this much longer, he thought. It was only a matter of time. Soon, maybe tomorrow, he would have to go to ground. He couldn't wait forever to get the assignment to cover the President, Prophet, Seer, and Revelator. Christ, it could be months. Going to ground was the only way he would have the time to finish this up right. Besides, he knew how to get the Prophet.

With the General Conference only two weeks away he needed more time to prepare. Going to ground was the only answer. Then they would know who he was. Once he pulled out of the routine, they would put him at the top of their list. They would begin to piece his schedule together with the killings. Why they hadn't done that already was a mystery to him. Just stupidity, he thought. He had all but given them his name. His schedule was there for them to see. He had even given them his blood type. He could have lead them on a wild goose chase, but he didn't. He had spilled his seed and nailed it to a cross for Mahoney to find. What the hell more did they want? He expected better from Detective Mahoney. Still, the guy was trying, he had to give him credit for that. He wondered whether killing Detective Mahoney was the right thing to do. He was the only cop the man could think of who could have stood up to him like this. The bastard hung up on me, the man thought. He hung up on me three times. He's got guts. Maybe I should let him live. Maybe not.

The man watched television and grinned at the KSL-TV report on the crash of the Gulfstream. I wonder, the man thought, if the money was in there. There was no mention of it in the broadcast. Never mind. He was satisfied. He was sure it wasn't there. He knew these people. And he had wanted them to know he knew. The touch with the red-neck in the trucker's hat was brilliant, he thought. He wondered if they actually opened three of the suitcases or just took off. Given the timing, he concluded, they just took off. If the suitcases were full of newspaper, or rocks, that's what they had to do. Either way, he had won again. If it was a sham, then they would go crazy wondering how he knew for sure. If it wasn't, and the money was actually in the plane, they had to be going crazy wondering what he'd do next. After all he had just burned up $100 million, and destroyed a $25 million corporate jet in the process. He also wondered how many men he had killed. Undoubtedly the pilot was a cop. Did they have other cops on board? Probably. At least one. Maybe two. He'd have to talk to Mahoney about that. Maybe tomorrow. Tonight, the man thought, Mahoney has some wreaths to lay. He will probably get drunk.

The man spent the rest of the evening guarding the front gates of Temple Square. It was definitely time to go to ground. This rotation of duty sucked. Kimball sucked. It's about time to kill that bastard. Tomorrow would be good. It's Sunday. Fuck the day of rest. So what if God gets pissed.

Sunday: Day Fourteen, Morning

Checking out of the Salt Lake Marriott, he regretted the short stay. He liked the Marriott. Every time he traveled across the country he always stayed at a Marriott. Unlike all other hotels throughout the country that were stocked with Gideon Bibles, every Marriott, even those in backwater states and depressing cities, were stocked with a complimentary copy of the Book of Mormon in every room. It made him feel at home. The Marriotts were devout Mormons and major contributors to the church. They dripped money. The church leaders had probably given every last Marriott a Second Anointing. With that much money, the man thought, anything was possible.

The man also cleaned out his apartment of everything he wanted to keep. It wasn't much, a few books on weapons, explosives, and guerrilla warfare; a history of the Vietnam war; a small stack of pornographic magazines; and the only good one-volume history of the Mormons called *The Story of the Latter-Day Saints*, by Allen and Leonard. This was his favorite book. He liked it because it was a first edition, published by the church; there was never a second edition. Ironically, the book was published under the direction of Arrington's church history department. The first edition sold out, and even non-Mormon scholars believed it to be the best one-volume history of the church. Yet it was later banned by the church, and never reissued. Its objectivity and frankness had rankled President Benson.

The man also took the rest of his arsenal from the back of his closet. He left behind some clothes, everything in the kitchen, and all of his furniture. He took a portable television set, a VCR, and some tapes. He also took three separate sets of false identity papers, bogus credit cards, and a metal box

181

full of cash. He closed the door and never looked back.

He drove to Midvale and parked along a main thoroughfare. He walked two blocks to an Avis rent-a-car outlet and rented a late model Oldsmobile. He presented his credit card. Life was easy. He drove the two blocks to where he had parked his own car, and transferred his belongings. He removed the registration and plates from his old car and abandoned it, leaving the keys in it and the doors unlocked. It wouldn't be there long.

Driving the Oldsmobile to Sandy, a suburb south of Salt Lake City, nestled between the entrances to Big Cottonwood Canyon and Little Cottonwood Canyon, the access point to the Snowbird and Alta ski resorts, he pulled up to an apartment house with a vacancy sign on the lawn. He had passed it days before. It was near Wasatch Boulevard, on a side street called Westwood. After paying the landlord a three month deposit, he transferred his belongings to the apartment at the end of the row. It would suit his needs. His name was now Walter Thomas, his car was rented in that name, and his papers were in that name. He had severed all ties to his former identity. He was not going back to his job. He was, however, going to work. His kind of work.

"Grant," said Mahoney, "what did you find out about those three names you were going to run from the list of the nine with B type blood?"

Grant just stared at Mahoney for a moment.

"Oh, shit!" said Grant.

Mahoney was actually amazed. Grant had said 'shit.'

"That must mean you haven't done anything with them."

"I'll get right on it. It's here someplace," Grant said, as he started searching through the papers on his desk.

Mahoney couldn't get angry with Grant, although he wanted to. He knew it was the lack of sleep that was making them careless. Not just Grant. Everyone, including himself.

Entering the names John David Sampleford and John Douglas Davies into his computer, linked to the church personnel database, he requested from the menu all possible information, including personnel records.

A flashing cursor and the words "Searching, Please Wait," were the only things showing on the otherwise blank screen. It took only a few minutes for the information on the first name to appear. Grant dumped it to the printer. Then the second name finally appeared, and it too was dumped to the printer. Grant ripped off the computer paper containing the information and began to read it:

JOHN DAVID SAMPLEFORD
Date of Hire: 03/22/82
Date of Birth: 08/16/49
Status: Married: 09/01/70 to Mary Shackleforth
                 Children: Jeffery 09/22/71, Lucy 03/12/73
                 Mission: Canadian Mission, '67-'69
                 Military: N/A
                 Education: BYU — BS Physical Ed. '74
Employment: Provo Police Department — '74-'78
                 Church Security Office — '78-Present

The report went on to list everything from grade point averages, extracurricular activities, employment promotions, reprimands, Temple recommend status, police record, and detailed references from friends and associates, including the complete transcript of Sampleford's missionary recommendation from his local Mormon bishop. The list included the names of next of kin, and complete church records for all of the members of the immediate family.

Grant moved on to the next name.

JOHN DOUGLAS DAVIES
Date of Hire: 11/12/84
Date of Birth: 03/16/60
Status: Married: No
                 Children: None
                 Mission: England Mission, '78-'80
                 Military: Army, Green Berets, '80-'84
                 Education: BYU — BS Chemistry '88
Employment: Church Security Office — '89-Present

In the ancillary material for Davies, under extracurricular activities at BYU, was the single entry: "Special Security Assignment, Restricted Access; Excelled above and beyond what was asked of him."

Under Temple recommend status was the entry: "Current." Behind that it read: "NOTE: First missionary partner in England disgraced; suicide; subject Davies found blameless; second missionary partner reported highest marks on Davies to Church Missionary Office; no subsequent blemishes recorded; exemplary performance following incident with first partner. Conclusion: no primary or secondary involvement in partner's disgrace. Highest recommend due to special service record for the Church."

Grant had a funny feeling about this one. He took the two reports and handed them to Mahoney.

"I don't think the first one is our man. But the second one could be. Some funny stuff went on in England. He also was trained as a Green Beret. He has a degree in Chemistry from BYU, and has never had any job other than with church security. He also did some sort of special assignment security stuff for the church while at BYU. And whatever it was, they loved it."

Mahoney grabbed at the printout on Davies and read it intently. He picked up the phone and called Kimball. Some assistant wanted to know if Brother Kimball was expecting his call. The smug little prick, Mahoney thought, had surrounded himself with smug little assistant prickettes.

"This is police department business. Put Kimball on the goddamn phone!"

"Well, I never . . . " was the only reply.

Mahoney, speaking into a phone having already been put on hold, said, "I'll bet you never . . . "

"Mr. Kimball here."

"Kimball, Mahoney. Check your assignment sheet for John Douglas Davies and tell me if he's on duty now, and if not, when he will be."

"You've got a copy of the assignment sheet."

"I know what I have got, Kimball, you twit! But it's in the task force room under a pile of other shit. Now, let me make this simple for you. Look at your fuckin' sheet and tell me what his schedule is!"

There was a very long pause before Kimball spoke.

"He was supposed to be on duty this shift, but he didn't show up. We had to substitute for him. We called his . . ."

Mahoney hung up. This was getting to be a habit, thought

Grant.

"Come on, Heber, let's go."

The two men drove to the address on the printout. It was a small grubby home in the avenues behind the Capitol. The area used to be grand in the early days, but in the '60s it turned into a hippie haven with large dilapidated mansions becoming communes overnight. The area never fully recovered, and pockets of it were still run down. This place was small and obviously unkempt. It appeared as if no one ever cut the grass or painted the fence. It had a used and seedy look. As they approached the front door, Mahoney pulled his weapon and held it at his side. Grant followed Mahoney's lead.

Mahoney stood to the side of the door and knocked. No answer. He knocked again. Still no answer. Trying the door Mahoney realized it wasn't fully shut. As he reached to turn the doorknob the door opened slightly and creaked as it did. Both men waited. Nothing happened.

Inside it smelled of mildew and grease. It wasn't filthy, but it wasn't clean. It had the look of a bachelor pad belonging to a bachelor with no girl friends whatsoever. In the bedroom Mahoney found several copies of smut magazines, and three foil wrapped condoms on the floor near the bed; they were the same brand as the one found hanging on the stop sign. A box of Kentucky Fried Chicken was also on the floor. It had a piece of chicken rotting in the bottom, covered by some bones and a half container of coleslaw. There were flies buzzing in the room, and something was crawling on the chicken. Mahoney turned on the light in the kitchen and saw three cockroaches scurry up the wall behind the faucet. Whoever lived here, David undoubtedly, Mahoney thought, hadn't stayed here much during the past 14 days. It had been fourteen days since the killings had started.

"Mahoney, come here."

Grant was standing in the living room looking down at some papers on the floor. There were several copies of the *Deseret News*, some open on the floor, and the rest in a stack by the side of a chair.

"So?"

"Well," said Grant, "they're not just copies of the *News*, they're copies of old papers. They're copies of the special editions the *News* puts out twice a year. Why would your average citizen be reading year-old newspapers covering the April and October General Conferences of the Mormon church?"

Mahoney smiled broadly.

"Let me guess. Either he's a slow reader who has trouble keeping up with the news. Or — we've found David."

Although Mahoney and Grant were elated to have gotten this close to their elusive killer, they were depressed by their discovery that the closets had been partially cleaned out, and all the toiletries were gone from the bathroom. They both agreed that the apartment should be staked out, but neither held out too much hope that David would return. Not now. Not after failing to show up for work. They now knew, and David knew they knew. The son-of-a-bitch knew we were getting close, Mahoney thought. Where the hell is he? Who the hell is he — in his heart? Does he even have one?

Sunday: Day Fourteen, Afternoon

Kimball hated to admit that the killer might be one of his security agents. It now seemed likely, but he had been hoping that it would turn out to be some rogue cop of Mahoney's. No such luck. Still, if it was Davies, Kimball was going to be the one to get him. Not Mahoney.

Kimball pulled the special file on Davies. It wasn't the file kept on the computer's personnel data base. It was the private files Kimball had on all hundred agents, cross-referenced by skills and special training. Kimball called it his "Danite File." It was stuff he never entered in the Church computer.

At the top of the list were fifteen names, names of operatives Kimball was sure would do anything asked of them. Davies' name wasn't among them. The next group, thirty in all, were still good men, men who would follow Kimball's orders as long as too many civilian laws weren't broken. Davies did not appear in this group either. The remaining fifty-five names were the loyal majority. Good men, he was sure. But they were not among his inner circle. Here is where he found the name John Douglas Davies.

Kimball remembered now. Although he knew most of his men, some of them were just men in uniforms of blue blazers and gray slacks who did their job. Looking at the black-and-white picture of Davies, Kimball nodded several times to himself. Of course, he thought, the guy with the weird eye. He had never made Kimball's top ten, although he had the background to do so. He was an excellent marksman; highly schooled in hand-to-hand combat; decorated for bravery; yet Davies had never been promoted above his initial rank after Green Beret training. He was either a follower, and that was good, or an individualist, and that was bad. His record indicated he hadn't been promoted because he never quite fit in. He was just a bit too strange. He vaguely remembered that Davies was somewhat unpleasant. Abrupt. Insubordinate.

When Kimball got his men together, Davies always sat in the back, alone, separated from the others. He had no friends Kimball knew about. Kimball never trusted a man without friends.

Scanning the detailed report on Davies, Kimball noticed that he was cleared of an incident in which his missionary partner had committed suicide after alluding to some "unnatural act." Sure as hell, Kimball thought, Davies was throat deep in that unnatural act. Cleared of all suspicion, my ass. If this guy wasn't playing find-the-soap-in-the-shower with his partner, nobody was. Davies was a good liar, thought Kimball. He was also a good actor. He could have used him among his most loyal men, but for this, and his aloofness.

He read the report on the special security detail assigned to Davies at BYU after his return from the Green Berets. Because of his training Davies had come to the attention of a few students at BYU who were carrying on the traditions of the BYU spy ring of the mid-60s. Recruited by a fundamentalist teacher, he reported directly to a contact in the office of the General Authorities.

The man thought about what he was doing and was pleased. He sat in his new apartment and thought about Lucy Snow, the only girl he had ever been in love with. She would like it here. She wouldn't like what I've done, but she would like it here.

David had met Lucy at BYU after his return from the Army. He enrolled in 1984 and she had entered the university, one year later, with a home economics major. He had heard all the jokes about home economics being the department at BYU that was the holding tank for Mormon girls waiting for returned missionaries and a wedding band. No use finishing college. Just marry, and get on with being a dutiful Mormon wife to your man. The drop-out rate in the home economic department was enormous. It was a matrimonial revolving door. Most women needed no more than a year to snag a husband and a future. Women had changed in the '70s and '80s. But in Utah, and especially at BYU, the women were still in a '50s mentality — *Beaver*

Cleaver and *Father Knows Best.* Among newlyweds there was a *Stepford Wives'* aura about the small apartments that housed the returned missionary and his obedient spouse, and extended onto the campus like a creeping fungus.

The man, during his BYU years, had never had normal sex with a woman. He knew it, but no one else did. Not even Lucy, who set her sights, unbeknownst to him, on becoming Mrs. John Douglas Davies. Lucy Snow Davies had a wonderful ring about it. She constantly told him that. She reminded him that she was a distant relative of Lorenzo Snow, the fifth President, Prophet, Seer, and Revelator of the Mormon church. It was President Snow who in 1899 brought the law of tithe to the Mormons. The church was broke and money was badly needed. Drought had ravaged the land and Mormons everywhere in Utah were starving. President Snow recounted that the prophet Malachi brought forth the Lord's message that Israel had robbed Him in tithes and offerings. He told them that God had also given them a promise that if they brought their tithes into a storehouse the windows of heaven would open and pour out a blessing so great that they would not have room enough to receive it. President Snow asked the saints to pay their tithe, and promised rain in return. They did, and one morning in August, so the story goes, a telegram was placed on President Snow's desk that read: "Rain in St. George." By 1907 the last Church debt was paid, and the ledger has been startlingly black ever since.

David was enamored of the story. He wished he had known it during his mission. He would have told it and re-told it. After one date with Lucy, in the quiet of her automobile's back seat, she offered herself to him. When he couldn't get an erection, she was furious. She laughed at him and taunted him with the story she had heard that his missionary partner was a homosexual. Obviously, she said, so was he. She threatened to spread the story on campus. He struck her, hard. Again, and again. He achieved his erection.

Three weeks later a ground's keeper at BYU found the decaying body of Lucy Snow, her throat cut open so deeply that her head was lying at a ninety degree angle to her shoulders. The campus went crazy. A direct descendent of Lorenzo Snow had been murdered on the campus of Brigham Young University. What was the world coming to?

Lucy Snow was as pure as the driven slush. She had a reputation for dating anyone who might be a candidate for marriage — anyone who might tolerate her endless chatter about being a relative of President Lorenzo Snow. Fortunately for Davies he was only one on a long list of suspects. And he could lie better than all of them.

Provo police and BYU security investigated and after seven months of rumors and innuendo concluded that the murder had been committed at the hands of a person or persons unknown, obviously non-Mormon, seeking to harm the church and the university because of its ever increasing growth and influence worldwide. The case was never solved. There were suspicions about David's involvement, but without proof, the returned missionary prevailed.

Two years later John Douglas Davies graduated, amid the continuing flap of wagging tongues that refused to let the ugly verbal rumors of his involvement and past die.

Ironically, because Davies' record was so outstanding, otherwise, and his service on special assignment so highly lauded, no one could bring themselves to write on his record even the slightest hint of the scandal. Davies surmised, as the years passed, that because the incident was so volatile, and involved a descendent of a church prophet and president, everyone was afraid of making a permanent record of it. The murder was not to be linked to a Mormon, at all costs. It never showed up on the file of the man who would later apply for employment, his first job application ever, to the security office of the Mormon church.

Davies also secretly believed that if any indication of the incident existed in his records, it might serve as proof, to an exceptional kind of man, that he was tough and capable. Later, when he subsequently met Kimball, he first thought this might be such a man. The pep talk carried allusions to loyalty and complete surrender to the authority of the church. Shortly, however, Davies came to know that Kimball was a sycophant, much inferior to himself. He would have to do it on his own.

Davies expected his promotions to come almost daily. When they didn't, he found fault with Kimball and the Church. But his disappointment and growing hatred began to focus on the leaders of the church — the men who couldn't see the real leader they had among them, for all the obsequious toadies who fell at their feet. It was the Green Berets all over again. When others were promoted before him, and given more money, and the favored position of being Kimball's lackeys, his plan began to develop.

No one would ever call him impotent again. He wasn't. He knew how to get an erection. It was easy.

Monday: Day Fifteen, Through
Sunday, Day Twenty-One

Mahoney and Grant were restless. They had been sifting through every possible lead pointing to the whereabouts of John Douglas Davies. So far, after three days of intensive searching, they were no closer than they had been when they found his apartment in the avenues.

The task force canvassed every real estate agent in town and made lists of apartments and houses for rent. They combed the rental ads in the newspapers, and planted stories asking the public to come forward if they had rented to a stranger in the past week. Davies was either the luckiest man alive, or a ghost who could come and go as he pleased. Over a hundred tips had been checked and rechecked. Nothing.

Mahoney often looked at the calendar and mentally checked off the days left till the Easter Sunday convocation of the General Conference of the Mormon church. Just over a week was left. Grant missed his family. Mahoney pined over his flagging hopes for a full departmental pension. The chief screamed at the members of the task force, Mahoney in particular. And the mayor screamed at the chief. It was a cluster-fuck.

The man spoke little of the language, but enough to be considered a friendly and well-mannered tourist by the natives of Sao Paulo, coupled with his generosity with the American dollar.

The last piece of church intelligence David had secured before leaving his post for good, was the simple fact that Apostles Martin X. Beck and Stanford Boyd Williams, upon having officiated at the opening of a new Mormon temple in Santiago, had been asked by the First Presidency to extend

their visit in South America by ministering to the faithful at
the Templo De Sao Paulo. High church officials had not
visited the Sao Paulo temple for several years. The faithful of
Sao Paulo rejoiced.

He had prepared well. No guns, no knives, no explosives.
He had booked first class passage directly to Rio De Janeiro
and had spent the next day motoring south to Sao Paulo. He
carried only one small flight bag that contained a white linen
suit, a fresh shirt and tie, and a toilet kit that looked
remarkably harmless.

Before leaving Salt Lake City, David had seen the articles
in the paper regarding new tenants. He was out of the
apartment within five minutes, taking only a few items,
including the large suitcase full of weapons, and the nylon
shoulder bag full of his personal belongings. He transferred
these, his box of money, and a few of his most prized books
to the trunk of his car. His second trip into the house was to
leave a note for Detective Mahoney on the bed.

Sure that his landlord had never seen his car, which he
parked around the side of his apartment, he drove away, and
never looked back. The car was now parked in the most
crowded part of the long-term parking lot at the Salt Lake
International Airport. As of this moment, his car was his only
address, and he was on "vacation" in Sao Paulo. The police
would not expect him to be out of town. They would never
check the airport parking lots. Instead, the man was sure, they
would concentrate on the motels in the valley, and in the
surrounding suburbs. Have fun chasing your killer, he
thought. Enjoy!

David, dressed in a new white suit, white shirt, and pale
blue tie, looked dapper in a slightly crumpled way, as he
stood leaning lightly on an umbrella he had purchased at the
airport, and had later modified in his rental car. It seemed an
affectation on this bright day, as puffy clouds drifted
overhead devoid of any threat of gray. Still, the umbrella and
the white suit appeared to be in keeping with the
surroundings.

A massive crowd has gathered on the large expanse of
lawn near the Templo De Sao Paulo, a modest but beautiful
building surrounded by palms and bright flowers with a
fountain spraying arcs of water toward the heavenly spire

topping the temple. It was the first outdoor ceremony the
local officials had planned. The apostles did not have the
heart to request the services be moved inside a local church,
nor did they relate completely to the terror other, more
geographically distant, church leaders felt in the wake of
local happenings in their beloved Zion.

The curious gathered along with the faithful, and among
them stood David, white suit, umbrella, and the Book of
Mormon clutched in his free hand. To all the world he looked
like a successful American businessman, working in Sao
Paulo, out on this warm Sunday to see two of his prophets
visit one of their fifty worldwide temples.

Following the services the crowds pushed in around the
apostles who were being shielded as much as possible by the
local Stake President and the local Bishopric. Sao Paulo was
not Salt Lake City. In this city of six million people the
Mormon population was little more than a curious cult. There
were no security guards, no local police, no terrorist
preparations. One of the apostles had mentioned the
"unpleasantness" now going on in Utah, and dismissed it as
an isolated case of a madman whose soul was lost. Many had
no idea what he was referring to.

As the crowd pushed and shoved to get near their
apostles, the man in the white suit pushed nearer the two
church leaders. As one raised his hand to wave to the crowd,
David lifted the umbrella and aimed its tip through the gap of
a man's legs in front of him and pulled a loop of nylon leader
encircling his index finger. A small, silent, puff of
compressed air propelled a dart no larger than the point of a
ballpoint pen directly into the calf of an apostle of the
Mormon church. The barrel of a modified air gun, handle
removed, was concealed in the black fabric folds, taped to the
umbrella's core. The apostle slowly reached down and
brushed his leg as if a bee had stung it. He then stood up, not
even looking at the spot he had brushed, and began waving,
once again, to the crowd that loved him so.

Within five minutes the man had left the crowd and was
in his rental car driving toward Rio De Janeiro. He had a
connection to make, and he would have to drive several hours
without stopping in order to make it on time.

Arriving at the airport with forty minutes to spare, the

man in the white suit returned the car, and entered a men's room in the main terminal of the airport. There he changed clothes in a toilet stall, and when he came out he dumped the suit, shirt, and tie, along with the umbrella, which he had ripped apart and bent in half, into a large wastebasket by the door. Nylon bag over his shoulder he headed for the gate and his flight back to Utah.

The death of this apostle would take some time.

Monday: Day Twenty-Two, Afternoon

Mahoney and Grant had slept in until late morning. It had been an order from the chief. They had gladly accepted his wise counsel. Mahoney left his apartment at 11 a.m., made several routine stops, arriving at police headquarters at 12:20 p.m. Grant was already there. So was the chief. So was every member of the task force. When Mahoney entered the day room he felt every pair of eyes in the place on him. Christ, he thought, if the chief hadn't wanted me to sleep in late he shouldn't have ordered me to. Fuck.

"Mahoney! Grant!" the chief yelled.

Sitting in the chief's office Mahoney felt like a bad kid waiting for the principal to paddle him. He wasn't sure what he'd done wrong, but he knew he must have done something.

"Look, guys," the chief said, "I know you've been working your asses off. I appreciate it. Really, I do. If I've been all over you it's because the mayor's been all over me. We've got less than a week until the General Conference, six days to be exact. If my reckoning is correct that will be Day Twenty-Eight by our nut's calendar. He said he has thirty days of hell in store for the church. And, I might add, for us. You both know that there are a lot of fat ladies in Utah, and we ain't heard a jack-shit one of them sing yet. I am not going to assume that this thing is going to result in another killing or two, and disappear into thin air come sundown on Tuesday, Day Thirty.

"From right now, we have less than six days till the Saturday conference, and less than seven till Easter Sunday and the main General Conference session. For all we know this ass could kill a person, or two, a day, and have wiped out his original targets plus a few for good measure.   Now, we

196

may not have stopped him, but we know a lot more about him, and he is no longer working from the inside . . . "

"Unless he's got a partner?" Mahoney added.

"Well, does he?"

"No, Chief, he doesn't."

"Okay, then, please let's get this son-of-a-bitch before the public gets us. The faithful in Utah are about to lynch us. There are public meetings and protest marches going on all over town. The anti-police groups are having a field day. I know you're trying as hard as humanly possible, and I wanted you to know that. But we've been lucky during the past week. Nothing's happened. You've finally gotten some sleep. Now here's the bottom line. I don't give a rat's ass if you don't sleep another wink between now and next Tuesday. If you haven't caught him by then, you won't need any sleep because I am personally going to kill both of you. Then I'm going to commit suicide. Do you understand?"

"Yes, sir."

"Yes, sir."

Both men walked back to the day room. Everyone was looking right at them. Mahoney smiled. He realized too late that it probably looked like a shit-eating grin on the face of a whipped old fart who needed a drink. Well, thought Mahoney, when you're right, you're right.

"Hey, Mahoney," called Candy from across the day room. "I just picked up a rumor from one of the press guys that Apostle Williams is sick in South America and nobody knows what the hell is wrong with him. He might die. He's in Sao Paulo, I think."

Mahoney had Number Two on the phone in ten seconds flat.

"What is it, Detective?"

"Have you heard about Apostle Williams?"

"Yes, we have heard that Brother Williams is ill. I have been assured, however, that he has the best of . . ."

"Why the hell didn't you call me and tell me. I thought we had an agreement about this kind of thing?"

"Surely, Detective Mahoney, you don't think this has anything to do with this Davies person?"

"I know it does! Doesn't it strike you a bit odd that nothing has happened here for the past week, and just when we think we're out of the woods, Apostle Williams becomes critically ill?"

"I think you're overreacting to this, Detective."

"And I think you're not reacting to it at all. Goodbye."

Mahoney had no idea how to call an overseas number, so he bluffed his way around it by saying, "Grant, get me the chief of police on the phone. Not ours, the one in Sao Paulo. That's in, ah, South America."

"Yeah, I know. Will do."

Mahoney watched in amazement as Grant picked up the telephone and dialed 00. He waited a moment and then said, "Operator, I would like to talk person to person with the chief of police in Sao Paulo, that's in Brazil."

Mahoney wondered how Grant knew Sao Paulo was in Brazil and all he knew was that it was in South America. Mahoney watched as Grant waited on the line for about thirty seconds and then said, "Just a minute."

Mahoney took the phone from Grant. The man on the other end said he was in charge of the police department. He spoke better English than Mahoney did. Shit.

"We are investigating a series of murders that have taken place in Utah, and . . . "

Mahoney stopped talking and pulled the phone away from his ear, covered it with his hand, and said to Grant, "He asked me 'What's Utah?'"

"Tell him," Grant said.

"Utah's a state in the United States, near Nevada and Colorado."

Mahoney listened again.

"Yes, Las Vegas is in Nevada. You've heard of that but not of Utah. Well, trust me, Utah is a state with about two million people in it, and . . . "

Mahoney listened again.

"You say Sao Paulo has nearly fifteen million people in it and it's just a city. Oh. Well. That's nice."

Grant was having a ball listening to Mahoney betray his chauvinistic American education.

Mahoney finally found the right approach.

"Well, sir, we need your help."

Mahoney finally smiled into the phone.

"Yes, we have had several murders, and as a detective

working on the case, I need to know exactly what . . . just a minute."

Putting his hand over the phone again, Mahoney asked Grant, "What the hell is Apostle William's full name?"

"Stanford Boyd Williams," Grant said.

"We need to know exactly why Stanford Boyd Williams is ill. We need to know . . ."

There was another pause, then Mahoney said, "Thanks, I will." He gave the Sao Paulo chief his Utah telephone number, spelled his name, and added, for good measure, that he was a homicide detective. Mahoney had the feeling that the man was not impressed.

"He said he would call me back."

"You handled that extremely well, boss."

"Fuck you."

The phone on Grant's desk rang twenty minutes later and Grant handed the phone to Mahoney.

"It's a friend of your buddy in Sao Paulo."

"Mahoney."

The man on the other end of the line identified himself as the head medical examiner in Sao Paulo. He was familiar with the case, since it was so unusual. He told Mahoney that Williams became ill an hour after a ceremony at the Mormon temple in Sao Paulo. He was taken to a local hospital, then transferred to another hospital two hours later when they couldn't seem to find the problem. Mr. Williams, he said, just kept getting worse.

By now Grant had lifted the other receiver and was listening. They were also taping the conversation.

The man in Sao Paulo described Apostle Williams as being very near death, and they weren't sure why.

"Doctor," said Mahoney, "I know this sounds strange, but did you, or could you examine Mr. Williams for an injection of some kind. Might he have received something like a shot, an injection?"

The man on the other end seemed incredulous. He admitted to being confused as to the cause of Mr. William's illness, but surely, he added, there wasn't foul play involved.

"I believe there may have been. Yes, I do," said Mahoney.

The medical examiner said he would call back.

Two hours later the phone rang again and the medical examiner, to his credit, sadly, and with a considerable show of regret, informed Mahoney and Grant that Mr. Williams was dead. They had examined the body completely and, because of Mahoney's suspicions, had located a small red area of inflammation on the back of the right calf. There seemed to be something in the wound, he said, and when they removed it, it appeared to be a hollow short needle with a slightly flared back end.

Mahoney asked him if it could have been a dart from an air gun. The medical examiner agreed that it could have been. He also added that their preliminary tests showed death by heart failure.

"Did you check for poison?"

Actually, the man said, they hadn't really had time to check for much of anything. They had run routine blood workups, but the man was seventy-six and very, very frail. Although not one of the oldest of the apostles by any means, he was one of the more infirm. Most of the leadership of the church had advised him not to make the trip to South America, but he insisted. He had been the driving force behind the temple at Sao Paulo, and was instrumental in the building of the new temple at Santiago. It was to be, in his own words, his last 'victory' for the people of South America.

The medical examiner on the other end of the phone expressed his sympathies again. He added that they would keep running tests because of the obvious foul play, but, in his opinion, a bad cold could have killed the man considering the state of his health.

"Mahoney," asked Grant, "what in heaven's name made you think he might have been killed by an injection?"

"I read thrillers and true crime stories like you do, Grant. You mean you never heard of the Bulgarian defector Georgi Markov and the umbrella trick?"

"Oh, my. Yes. Now that you mention it. Didn't he die a horrible death from some poison that was hardly detectable?"

"It was a poison called ricin. It was put in a metal pellet and injected into his leg as he stood waiting at a bus stop on the Waterloo Bridge in London in 1978. He felt a pain in his leg, turned around and saw a man bending down to pick up an umbrella. The man apologized and hailed a taxi. Four days later the man was dead with the highest white cell blood count ever seen by the doctors who treated him. The case was never solved. Ironically, two weeks before Markov's death another Bulgarian defector in Paris, a guy named Kostov, I think, was jabbed with an umbrella. He was ill for two days but he recovered. Apparently the pellet lodged well away from any blood vessels."

"And you think this was the same thing."

"Jesus, Heber. The man had a dart in his calf and twenty-four hours later he's dead. What do you think?"

"But, it took four days for Markov to die?"

"Maybe our friend David didn't care whether Apostle Williams died or not, just that he went through hell, and proved to us that no one is safe. Then again, everyone in the Mormon community knew Williams was hovering near death anyway. Markov was a healthy man. Yeah, I think David did it. He knew Apostle Williams was feeble, and, knowing our boy, he probably did it with a fuckin' umbrella."

Monday: Day Twenty-Two, Evening

When the man woke up in the early evening he had yet to hear the news that Apostle Williams was dead. It took him a moment or two to realize that he was in a motel near the airport. It was a sleazy place with a waterbed and yellowing sheets. He knew he would have to change motels every day now. Tonight he would stay someplace nice. Someplace deserving of his abilities. He turned on the black-and-white television set and watched a piped-in porno movie for a few minutes. Porno movies twenty-four hours a day. Interesting. Finally, he found the news. When he heard that Apostle Williams was dead he was amazed. He was sure it should have taken longer. Two days, maybe three. Twenty-four hours was better than he could have hoped for. He thought that they might be able to save the old codger, although not without some serious damage. The man expected an extended coma or a drawn out death. Mahoney must be furious, he thought. And the church leaders must be on their hands and knees praying that they're not next. David was sure each was hoping that one of their rivals or enemies would be next. He could hear them quietly saying to themselves, Anyone but me, Dear God. Anyone but me. Even Apostles are human.

He had one quick thing to do before he could eat and find a woman for the night. Finding a woman was getting harder, he thought. When you beat up a prostitute while you're fucking her, word gets around. He would have to be careful. Either that or he would have to kill them when he was through. So far, paying them extremely well, triple the usual rate, usually got him what he wanted voluntarily. The whores in Salt Lake City were used to a little rough stuff from time to time.

He picked up the telephone and dialed a number he knew

by heart. When the person answered the man said he knew
who the killer was. He said he didn't want the police
involved, but was willing to meet. Come alone. Would west
of the Salt Palace in the parking lot of a small strip club
called The Golden Spike be okay? Good. Remember, come
alone.

Warren Kimball, chief of security for the Church of Jesus
Christ of Latter-day Saints had agreed to meet in one hour.
He would show that ass Mahoney a thing or two.

The Golden Spike was a small club with a large parking
lot. The man was there in twenty minutes, the time it took to
drive from the motel near the airport to the area west of the
Salt Palace.

He parked at the back of the lot, toward the shadows, and
leaned back to watch the patrons. He stayed still and quiet
watching one person after the other park and enter the bar.
Finally, when the hour was about up, a new car entered the
lot, parked against the front wall, and Mark Kimball got out.
He stood in the parking lot, looking stiff and uncomfortable,
for nearly five minutes. Then he entered the club. He didn't
even look around much, the man thought. Stupid idiot.

The man reached to his side and lifted up the large
crossbow. He slid to the passenger's side and placed the
crossbow's front end on the floor. He placed one foot in the
metal D-ring, and with both hands pulled quickly on the
bowstring until it caught in the trigger notch. He placed a
long bolt in the rest and notched on the bowstring. Then he
waited.

Finally Kimball came out of the door, looking angry and
upset at not having found anyone wanting to talk with him
about the identity of the killer. As he stepped toward his car,
the man opened the door on the passenger's side and stepped
out.

"Are you Kimball?" he asked quietly.

Kimball turned with a start, then said, "Yes. Do you have
some information for me?"

Jesus, was this man stupid, he thought.

It was dark in the section of the parking lot in which
David had parked, and now stood. The light from the
overhead lamps illuminated only the front of the bar and

spilled onto the parking lot about halfway.

Kimball, cocky as ever, took one step forward as the man aimed and pulled the trigger. The steel bolt entered Kimball's left eye socket and drove deeply into his brain, its tip cracking the back of his skull.

The man pulled out of the parking lot before Kimball's body had stopped twitching.

Mahoney was still at the office when the call came in about Kimball. He hated the little rat, but he didn't wish him dead. Grant was thunderstruck. Both men knew anyone could be next, following the death of Toni Dannly. She had broken what pattern there was, and everyone they knew was at risk the second she died. Somehow, they had never dreamed it would be Kimball.

Mahoney had hoped Dannly was an aberration. Something the man did to vent his anger at the media, or because Dannly had called him a maniac. His hopes remained high as the man settled back into a pattern of killing the apostles of the church. It wasn't good, but it was a pattern, at least. It was something to track, something to plot, something to lean on. Breaking the mold sent them all in different directions.

Grant was thankful his family was still safely tucked away. Mahoney worried momentarily about his own mortality. As the game neared its end the man, David, wouldn't need Mahoney any more. Mahoney made a mental note to start some serious worrying on Day Thirty — eight days away.

Grant hated this section of town. He had only been here to investigate murders or muggings, and to ask questions of the dregs of the earth. This sickening area, he thought, should not exist in Zion. It was a blight on the beauty of his beloved Utah.

He stood over Kimball and felt his stomach knot up as his gaze fixed on the long bolt that had entered Kimball's eye socket and ripped into his brain. No man should die like this, Grant thought. Especially, a Mormon.

Mahoney told the policemen on the scene to make sure the "arrow" in Kimball's face was dusted for prints before it was removed or disturbed. Grant looked at Mahoney like he had gone nuts.

"Do you really think we'll find prints? We never have yet."

"Yes, I do. In fact from now on we'll find his prints all over every fuckin' place he goes. He knows we know who he is now. He doesn't have to be careful any more."

After questioning everyone who came forward, and a few who didn't, the detectives had nothing. No one saw a damn thing. True or not, there was little more to do in the dimly lit parking lot of The Golden Spike. Grant and Mahoney crawled into their car and drove off toward headquarters.

"Has it occurred to you that this place is called The Golden Spike, undoubtedly after the Golden Spike ceremony at Promontory Point, and that Kimball was killed with a bolt from a crossbow — a spike?"

Grant didn't respond.

"Grant, you look ill."

"I'm not sick, I'm just disgusted. This shouldn't be happening in my town. To my church."

"If there is anything to this blood atonement stuff," Mahoney said, "our Mr. Kimball is now a sinless man."

"For God's sake, Mahoney!"

"Listen Grant, it's about time you met a friend of mine. Take a left."

The two detectives sat in Maxwell Jackson's living room, while Max played bartender. Grant asked for a decaf Pepsi. Jackson finally pulled up a chair and sat across from the men.

Mahoney hadn't brought Grant to see Jackson out of meanness or spite. He just wanted Grant to be a little more broad-minded about police work as it related to the church. It had been the same for him. Early in his tenure with the Salt Lake City police department he had been assigned to investigate the murder of a monsignor. He was younger then and his own upbringing in the Catholic faith made it very difficult to be objective and to view the clergy from the perspective of a good cop. He tended to be a bit soft on those with the authority of the church. Grant, he felt, was doing the same thing.

He knew Jackson would start easily and would never attack the Mormon church for the sport of it. He would just talk its history and evolution.

Jackson started talking about the doctrine of blood atonement because Mahoney had recounted their brief confrontation in the car. All Mahoney was trying to say, Jackson told Grant, was that blood atonement was part of Mormon history, and history is nothing more than how we get from point A, on a time-line, to point B. The process might be rougher than hell, but the product that results is very special. Mighty oaks, Jackson thought. Mighty oaks.

"Detective Grant," said Jackson, "you just have to know that in discussing church history we are not condemning the modern day Mormon church. However, we must not change the past because it doesn't agree with today's beliefs."

To Grant's credit, Mahoney noted, he nodded and kept his mouth shut. The only thing that worried Mahoney was the penchant of all faithful Mormons to listen politely and then say, without batting an eye, "Well, that's your opinion. But I have faith in the church, and I know it is the one true church." End of story. End of discussion. End of argument.

Jackson made his case on blood atonement. He pulled original church documents off the shelf to allow Grant to read the words of his past apostles for himself. He pointed out, not unlike Mark Twain might, that present proclamations stating that blood atonement was never a doctrine of the church are greatly exaggerated. He pointed out a section of a speech that a member of the First Presidency had preached openly in the Tabernacle in the early days of the church. He justified blood atonement by stating that Judas had been killed, and was kicked until his bowels came out.

Jackson showed Grant a sermon by Brigham Young in volume four of his *Journal of Discourses* in which the prophet proclaimed that there are sins that must be atoned for by the blood of the sinner.

"Detective Grant, let me assure you," continued Jackson, "I do not have an argument with today's Mormon church. I was a Mormon. I only have problems with the rewriting of history — revisionism. Have you ever wondered why Utah has always had the choice of a firing squad as part of its death penalty? It isn't there just for the fun of it. Early in Utah's history the condemned was given, not two, but three choices of how to die — hanging, shooting or beheading.

"Let me read you something," Jackson opened a copy of volume one of the *Doctrines of Salvation*. "This is from the writings of Joseph Fielding Smith, the sixth president of the church, and it refers to the territorial provisions for capital punishment in Utah: *This law, which is now the law of the State, granted unto the condemned murderer the privilege of choosing for himself whether he would die by hanging, or whether he would be shot and thus have his blood shed in harmony with the law of God; and thus atone, so far as it is in his power to atone, for the death of his victim. Almost without exception the condemned party chooses the latter death.*

"Apostle McConkie, as late as 1958, explained that as a mode of capital punishment, hanging does not comply with the law of blood atonement. The blood is not shed."

Jackson went on to tell Grant about the rewriting of some of the history of the church. He told him everything from the fact that early pictures of the golden spike ceremony at Promontory Point in Utah showed railroad workers holding bottles of booze in outstretched hands raised in triumph at the linking of the rails with the east. He showed him a copy of the photograph. He then showed him a publication by the Mormon church showing the same photograph — only in this photograph the bottles of booze had been airbrushed out.

Good old Max, thought Mahoney. He's relentless.

Jackson then mentioned the *Word of Wisdom*, the sacred doctrine of the church, prohibiting liquor, tobacco, and hot drinks, among other things. He showed Grant early writings by the prophet Joseph Smith asking Brother Markam to get a pipe and some tobacco for Apostle Willard Richards. He showed him the same document in which the phrase "a pipe and some tobacco," was replaced with the word "medicine" in a more recent printing of the church's seven volume *History of the Church.* He pointed out that in Nauvoo, Illinois, Joseph Smith sold liquor, and that Brigham Young once counseled Mormons on their way to Utah to make beer as a drink, and that the first bar-room in Salt Lake City was the Salt Lake House, owned by President Young and Feramorz Little. Brigham Young also built a distillery and employed a man to manage it. He closed it down, because, as he said, whisky ". . . came here in great quantities, more than was needed."

By the time Jackson was through with Grant, he had loaned him several books written by Jerald and Sandra Tanner tracing the changes in Mormon doctrine over the past 150 years. Grant had the books under his arm, and a very confused look on his face.

During the drive back Grant said nothing until they pulled up next to where Mahoney's car was parked. As Mahoney got out, Grant pushed the books over and said, "I don't know if I believe all this — I hadn't heard much of the stuff Mr. Jackson was talking about. But it is interesting. See you tomorrow."

Tuesday: Day Twenty-Three, Morning

Grant looked across his desk at Mahoney and waited for him to finish a container of coffee.

"Why did you take me to Mr. Jackson's last night?"

"You're a good cop, Grant. I don't want you to make the same mistakes I did. I don't want to step on your religion or your faith. Personally, I can't buy the doctrine of the Mormon church, but it is, nevertheless, a great church that does great good. You shouldn't lose that. But you must not let your reverence for its leadership get in the way of doing your job. Privately, and in church, you can believe that these men are true apostles of God. But on the job, here and now, you had better realize that they are just men, like you, who make mistakes and do foolish things. Don't let them intimidate you, Grant. Don't ever let them keep you from doing your job. Either that or you should quit and join church security. Personally, I think you're too good a cop for that."

"What have I done wrong?" Grant sounded almost pathetic.

"You haven't done anything wrong. Believe me. But I am concerned about what you haven't done, or might not do in the future."

"What do you mean?"

Grant looked around the day room somewhat self consciously, but no one was paying any attention. And Mahoney, bless him, thought Grant, kept his voice low.

"Well . . . you jumped in and did one hell of a job figuring out the strength of the church security force. That was good work, but I had the feeling you did it because it was a puzzle and you like puzzles. You didn't do it because you wanted to break Kimball in half. That's why you should have

209

done it. You and I both know the son-of-a-bitch was stonewalling from day one. Literally. But he was a Mormon, and so your killer instinct never surfaced. I want you to remember that there are bad Mormons just as there are bad Catholics and bad Boy Scout leaders. When you investigate these people, even if you have to interrogate the Prophet himself, you must suspend your faith and belief that he is a true apostle of God, and deal with him like any other human, warts and all. You need to stop saying Yes, Sir, and start demanding what you need.

"A man far wiser than I am once told me that if you are a professional pool player, and you are going to play straight pool to fifty points against your sick old grandmother, you should try to beat her fifty to nothing. That's what being a professional is all about. If you want to make your grandmother feel good, and throw the game her way, you should retire as a professional, and take up pool as a hobby."

"What about the blackmail idea?"

"You get an A for that. All I want is that you approach everything you do in this job with that same killer instinct. You can't turn it on and off depending on whom you're dealing with. If you do, you will turn it off at the wrong time, and people will lose their lives."

The phone rang.

"Mahoney."

Mahoney listened a long time, nodded twice, and said thanks before hanging up.

"That was the medical examiner in Sao Paulo. The dart was filled with ricin, a copy of the method used to kill Markov. The dart was drilled at the end and ricin placed in it. The top was sealed with a smear of chocolate. When it went in his leg the smear was dissolved by the body heat, or pushed out of the way by contact with the skin, and ricin was released in the bloodstream. He said a millionth of a gram is a fatal dose for an individual. The old man was weak and frail as it was. Shit."

Mahoney looked at the piece of paper in front of him. Typed on it were the names of the victims to date:

— Mr. John Williamson; Mormon, St. Paul, MO; Rifle Shot

— Apostle G. A. Fielding; Church Ad. Bldg.; Bomb

— Apostle Mark Banner; Emigration Canyon; Blood Aton.

— Toni Dannly; KSL-TV Anchor; Home; Knife & Rape

— Apostle William M. Randall; Huntsville; Sharps Rifle

— John Carpenter; SLC Police Pilot; Air Crash

— Fred "Dufus" Dupree; SLC Police Patrolman; Air Crash

And at the bottom of the list, handwritten below the neatly typed list, Mahoney had scribbled in:

— Warren Kimball; Church Security; Golden Spike; X-bow

— Apostle Stanford Boyd Williams; Sao Paulo; Poison

At the bottom of the list he scribbled the following:

Nine good people. Who's next?

Mahoney was tempted to add his own name to the list with a question mark behind it.

Tuesday: Day Twenty-Three, Afternoon

The phone on Mahoney's desk rang. Mahoney nodded at Grant and kept reviewing the task force reports on new rentals in the city. Grant reached over and grabbed the phone.

"Detective Grant, may I help you?"

"I would like a meeting with you and Detective Mahoney," said Number Two in a voice somewhere between Charlton Heston and God, "in my office in one hour."

"No, Sir. I'm afraid not. Detective Mahoney and I have too much to do right now to go to meetings with anyone. Whatever you have can be said over the phone."

Mahoney's head slowly turned toward Grant as it began to sink in that Grant was actually saying this to Number Two.

"See here, Detective Grant, do you realize just . . ."

"Yes, Sir, I do. But we have had nine killings in the past three weeks, and the time for meetings is over. Now, what did you want to see us about — the phone will have to do."

Mahoney hadn't taken his eyes off Grant as he listened to Grant's end of the conversation. He wanted, badly, to reach over and pick up the extension, but he was afraid he would cramp Grant's style, which, he thought, was developing rather nicely. He also wanted to stand up, walk over, and kiss Grant. Maybe not, he thought.

Grant actually thought he could hear huffing and puffing on the other end of the line, but it was mostly silence. Just when he was about to ask if Number Two was still there, the Second Counselor to the First Presidency broke the silence.

"I want you men here to meet the man who will take over Mr. Kimball's role and serve as acting head of church security. I want a new reporting sequence initiated and the three of you need to discuss it in detail. I would like to be present."

"That's impossible, Sir." Grant said. "It would be unwise for you to leave the Church Administration Building, and we are not coming over there right now. Please send your man over with some identification and have him ask for me or Detective Mahoney. We will be happy to talk with him and then turn him over to an officer in the task force.

"And, Sir, we are all very sorry about Mr. Kimball. You'll be hearing from us soon."

And Grant hung up.

Mahoney had a slack-jawed, slightly stupid expression pasted on his face. He couldn't believe what he had just heard. He was delighted, but he couldn't quite believe it.

"Was that who I think it was?"

"It was Number Two," was all Grant said.

Mahoney suppressed a grin and managed a most serious and professional expression.

"Did you get a good night's sleep last night?"

"Very good. How about you?"

"Me too. Want a donut?"

"You don't have any left."

"I'll go buy you one."

"Thanks, no. But you might pick up an extra one tomorrow morning."

Grant looked down at the papers on his desk and started to riffle through them. Mahoney wanted to buy Grant a drink — and toast this partner of his. Hell, he wanted to get drunk with the guy.

"Grant!"

At the sound of the chief's bellow, Grant sat bolt upright and pushed his chair back in one smooth motion. He headed for the chief's office, and Mahoney, although not summoned, followed behind. A warped and somewhat uncomfortable paternal instinct, Mahoney reasoned.

Grant entered the office first and stood in front of the chief's desk waiting to be told to sit. Mahoney entered the office and slouched in a chair to the right of where Grant stood. Seeing Mahoney sit, Grant sat down immediately.

"Am I to understand that you told the Second Counselor

to the First Presidency of the Mormon Church that you would not meet with him in his office!?"

"Yes, Chief. I did."

"Just why in hell did you do that!?"

"Sir, we just don't have the time to run back and forth between the church offices and this office, and still get our work done. We don't need a meeting to introduce us to Kimball's successor. What we need is to find David before he kills someone else."

Grant's words were running together a bit and his voice was a half-octave higher than usual. He actually sounded confident and scared at the same time.

Mahoney had his hand over his mouth and chin trying to keep from smiling every time the chief bellowed something. The chief and Mahoney went back a long way and they knew each other like two whores in a whistle-stop town. Mahoney was marveling at the chief's control. He looked furious.

"Well, Detective Grant, just when did you decide that you would be the person who determines whether or not this office meets with the First Presidency of the Mormon Church!?"

Grant's confidence seemed to be ebbing away, and his eyes kept moving between the chief's desk and the floor in front of him. After a short pause, which felt like eternity to him, he said, "It just happened, Sir."

"Why?"

"Well, Sir, I started thinking last night that I have two choices. I can either try to be the best cop I can be, or work toward becoming a member of the General Authorities by the time I'm seventy or so. I decided that what I really want to be is a good cop. And, Sir, we just don't have the time to run back and forth doing church public relations. When it's substantive, sure. But most of the time it isn't. I guess I just got carried away."

"Well it's a God dammed good thing somebody finally had the hard-ball nuts to do it!"

Grant looked thunderstruck. Mahoney started to chuckle. The chief's frown and foreboding stance softened and he started to laugh one of those airy, spasmodic laughs from the belly that makes the muscles in your stomach hurt the next day.

At first Grant just stared at the two men, and then he began to realize he was among friends. He felt very good.

"I guess Number Two called you," Grant said.

"Yep. I'd say about ten seconds after you hung up on him. He yelled at me about how insubordinate my men were, and how rude you were in particular. He demanded a meeting in his office in one hour."

No one spoke for about ten seconds.

Mahoney could hardly keep a straight face.

The chief, Mahoney knew, was not about to be the first guy to speak. Mahoney knew that the first guy to speak was going to lose.

Grant sensed that he should tough it out; Mahoney could see that. But the silence was maddening. Grant couldn't take it any longer.

"Sir? What did you say?" Grant said quietly.

"I told him that whatever Detective Grant discussed with him had the full approval of my office."

"And what did he say?" Mahoney quickly asked, setting his old friend up for the punch line.

"The son-of-a-bitch hung up on me."

The wheezing laugh started again in the chief's belly, and sounded for all the world as if the old man was having a heart attack while simultaneously letting farts.

Mahoney laughed. Grant laughed. The chief recovered.

The chief finally told the two men to get the hell out of his office and go to work.

When Grant walked out everyone in the day room was looking at him. Most of them were smiling. As Mahoney left the chief's office he nodded at his boss, and his boss nodded back. Mahoney felt very good.

David had changed his location and was now staying the night, one night only, at the Brigham Street Inn, a restored Victorian mansion on South Temple. Months ago, when planning his assault on the church, David had reserved a $400 suite at the Doubletree, also on South Temple, but much closer to Temple Square. The suite had been reserved for Thursday and Friday, the two days before the General Conference, Saturday and Sunday, the days of the conference, and Monday and Tuesday, the two days following the conference. Days twenty-five through thirty. He had made the reservations far in advance because of the difficulty of getting rooms in Salt Lake City during conference. Many Mormons stayed with relatives, but thousands, those not from Utah, flooded into the city and rooms were as scarce as coffee pots in the Temple. He had sent a cashier's check for $3,000 to cover the suite's six-day rate, plus, his letter stated, an additional $600 to be credited to his account for miscellaneous expenses. The name he gave was John Sample. Mr. Sample, the letter said, was a Mormon businessman from Colorado who would be attending the General Conference and conducting business for his firm, Sample Enterprises, Inc. The letter was signed by his secretary, Ms. Freeman. The confirmation of the reservation was to be sent to a post office box number in Grand Junction. Mr. Sample, who would be traveling, would pick up the confirmation there. It was the same post office box David had used for years.

Tomorrow he would stay at yet another motel or inn. Then, on Thursday, he would check into the Doubletree as John Sample. He would remain there until his work was over. Tonight he would eat well at La Caille at Quail Run, a chateau in the style of an 18th century French maison, one of Utah's finest restaurants. It was about time he indulged himself. He had done such good work, he deserved a break today.

Wednesday: Day Twenty-Four, Morning

Mahoney couldn't have been more pissed off. Grant was away from his desk, he hadn't had any coffee yet, and an entire box of powered sugar donuts still sat unopened on his desk. He had only just sat down and the damn telephone was ringing.

"Mahoney." His voice was as gruff as he could make it.

"Good morning, Detective Mahoney, I've missed you. Have you missed me?"

Mahoney thought about hanging up, but at this late date he couldn't afford to. He had to pump David for all he was worth.

"If it isn't David the asshole. I can't say I have. Why did you kill Kimball — wouldn't he give you a raise?"

"Things are never that simple, Detective Mahoney. Besides, I feel no need to explain why I select someone to die. I didn't call you to talk about that, but now that you've brought it up, I will share something with you I think you might find interesting."

"Interest me."

"You are a man of few words, Detective Mahoney. So am I when it suits me. And it suits me now, so I hope you have your tape recorder on."

Mahoney looked fleeting at the red light glowing on the machine he had reflexively turned on to record the phone conversation — but he said nothing.

"Remember the money. Well, I want it. But there are some changes. Instead of that rather ungainly number of suitcases filled with twenty-dollar bills, I would like one small black suitcase, the kind that fits under an airline seat, filled with twenty-dollar bills. You should be able to get at

217

least $500,000 in it. Be sure you do. Same rules, random numbers, used bills, no marks, and that means invisible markings as well. I will check. In addition, I want you to purchase, with the rest of the $100 million you have on hand, since you didn't send it the first time, $95 million in high quality diamonds, nothing over five carats. There should be enough room in the suitcase to tuck that packet on the side. If not, keep a few thousand dollars for yourself. Just make room for the diamonds.

"I want the suitcase in the Tabernacle during both sessions of conference on Saturday and on Sunday. I will call you with instructions on how to deliver it. Any tricks, any deviation from my instructions, will result in hundreds being killed on Sunday. By the way, I may still kill more apostles, then again I may not, but I will spare the president if my demands are met. By the way, Detective Mahoney, I now know where Detective Grant's family is hiding. If the church doesn't pay the money, and provide the diamonds, I am going to throw in a bonus just for you. I'll kill Detective Grant's family on Saturday evening. I would advise you not to fuck around, Detective. Goodbye."

Mahoney tried to break in and keep the conversation going, but the phone went dead. The call was traced to a phone booth on the University of Utah campus. When police arrived, no one was there, but several students had seen a man near the phone booth. None could remember what he looked like. "Just another guy," one student said.

Candy walked up to Grant and Mahoney and said, "There's some guy, a stiff sort, here to see you. He says you know him — he's with church security — his name is Heber Lakewood."

Both Candy and Mahoney grinned.

"Jesus, Grant, how many 'Hebers' are in your church anyway?"

"Too many. Bring him in, Candy," Grant said.

"Heber Lakewood, Gentlemen. Chief of Security for the Church of Jesus Christ of Latter- . . . "

Mahoney interrupted.

"Don't you mean 'acting chief of security' Heber?"

"You can call me Mr. Lakewood, Detective Mahoney. I

understand you're going to brief me on your progress?"

"You understand wrong," said Grant. "What we are going to do is give you to the task force, and they will be delighted to have you help them sift through reports and paperwork on the killer. Maybe you can find something we've overlooked. Go back through the door you came in and take a left. Ask for a man named Draybeck. He's expecting you."

"Now just a minute. I am not here to . . ."

"Then leave," said Grant. "Either you do what we need done, or go back to Temple Square and play with your schedules."

Even Mahoney wondered if Grant was carrying this new found enthusiasm for being a hard-nosed career cop a bit too far.

The man turned and left. Grant and Mahoney watched him hesitate as he went through the door. If he turned left he would find Draybeck. If he turned right he would be leaving.

He turned left.

The kid's okay, thought Mahoney. Maybe I ought to start acting tougher. It could be embarrassing if I lost my reputation to a Mormon cop.

Wednesday: Afternoon, Through Thursday: Day Twenty-Five

Wednesday afternoon and Thursday turned into each other. The hours compressed into one short day. The time passed quickly. Mahoney and Grant, along with most members of the task force, felt as if they had played two back-to-back NFL Monday Night Football games. They ached and felt numb at the same time. Mahoney actually believed he needed to go to Lourdes. It would take a miracle for him to sleep more than two hours at a stretch. By the time Wednesday afternoon faded, it had slid into Thursday. Two days of grunt-work were nearly the same.

Grant was taking the threat to his family rather well. Neither he nor Mahoney believed that David knew the location of Grant's family, but to be on the safe side Mahoney had the chief call his friend at the Federal Witness Protection Program. The favor was extended a bit. Grant's family was moved within four hours, and Mahoney felt much better. This time even Grant didn't have the telephone number.

Early Wednesday evening Mahoney and Grant had dumped the task of getting $95 million dollars in diamonds, and $500,000 in cash, directly into Lakewood's lap. It seemed the ideal thing for the acting chief of church security to do. Mahoney's advice, as old as politics itself, was to pay the two dollars. He wondered what the church leaders, those who were still alive, would decide to do. He found himself wondering if they could reach a unanimous vote on the issue. Cynically, Mahoney believed that a unanimous vote was impossible. He shared his feelings with Grant.

"Let's assume for a minute, Grant, that you are the president of the church. Your vote is all powerful providing that the entire Council of Twelve Apostles doesn't vote you down. If eleven of them do and one doesn't, if I understand your church structure correctly, then the president gets his way. If all vote against him, the Quorum of Seventies gets into the act.

"Now, if you happen to be the senior member of the Council of Twelve Apostles, would you vote not to pay in the hopes that your succession as president and prophet would come that much sooner? And what of the council members lower on the seniority scale? Could it be that they feel fairly safe from the threats made by David, and realize that bumping off the most senior members of the church leadership moves them up the ladder rather dramatically?"

"Boy you're cynical," said Grant. "You don't really believe any of them are thinking like that, do you?"

"Well, my friend, I find it hard to accept that Lyndon B. Johnson never wondered what it would be like if JFK were dead. The fact that he found out doesn't make him a bad person. All it makes him is human. Can you tell me that it has never crossed your mind what would happen to your career if two or three of the senior detectives in this department, including me, quit, took jobs someplace else, or died?"

Grant smiled. Too broadly for Mahoney's taste.

"These men may well be saints. However, they may just as easily be ordinary men in extraordinary circumstances. Ordinary men have burning ambitions. Maybe saints do, too.

"Frankly, Grant, I believe it will be a very cold day in hell when they unanimously decide to pay. You know yourself that there is an ultra-conservative and a moderate faction doing battle within the church hierarchy. It has been that way for 150 years. Do you really think a crazy killer can change that?"

"I wish I could say yes. But I can't."

Grant looked sad. Being away from his family was taking its toll.

The bright spot Thursday morning was that Draybeck kept the new acting security chief, Lakewood, out of their way. To Lakewood's credit he turned over the decision on the diamonds and the money to Number Two, and returned to work at police headquarters. Vertical delegation, thought Mahoney.

Draybeck put Lakewood on the rental printouts, and had him calling all over town. He was still placing calls at 11 a.m. when he connected with a landlady who did remember a new tenant renting an apartment to someone who matched David's "average" description, as well as the time frame the police were working. Lakewood went with Draybeck to the apartment that David had vacated days before. They found a few books and some odds and ends, but nothing to indicate the killer would be back, or where he had gone.

When the two men returned to the day room, Lakewood suggested they shift their search to the hotels and motels in the city, now that they knew David was no longer in his apartment. They would stake it out, but it was obvious to the men that David was not going to return.

At first Mahoney jinxed the idea of the hotel and motel search, based on what they knew about David, and about the city at conference time. David, Mahoney reasoned, would have new I.D., and it would be good. He would probably be staying at one of the hotels, from the day before conference, until the Monday after conference. They knew from past experience that the hotels and motels in Salt Lake City were full to capacity during that time. Everyone in every hotel or motel room in the city could be a suspect. It was a nightmare.

Grant was the one who added the twist that made Mahoney sit up and take notice. What if, reasoned Grant, David needs a base of operations now, and made his reservations a long time ago? He would have had to do that in order to get rooms. What if he's already checked in, and what if he isn't checking out until Day Thirty, as he said in his initial letter? Grant had everyone's attention.

"Most of the people who stay here for the General Conference arrive on Friday evening and leave Sunday night, with a few staying until Monday to shop and sightsee. I believe that those registering for a stay beginning Thursday, and not leaving until Tuesday or Wednesday, would be a rather small percentage of those holding rooms. What do you think?"

Lakewood jumped in and asked to follow up on the extended reservations idea. He seemed genuinely enthusiastic. Mahoney and Grant both nodded 'yes' as Draybeck smiled. Not such a rotten prick after all, thought

Mahoney. Kimball could have done worse than have this guy working for him.

The rest of Thursday went like Wednesday. Fast and hard. Nothing easy. With Lakewood's help some routine changes had been made. With the death of two more apostles since the initial assignments were made, the freed up bodyguards were assigned as additional backup for the Prophet, and for the senior apostle of the Council of Twelve Apostles, as direct successor to the Prophet. Both Mahoney and Grant believed that if David wanted to make a last minute splash, killing either, or both, of these two men was the way to go. The men absolutely agreed on one thing. David couldn't be trusted. He could just as easily kill the president of the church at the Saturday morning session of conference as not. The money and diamonds, both men believed, still had little or nothing to do with it.

The church wouldn't give them unlimited access to the Tabernacle, but Lakewood assured them church security had it under control. Before the doors opened on Saturday the place would be swept electronically, with metal detectors, and sniffed by dogs for explosives and gas.

Mahoney had no idea what was going down, but he knew it was going to be a weekend he would never forget.

Friday: Day Twenty-Six, Morning

Mahoney showed up on Friday morning without coffee or donuts. He looked naked.

"Candy, send out for some coffee and donuts. Quickly."

"What kind of donuts?"

Mahoney lifted his eyes and looked through her.

"Just kidding, boss. I'll get them myself."

Mahoney put his head down on his arm and went to sleep. Grant knew better than to say a word, although he was curious about how Mahoney could have made it into the station without stopping to get his morning fix. He'd ask later. Much later.

Mahoney didn't move for the better part of twenty minutes. When Candy's arrival was announced by the crinkling of a paper bag and the soft clunk of paper containers of coffee being set on his desk, he rolled his head and peered over his elbow at the box of donuts. He slowly raised up and began to drink some coffee. He opened the donuts and stuffed the better part of one into his mouth. In a muffled tone, spewing small explosions of white powder, he said, "Help yourself," to no one in particular. Grant reached over with a Kleenex and took two donuts. Mahoney looked hurt.

By mid-morning Lakewood had informed Draybeck that he was following up on leads from his list of extended hotel and motel reservations. Draybeck passed the information on to Grant.

"Lakewood says he's following up on the reservation thing. Said it was a surprise to him but there were only twenty-seven reservations that extend from Thursday through either Monday or Tuesday. All of the others were from Friday through Sunday or Monday. Maybe he'll get lucky."

"Tell the kid," Mahoney said, reflecting on the fact

that Lakewood looked pathetically young, "to be careful. This is one reactionary son-of-a-bitch we're dealing with here. If Lakewood sniffs out a possible, tell him to call here for backup and we'll be there in minutes. Tell him he's doing a good job."

Draybeck just nodded and went back to the task force area to speak with Lakewood; he had left him on hold.

The man was eating a western omelette, french toast, and a dish of sliced bananas in cream. A pot of steaming coffee sat next to his half-full cup. He poured hot coffee to fill the cup and opened the morning newspaper to the section outlining the upcoming conference program on Saturday and Sunday. There was nothing in it to indicate any major change in tradition. The church leaders would be there, and the public would be allowed in on a first come, first served, basis. Business as usual. Bullshit! the man thought. Behind the scenes it was probably like preparations for D-Day. Business as usual, my round ass.

The news in Sunday morning's newspaper would be of another sort, the man thought. He was confident of his plan. Simplicity was always the best approach. Besides they would never expect it. He had gone through the plan a hundred times in his mind. He had made contingency plans for everything that could possibly go wrong. He was sure Saturday would be the day he would bring the Church of Jesus Christ of Latter-day Saints to its knees. He might not live to get away. He may never get his hands on the money or the diamonds. But he would accomplish his task. He was sure of that. He smiled, fleetingly, at the thought that he might just accomplish his task, get the cash, and the diamonds, and end up killing Mahoney and Grant in the process. Maybe he would get lucky. Why not? After all, he was doing God a favor.

Lakewood had divided the reservation list into concentric circles, starting first with those closest to Temple Square and working outward. He was sure the killer, if he was staying in a Salt Lake City hotel, would want to be as close to the action as possible. It was Mahoney's idea, but he agreed with it, and now it seemed like his very own.

He had already shown John Douglas Davies' photograph to the desk clerks of eight hotels not more than a half-mile away from Temple Square, including the staff of the Hotel Utah Build- Building, which was probably a waste of time. The man would not return there.

At the ninth hotel, the desk clerk said the photograph might look a little like one of their guests. Maybe. He couldn't remember which one, but he did think it was vaguely familiar. Lakewood had only one name on the extended reservation list at this particular hotel, the Doubletree. The name was John Sample. When he mentioned it, the desk clerk said, "Yes, John Sample, I remember his name. But I have no idea if John Sample is the one in the picture. The picture looks familiar, and I remember seeing the name John Sample, but I couldn't say if there is a connection. Is there a problem with Mr. Sample we should know about?"

Lakewood shook his head no and said, "Just routine. By the way, which room is Mr. Sample in?"

Lakewood rode up the elevator heading for Mr. Sample's room, wondering if Sample could possibly be David — could possibly be the killer. It was a long shot, but Lakewood was willing to take it. He knew he would be a hero to his church if he could capture this guy all by himself. He liked Mahoney and Grant now that he had been around them and saw their dedication to stopping the killer, but he was head of church security. Acting head, he realized, but only for a while. Soon the job would be his.

When the elevator stopped, Lakewood thought about taking his gun out, but with most of the rooms in every hotel filled with Mormons, it would create a hell of a stink if he scared the bejesus out of some rich Saint. Besides, he was sure John Sample wasn't the man. After all he was staying in a $400 a night suite. That's something no crazed killer would ever do, he thought. Just question him and leave. That's what he'd do.

Lakewood knocked.

"Who is it?" The voice behind the door was level and calm. Lakewood thought that a good sign, and relaxed a bit.

"My name is Heber Lakewood, Chief of Church Security. I'm just making a routine check. Could I talk with you?"

The door cracked slightly and Lakewood heard the man

behind the door say:

"Give me a second to get my robe in the bathroom, I'm not presentable. Just got out of the shower. You know how it is. Just a second, then come on in. I'll be glad to help in any way I can."

Lakewood stood there for a few seconds, wondering if he was doing the right thing. Just to be on the safe side, he took his automatic from its holster and held it down at his side, pressed into the fabric of his trousers. He used his left hand to push the door open.

Jesus, he thought. What a beautiful suite! The doorway opened into a large foyer. In front of him to the left was a closet and further on a large wet-bar. To his right, and in front of him, was the slightly open door of what Lakewood assumed was the bathroom. Beyond was the vast expanse of the expensive suite. He could hear water running in the bathroom sink. He took a few steps into the room and the door behind him started closing by itself. Lakewood turned to his right and glanced at the closing door, then he turned back toward the open bathroom door. He peeked into the bathroom. It was empty. Just then a naked John Douglas Davies stepped out from behind the closed half of the open sliding closet door behind Lakewood. Before Lakewood could complete his turn, Davies brought his left hand around, and placed it over Lakewood's mouth, simultaneously using the Ek-Warrior in his right hand, he cut Lakewood's throat from ear to ear.

With his mouth still covered, the sound of death through a gurgle of blood could be heard escaping from Lakewood's neck. The man leaned his naked body against his victim's back and placed his mouth next to Lakewood's ear, just above the bloody gash. He knew Lakewood was still conscious. As he felt the life starting to slip from the body, the man said softly, "My name is David. It was nice of you to come and see me."

As the last sign of life ebbed from the slack body of Heber Lakewood, acting chief of security, the man turned and dragged him into the bathroom, throwing him, uncere-moniously, into the bathtub. His head cracked against the tile wall and thumped again as it hit the rim of the tub. David pulled a towel from the rack and walked out into the foyer.

He turned on the hall light and looked at the puddle of blood, and the smear marking his trail into the bathroom. He draped the towel over the main stain, then returned to the bathroom. He dipped his forefinger in Lakewood's blood and wrote something on the tile above the tub. He then washed the blood from his hands, arms, genitals and legs.

The man knew he might not have much time. There could be others. He was dressed in three minutes and had stuffed everything he owned into his black nylon shoulder bag. He left the Ek-Warrior on the floor where he dropped it, and retrieved a new one from his suitcase, along with a Velcro scabbard he attached to his belt. He tucked a loaded automatic into his belt at the back and put on a blue blazer to cover them. Placing the suitcase on the collapsible cart the man was careful to roll it over the clean part of the towel covering the stain on the floor in the foyer. Once outside the hotel he calmly entered his rental car and drove the 117 miles to Wendover. Crossing into Nevada he would have the solace of gambling, a safe night's sleep, the whores across the railroad tracks, and the memory of Lakewood's warm blood sticky on his naked body.

Friday: Day Twenty-Six, Afternoon

Arrangements for the April conference were final as far as the leaders of the church were concerned. Mahoney and Grant weren't so sure.

Mahoney was pissed that Number Two wouldn't give them complete access to the Tabernacle. It was something, he was sure, having to do with secret tunnels and internal security. People would be killed and Mahoney would be blamed. Life sucks, Mahoney thought.

"What do you hear from Lakewood?" Mahoney asked Grant.

"He hasn't called in since morning."

"Well . . . see if you can track him down. Maybe we can get some cooperation from Number Two through Lakewood. We have to try everything we can now that you have personally pissed off the Second Counselor. Welcome to the privileged class of the gentile in Utah."

"It's not like that, Mahoney. Number Two understands. I'm sure he does. I'm really sure he does. I know it. He does."

"Jesus, will you listen to yourself! You sound like you're trying to assure yourself that you haven't been excommunicated."

"They'd never do something like that."

"They've done it for much less than telling Number Two to stuff it."

"I didn't tell Number Two to stuff it."

"He thinks you did."

"Jesus."

Candy interrupted Grant's self-flagellation with a message from dispatch; they had just received a call that a dead man had been found at the Doubletree. It was a church security agent. Grant and Mahoney thought Lakewood at the same instant. Both men were at the Doubletree in record time.

229

* * *

Viewing Lakewood's body deeply saddened Mahoney. It was curled up in a fetal position, of sorts, resting in a pool of its own blood, a rivulet of which had managed to flow from Lakewood's slashed neck, around arms, elbows, and legs, into the drain hole near his feet. On the white tile above Lakewood's body the killer had printed out: NEXT TIME MAHONEY, DON'T SEND A BOY.

Grant read the words, and knew that David, the cold and calculating killer, was pushing Mahoney's buttons. He could see Mahoney's reaction as his partner finished reading the neatly printed words with their slightly runny bottoms. Grant knew that Mahoney felt responsible for every man in the department, especially those younger than him. He was supposed to be wiser, and smarter, and more careful. A father figure. Yet Grant could see guilt washing over Mahoney's face and eyes. Grant knew that Mahoney was mentally adding up the bodies. As Mahoney had once told Grant, when they first met, there are times when you can't prevent shit from happening; all you can do is count the bodies and keep the records.

Saying that the church leadership was in a state of panic following Lakewood's death, was like saying the Titanic would experience a slight delay. It was true as far as it went.

Mahoney and Grant, along with the Chief, sat in a small conference room in the Church Administration Building, one they had never been in before. To their amazement they watched, as one by one, in what Grant viewed as a surrealistic parade, the surviving members of the Council of Twelve Apostles filed into the room like good, gray elephants, trunk-to-tail. All were there but for those who had been killed, and Martin X. Beck who was on emotionally shaky ground in Sao Paulo following the death of Apostle Williams.

Grant's eyes studied the serious and aging faces of the men as they sat around the front of the table. Today they looked very old. They left three chairs empty at the center of the arc, and Grant found himself holding his breath in anticipation. Despite pangs of sympathy, Mahoney just wished the old farts would get on with it.   He had work of his own to do. And there was little time in which to do it.

The door opened to the side of the room and the Prophet and his First and Second Counselors entered. The seated apostles stood, waited for the three members of the First Presidency to find their seats, and then all sat as the Prophet sat. Grant actually found himself short of breath. He was finally in a meeting with the head of his church, and a living prophet of God on earth. Mahoney wouldn't understand, but despite his new found detachment, Grant was still in awe.

Mahoney knew what Grant was going through, and he maintained a respectful posture. His thoughts might be irreverent, he admitted, but he was not about to blow this meeting, nor could he find it in his heart to embarrass Grant. Not now. Mahoney was sure the chief would be neither help nor hindrance. He appeared to be a seated pillar of salt frozen in his chair.

Both Mahoney and Grant thought that Number Two would run the meeting. Mahoney was pleased, and Grant was astounded, when the first words spoken were from the Prophet himself.

"Gentlemen, there has been too much tragedy and pain to let words and past mistakes get in the way of what is needed. Chief, Detectives Mahoney and Grant, you have full authorization from me to deploy your men as you see fit, wherever you see fit, as of now. It is obvious to me that our own security is ideal for public relations and guest services, but is woefully inadequate in dealing with a crazed killer."

The Prophet nodded to Number Two and Number Two pushed a small white box across the table. It skidded to a stop within arms' reach of Mahoney.

"In this box are six lapel pins that will assure you access to every square inch of all buildings and property owned by the Church. If you need more please ask. They are to be returned when this is over. Do you have any questions?"

Mahoney started.

"Does this include the Temple?"

"Yes it does. All sacred Temple activities have been suspended for the duration of this attack on us. You have complete access to everything. I repeat, everything. A church security guard may accompany you into some areas, but you will not be denied access to anything."

"Do you have any other requirements?" Mahoney asked.

"No," said the Prophet, "just catch this man and end this thing. Do what you have to do. And God bless you."

As the last word passed his lips, the Prophet stood. So did everyone else. He turned and walked out, and the rest followed in complete silence. Grant had moisture rimming his eyes. Even Mahoney found himself thinking that there was something very special about this man. Power, maybe. Divinity, maybe — maybe not. But there was something. There was sure in hell something.

Grant hadn't said a word. The chief hadn't said a word. Mahoney hadn't said much. But they had what they wanted — finally. Maybe now, Mahoney thought, they could stop this bastard.

Mahoney and Grant put the lapel pins on before returning to the station. They took a detour through Temple Square and into the Tabernacle. Preparations were frantically underway inside the Tabernacle in anticipation of the two sessions Saturday and the two sessions Easter Sunday. The Mormon Tabernacle Choir had rehearsed earlier, and the great organ had been adjusted and pampered. Now, those left inside the building were doing their jobs; cleaning staff polished and swept and dusted; security staff on their hands and knees sighted under long rows of benches, looking for explosives and aberrations of any sort; uniformed guards patted and probed the clothing of those who entered; and a clerk posted the name as someone arrived and logged it out again when the same person left.

Much to Mahoney's gratification two burly security agents braced Grant and himself the second they tried to enter the Tabernacle. Seeing the lapel pins they asked for supporting credentials, and once viewed, moved aside immediately. The clerk logged them in by name and time.

They had already been through a preliminary check as they had entered the outer gates. Mahoney noted the door-like frame of a metal detector as they first entered the Tabernacle. When the metal detector buzzed at their unseen weapons, the guards nodded, waved them past, and resumed their place at the front doors of the Tabernacle.

Mahoney and Grant walked all through the Tabernacle,

snooping into every corner and alcove, and behind every rail and bannister. Mahoney then headed directly toward where two stationary guards stood. He wanted to see what was being protected.

The first guard Mahoney confronted was guarding nothing more than the area in which the First Presidency and the Council of Twelve Apostles would be sitting. The church had assigned security to stand guard over the actual seats and seating area on a twenty-four-hour watch.

The second guard Mahoney confronted, reflexively said no one could pass beyond him. Mahoney placed his finger on the lapel pin and tapped it. The guard looked and then pulled out a walkie-talkie and pressed the button.

"Central — this is Agent TB6 — I have two men here with unrestricted buttons — cops — do I let them pass? Over."

The radio immediately crackled back.

"TB6 — just where were you when the word came down? The answer is YES — and please give them an apology for the delay. But if you weren't sure, it was wise to check. Good job. Over and Out." The guard puffed his chest out a bit and nodded for them to pass.

Mahoney and Grant both noted that good old TB6 was a bit pissed off at first, and never did offer an apology. But he did his job. Mahoney found himself speculating that sometime in the man's past he had been a cop. He had probably loved it, and he had been kicked off the force for some violation — taking bribes maybe. He became a private security guard, and now cops rankled him. Poor bastard, thought Mahoney, who could blame him? No one in their right mind would want to stand around all day guarding what amounted to a meeting hall in the middle of Temple Square. Lordy.

Passing the disgruntled guard they opened a small mahogany door that revealed an undersized flight of stairs leading down behind the seating area of the First Presidency. As they arrived at the bottom of the stairs, which was illuminated by a single, bare, 40 watt light bulb screwed into a socket on the side wall, and covered with a bent wire guard, Mahoney placed his hand against another carved and polished mahogany door, found the old thumb latch on the door handle, and pushed as he pressed it. The door was heavy and moved slowly. It creaked as it opened inches to let in a muted stream of light that looked otherworldly. Jesus, Mahoney thought, I'm actually getting spooked.

Grant had been following close enough to Mahoney that twice he had stepped on his heels. Mahoney mumbled a rebuke both times. Grant mumbled back something Mahoney took to be a nervous form of "Sorry 'bout that." Mahoney couldn't see Grant's face, but had he been able to he would have been amazed at the size of Grant's eyes. In effect they had nearly doubled in diameter; in reality they had just opened very wide and were bulging a bit. Grant was scared shitless, and he couldn't understand why. He was flooded with conflicting feelings of privilege and fright at the prospect of gaining entry to the secret tunnels he had heard about all his life.

As the door softly creaked, Mahoney stopped dead still. Grant bumped into him, jumping at the creepy sound. Mahoney blamed Grant for scaring him and let go of the door handle. Turning, he looked directly into Grant's bulging eyes.

"Good evening, friends," said Mahoney in a low and menacing voice, "This is Raymond, your host, welcoming you in to the Inner Sanctum."

Grant looked stricken and after his heart had recovered he whispered to Mahoney, "Who's Raymond?"

"You young guys don't know shit from Shinola, do you? You probably don't even know what Shinola was! Jesus, Heber, Raymond was the host of one of the most frightening radio shows ever to waft over the Blue network. People like Boris Karloff and Richard Widmark would drive stakes through your heart while you listened in the darkness. You'd be buried alive, and your eyes would be plucked from your head by ravens and magpies."

Grant's eyes kept getting bigger, and the strange light spilling in from the cracked door seemed greenish and thick. Grant whispered again, "Why are you telling me this now, for heaven's sake?"

"The creaking door!" rasped Mahoney.

"What about it?" asked Grant.

"Jesus you're young," said Mahoney. "The creaking door was the trademark opening and closing of the show. It sent shivers up and down your spine!"

At that precise moment the door flew open with a guttural sound that damn near sent Grant and Mahoney around the bend. Mahoney snapped around and Grant grabbed the back of his coat and tugged so hard he nearly opened the seam. Standing, silhouetted in the doorway, backlit in the greenish light, was a monster looking for all the world like James Arness' *The Thing*.

"Can I help you?" The Thing asked. As it spoke it stepped back into the hallway and light spilled onto the front and pasty face of an average sized, bald, security guard, who would have been amazed had he known what Mahoney and Grant had been thinking and feeling. Mahoney toughed it out.

"Thank you, yes," said Mahoney, "I'm Detective Mahoney and this is Detective Grant from the Salt Lake City police department. We have unrestricted clearance and we are checking out security for the First Presidency."

Grant was thankful to be out of the alcove-like stairwell and into the fluorescently lit interior of a long, wide corridor, carpeted in a deep pile that was hunter green. Greenish light. Mahoney and his blasted radio show! Darn him!

Mahoney was standing next to the bald man and marveled at the gloss of his head. It looked like it had been polished with Lemon Pledge and a shoe shine boy's rag. He noticed that the guard's right ear had once been pierced and was now nearly healed over. Was this guard once a hippie in the '60s rebelling against war and sniffing flowers? How, Mahoney wondered, did he ever become conservative enough to be embraced by the church and become a trusted guard in the secret tunnels beneath Temple Square?

When the guard nodded at Mahoney, he and Grant proceeded down the long corridor. They could see another guard standing at the other end. By the time the self-conducted tour of the tunnels was over they had entered into an elevator that took them into the Hotel Utah Building, then retraced their steps and backtracked into an offshoot tunnel that connected with the Temple itself. They finally returned to the bald security guard's post. Mahoney asked if there was another way to enter the Tabernacle besides the claustrophobic stairs he now thought of as the "Inner Sanctum."

Pointing to a panel that looked for all the world like a
normal section of the wall, the bald guard pushed an inset
button and the panel opened to reveal an elevator just large
enough to hold four or five men, or two men and someone in
a wheelchair. Naturally, thought Mahoney. The elders of the
church were very elderly indeed. He remembered several
times when a frail and infirm President and Prophet spoke to
the multitudes from the Tabernacle. There had to be an
elevator. The staircase was left over from an earlier time in
the history of the Tabernacle and the labyrinth beneath.
Besides, Mahoney thought, no prophet of God, self-
proclaimed or otherwise, in this modern age, would put up
for long skulking back and forth through the Inner Sanctum.

The two detectives rode the elevator up and back down
again. Mahoney got out and looked around again, then
headed for the stairs. Grant pointed to the closed elevator
door, but Mahoney ignored him and entered through the
squeaking door. Suddenly Mahoney remembered that when
the Inner Sanctum first went on the air it was originally called
The Squeaking Door. As he climbed up the miniature
staircase with Grant hovering on his back, Mahoney heard the
door squeak as it closed behind them, undoubtedly from an
assist by the bald guard.

Mahoney found himself thinking, "Now it's time to close
the door of the Inner Sanctum until next week when
Palmolive Brushless and Palmolive Lather Shaving Cream
bring you another Inner Sanctum mystery. Until then, good
night and pleasant dreams."

In his head, Mahoney, once again, replayed the sound of
the door squeaking shut. He would have shared the program's
closing with Grant, but he knew it would not have been
appreciated. He kept it to himself and relished the sound and
the dimness and the terror of the unknown as it was meant to
be experienced — in the human mind of a solitary listener
savoring the confrontation of his own fears.

Mahoney and Grant left the Tabernacle and returned to
the police station. Grant was very happy to be above the
ground. Mahoney was smugly nostalgic. Age has its rewards.

Friday: Day Twenty-Six, Late Evening

The man was delighted it was Friday night. He believed the church officials, and the police, would expect him to infiltrate whatever they expected him to infiltrate on Saturday, and then do his dirty deeds on Sunday, the main culmination of the semi-annual conference. Idiots, he thought. He would do it all Saturday. They wouldn't be expecting that. They would believe they had one more day to plan and make ready before he struck. Fucking idiots.

Spread out before him the man scanned the personnel lists of the security force of the Mormon Church. He had acquired not only the rosters, but the home addresses and telephone numbers of each agent and guard. He had a supplementary list of all their assignments, both floating and permanent. He wasn't interested in the temporary or floating assignments, like those he had from time to time. He was interested in the few permanent assignments for this period only, and especially for Saturday. He went over and over the rosters and concluded his plan. It was all over but the killing. Soon it would be time to celebrate his success. Sunday. Sunday he would celebrate.

The plan was not elaborate. Elaborate plans, the man believed, resulted in elaborate prison sentences, or even worse, a Gary Gilmore death in front of dirty sandbags in a warehouse where strangers watched you die. Simplicity was the answer. Do it now and do it fast.

Over a month ago he had taken steps to complete the one diversion he would need for Saturday's blood atonement. He had placed a small plastic explosive charge underneath the main circuit breaker box in Temple Square. He had shaped it

237

and fixed it to the underside of the box, well out of sight of
prying eyes. He had placed it in a gray metal box identical in
size and coloring to the metal of the circuit breaker box. It
was, however, only two inches high. It was self-contained
and would be detonated by radio control. He had taken the
precaution of placing the plastic, the detonator, the fuse and
the control in the flat box before painting it. He had enclosed
the plastic in several layers of Saran Wrap to mask its odor
from sniffing dogs. He had sealed all of the internal edges of
the box with silicon caulking, and caulked the outer edges of
the closed box to form a perfect water-tight, air-tight, sniff-
proof seal. He then spray painted the box the exact shade of
mottled gray used on the circuit box. Using epoxy ribbon he
had affixed the flat box to the underside of the circuit breaker
box and pushed it in place. He passed it often making sure the
epoxy had hardened properly and the box looked exactly like
an extension of the main unit. Once satisfied, he never
returned. No one would toy with the box. After all, who
notices the size and configuration of a circuit breaker box on
a wall amid the electrical trappings of a major facility. An
antenna protruded from a caulked hole at the back of the box,
and was invisible from the front.

There was nothing else he needed to do tonight except
kill three people and get some sleep.

Working late, Mahoney and Grant made out the
assignment sheet for the conference sessions Saturday and
Sunday. They did the best they could with what they had.
Every guard and security agent, no matter where he might be
located, or what job he had, would be attended by an out-of-
uniform policeman or detective, dressed to fit in — blue
blazer, gray slacks, white shirt, rep tie, and a shoulder holster.
No one would be stationed alone, and each team would be an
agent or church guard, coupled with a policeman of one kind
or another. All police shifts matched the security shifts and
police were instructed to be in place at precisely the same
time as their counterparts from church security.

Mahoney and Grant would both serve as floaters, roaming
the entire Tabernacle, Temple, Temple grounds, tunnels, and
all access routes to and from each of them. For the first time
in the history of the church, police were given waivers to

enter the holy Temple accompanied by church security. Mahoney and Grant could do so alone. Grant couldn't believe it. He had his own Temple recommend, but Mahoney, an out-on-the-edge reprobate Catholic, could actually roam around the Temple alone, and enter any room he wanted. Unheard of! Grant thought. Sheeeeeeeeeee-it! Grant actually surprised himself. This was past weird.

David approached the house with the confidence of a top salesman strolling up after having been invited to exhibit his line. He was dressed in a nondescript manner, his contact lens was in place, and in his hand was a small black duffle bag. He knocked at the door and as it opened he withdrew a 9mm automatic from his pocket and pointed it at the man standing before him. Saying nothing he motioned with the gun quickly and stepped in, forcing the man back into the room. On the couch in the living room sat an attractive woman watching television and knitting somewhat absentmindedly. At the sight of the gun, and the man, she tensed, but didn't move. Just then a young boy, about five-years-old came running in to the room from the kitchen and stopped dead in his tracks to stare at the man with the gun.

The owner of the house started to speak and the man calmly struck him across the side of the face with the automatic, dropping him to the floor. He looked at the boy and pointed the gun directly at him and said, "Sit with your mother and keep quiet or I will kill your father."

The man set the duffle bag on the floor and ripped open a Velcro seal to remove three plastic restraint strips, the kind often used as temporary handcuffs to bind prisoners and the mentally ill. They were about an eighth-of-an-inch wide and twelve-inches long. He had purchased them at a Radio Shack where they were offered as devices to bind up loose cords running from computers and television sets. They came in several sizes. He tossed one to the woman and she flinched, nearly paralyzed with fright. The boy was shaking and tears were welling up in his eyes.

"Put your boy's hands behind him and wrap the plastic strip around his wrists. Place the end through the opening and pull it tight. Do it now or I'll kill your husband and then the boy. All I want is to rob the place, and you have to be tied up before I can get what I want and leave."

The man on the floor raised his head, blood from his jaw had made a small puddle on the carpet. He started to say, "No, don't help . . . " when the man with the gun kicked him violently in the ribs. The woman immediately told the boy to put his hands behind his back. She had the boy's hands secured in less than thirty seconds.

The man kept the gun on the woman and told her to sit on her hands. She did. He kicked the man in the ribs again, and he reeled in pain. She raised from the couch, but fell back and obediently put her hands under her thighs as she looked into the black hole at the end of the automatic. Keeping the gun leveled at the woman, the man knelt beside the husband, abruptly hit him on the head with the pistol, then raised it just as abruptly to point it, once again, at the woman's face. Her agony was telling. She loved her husband, and his pain was hers.

He took one of the plastic strips and set it on the man's back, then grabbed his hands, one at a time, and placed them behind him, overlapping at the small of his back. He placed the plastic strip under the hands and, hardly looking, used his gun hand to hold the opening as he threaded the end of the strip into its closure and pulled it tight.

The husband and his son were now secure.

"All right, lady," he said, "we can do this the easy way or the hard way. The easy way is simple: you stand up, come over to me, turn around, place your hands behind your back, and I put this last restraint around your wrists. Then I can get on with my business and leave. The hard way . . . well, you don't want to hear about the hard way. Which is it going to be?

The woman rose almost immediately, walked over and looked in the man's eyes. She was sure he was telling the truth. He just wanted to rob the place. Why would he kill them? She put her hands behind her back and turned to face away from him. As she turned she muttered, "We have very little of value."

David did not reply.

When she was manacled with the plastic strip he led her over to where her husband was and told her to lie down next to him on her stomach. She was momentarily relieved for she thought he wouldn't rape her unless she was on her back. He then told the boy to join his parents, face-down, on the floor.

Setting the gun on the end table he walked over to the man and knelt between him and his wife. Almost too quickly to comprehend he pulled an Ek-Warrior from a sheath tucked in his belt at the back, grabbed the man's bald head with the flat of his hand and pulled it sharply back. He drew the knife across his throat and dropped his head back onto the rug. He leaned over to the woman and grabbing her long hair, did the same. They were both dead within ten seconds of each other. The boy had reared up just enough to see his mother die, and began to crawl frantically toward the kitchen. Oddly, the man thought, he didn't scream or cry out. The man hated this part of his job. He didn't like kids, but he didn't like killing them. Still, it was necessary. Taking three steps across the rug he was on the boy, lifting his head by a thick shock of black hair. The knife cleanly cut the boy's throat and there was no sound other than the gurgling of blood and the sucking of air into the open throat of a five-year-old. Wiping the knife on the boy's trousers, the man walked to the front of the house and pulled down all the blinds, turned out the lights, locked the door, and turned off the television. He pulled the blinds at the sides and the back of the house and locked the back door. He unplugged the telephone and tossed it into the recesses of an overstuffed chair. He walked into the bedroom, set the alarm clock for 4 a.m., and reclined on the bed. Fluffing the pillows, he found a comfortable spot and was asleep in five-minutes. It had been a full day.

Saturday: Day Twenty-Seven,
Early Morning

When the man awakened at the buzzing of the alarm, he sat up in bed and stared at his unfamiliar surroundings as if wondering what he was doing there. He rose, entered the bathroom, and stripped off his clothes. Returning to the living room, and stepping over the body of the young boy, he picked up his duffle bag and took it with him into the bathroom. From it he pulled an unopened box he had purchased the day before and opened it. He removed a new, sleek, black, electric hair trimmer, and plugged it into the wall socket next to the mirror. Without hesitation he ran the clippers over his head creating images in the mirror not unlike those he remembered of Elvis Presley getting his first Army haircut in May of 1958. He hadn't seen the images at the time, but had seen them repeated on television a dozen times since. The hair cascaded into the basin and soon there was nothing but fuzz left on his head. Taking a razor and a can of Edge shaving gel out of the medicine chest, the man scooped the hair from the sink with his free hand and turned on the hot water. He splashed it on his fuzzy head and began to spread gel from ear to ear and down the back of his head.

Moments later his head was clean and shiny and he stepped into the shower and turned on the water. By 5 a.m. he was dry and, enjoying a quick look at himself in the foggy mirror, realized that he didn't have to comb his hair on this very special day. He walked naked into the living room and looking down at the three dead bodies, focused on the bald head of the man. Perfect, he thought. Just perfect.

Within the next half-hour the man had dressed in the husband's work clothes, blue blazer, gray slacks, white shirt,

242

rep tie, and shoulder holster. In it he was about to place his own 9mm automatic. He wanted to take the Beretta but at first felt that its attached xenon tactical light was too bulky. He quickly removed the light and switched guns. The Beretta, he reasoned, was fitted with an extended clip that held twenty rounds. It crossed his mind that he just might need the extra bullets.

He placed his Ek-Warrior in the sheath centered at his back between the slacks and his shirt. He removed a small black remote control device from the duffle bag and placed it in his right hand jacket pocket.

The dead man on the floor was about an inch shorter than he, and so he adjusted the pants down about a half-inch to split the difference and was pleased the cuff line was nearly perfect. The clothes fit well. It wasn't a tailored look, but it would be considered a very good off-the-rack fit by anyone who took notice. With the newly acquired bald head the man looked remarkably like his dead alter ego. He checked his contact lens, put on a pair of sun glasses, and the illusion was complete. With the dead man's security ID card, complete with photograph, clipped to his jacket pocket, the look was nearly perfect.

He removed the contents of the dead man's pockets and filled his own with what he needed. He took the wallet intact, along with its driver's license and credit cards. He located the bald headed man's assignment sheet and compared it against his for any last minute changes. It was the same. He knew exactly where to be and when.

The man took a chance that Mahoney would already be at work, gearing up for this threat to the saints. Walking into the kitchen, stepping over the bodies of the mother and the boy, he opened the refrigerator and drank directly from a half-gallon carton of orange juice. Breakfast over, he returned to the living room, opened the duffle, and withdrew a portable cellular telephone, turned it on, and hearing the dial tone punched in the number of Mahoney's desk at police headquarters.

"Mahoney."

"I thought you might be at work, asshole. Here is what I want you to do. Put the diamonds and the money in the bag and have the President of the church carry it with him. If he doesn't like it tell him he will die. Maybe I'll let the poor old codger live if I get what I want. Or, maybe not. At any rate I will kill him if he doesn't have the bag. Wherever he goes, or whatever he does from this moment on, I want him to be holding that bag. If he goes to take a dump, he is to take the bag with him. If he doesn't, he's dead, and so are a lot of his friends. Two days of carrying that bag shouldn't kill the old fart. I know he's not used to carrying things on his own, but this is a requirement. I'll see you tomorrow. Or maybe today. Goodbye."

The man hung up. He threw the telephone on the sofa, picked up the duffle bag, and left the house, locking the door after him. He entered the bald man's car and drove off toward Temple Square.

The case with the money and the diamonds had been ready for some time. At first Mahoney and Grant thought they'd booby-trap the briefcase. If they did, reasoned Mahoney, and the man opened it in the presence of the Prophet . . .

Nothing doing.

The briefcase was in the police safe now, and Mahoney and Grant decided to take it immediately to Temple Square and meet with the President of the church. They called the Church Administration Building to inform them they were on their way. The President of the Church was already there, Mahoney was told. Waiting. The poor bastard.

Mahoney and Grant entered the Church Administration Building with Grant clutching the case as if it were worth millions. It was. Both men now carried 15-round automatics. The extra fire power was comforting. The stuff they carried was real, and it belonged to the church. The diamonds had been secured by the church from diamond merchants on 47th Street in New York City. A worker from the Church's Visitor's Center in Manhattan had received the transferred money, and the purchase was made in one day from several vendors. The most difficult part of the transaction was the gut wrenching suspense incurred when the diamonds were routinely sent overnight special by Federal Express. When it arrived the church leaders breathed easier, and the worker at the Visitor's Center recovered from a pre-heart-attack state.

The cash had been added and the police took possession of the briefcase. Now, it was back, safe, if not totally secure, in the belly of the church.

The faithful had already started lining up along the high gray wall surrounding Temple Square before 5 a.m. By 7 a.m. thou- sands of people, Mormons all, were waiting patiently to see their leaders and hear the litany of their faith. Security agents and guards, along with their designated policemen, were to meet at their assigned posts routinely. Business as usual except for the pairing of a policeman with each agent and guard. The only individuals being let into Temple Square before the morning session was slated to start were those with the special lapel buttons, those with security cards clipped to their jackets, and policemen with similar authorization. By 8 a.m. all church security workers had entered the grounds and had found their stations. Policemen were searching out their posts and introducing themselves to those they had been paired with.

At precisely 7:58 a.m. a bald security agent entered the front gates of the Temple Grounds in something of a rush. He nodded to the guards at the gates and pointed to his security badge, while at the same time mumbling something about being late. He was obviously in a hurry. He was wearing sun glasses, but was removing them as the guard looked at his badge. There seemed to be recognition by the guard at the gate, but it was fleeting and in the press of business the bald man was ushered through without delay. He moved directly to the Tabernacle and entered. It was still dimly lit and a security guard forty yards from the door yelled out a pleasant morning greeting to the bald man, and the bald man waved his hand to return the greeting, then moved on to the elevator near the stands where the leaders of the faithful would soon sit. Descending in the elevator, the bald man, his eye slightly irritated from the contact lens, blinked rapidly, then thought briefly about his plan.

He knew that old Charlie would be at the Hotel Utah Building's end of the long corridor, and was never late. He would already be in place. From his end old Charlie could hardly make out anyone, but would be able to see the bald head and would wave with the friendship of a man frozen in rank greeting a peer, both disgruntled at their lot in life.

As the elevator door opened the man could see a police officer about half way down the corridor heading toward old Charlie. As he exited the elevator, the policeman stopped, turned around, and started back. Perfect.

When the policeman approached the bald man, he said, "Thought you weren't going to make it. I was about to ask the other guy what was up."

"Sorry," the bald man said, extending his hand, "I got caught in a struggle for my usual parking spot. Someone slipped in and I had to argue them out of it."

With that the bald man peered over the shoulder of the policeman and waved at old Charlie, which brought an enthusiastic wave and hoot from the other end of the corridor. There was another man standing next to Charlie; a policeman, thought the man. No problem; he was assigned to Charlie just as this man was assigned to him. His very own policeman witnessed the exchange, smiled broadly, and then reached out to take the bald man's hand. They shook hands warmly and introduced themselves as if to say, We're a couple of professionals and we can handle anything they throw at us. Sure, the bald man thought.

"Nice to meet you. Glad we'll be working together. Can always use the help, and the company, on days like this," the bald man said.

"Oh, you mean the threats. Yeah, that's tough," said the cop. "We'll get the bastard if anyone will."

"You can bet on that," said the bald man. He was watching the policemen stealing looks at his ID badge, and then back at his face. He seemed satisfied. The bald man took great pleasure in the stupidity of most people. If the policeman had done his job and just grabbed the security badge and really inspected it against the bald man's face, he would see that this was not the same man. But he didn't. People were funny that way. They didn't like confrontation. He had seen the general facial structure, the bald head, and that was enough for him. Besides, old Charlie knew him. This was his partner for the day — it surely was — the stupid old fart.

"Call me Jack," the bald man said as the policeman stole another quick look at the badge seeing the name John Warthington printed in large letters under the photo.

"All right, Jack. I'm patrolman Lance Davidson. You can call me Lance."

Lance, thought the bald man. Good god. Lance! And a patrolman yet; not even a detective. How good could it get. Now he would wait, and soon it would be over. Lance would be dead, and so too, most likely, would old Charlie and his sidekick cop.

"Lance," the bald man said, "who's the other guy with Charlie?"

"His name's Walter Something-or-other. I forget. He's usually on nights, and I'm on days. But I've seen him around the station. He's okay."

"Good," said the bald man, "we can't be too careful."

Lance, the cop, looked pleased and puffed up with professional pride. The bald guy, he thought, was his kind of security cop.

Saturday: Day Twenty-Seven,
Mid-Morning

By the time the Tabernacle was full, Mahoney and Grant had walked throughout the ancient hall. Mahoney thought it looked much bigger on television when the great Mormon Tabernacle Choir broadcast its Christmas show. He usually watched it, and now recalled that the pictures on television were undoubtedly taken with a zoom lens capable of tight shots on the organist, the choir, and the dignitaries sitting near the front. The zoom lens also had the capability of wide angle shots from the rear of the Tabernacle, and that is where the deception came in. The Tabernacle looked twice as large on television as it did in reality. Not unlike the covering shots in football stadiums, the Tabernacle seemed to grow as the lens elements changed from closeup to wide-angle and distorted reality into a massive image that the viewer took to be fact — the wide flattened view of thousands seated before the gilded pipes of the great organ.

Standing in the back of the Tabernacle, Mahoney realized that the old wooden structure, held together with wooden pegs and glue, was only a modest sized auditorium. He and Grant walked through the crowd to the front where the access doors to the tunnels were located. Security agents and guards watched them and nodded as they passed, their eyes moving from face to security badge and back to face. Mahoney didn't like this; it was a goddamned fishbowl.

"Grant," Mahoney said, "stay here at the door to the elevator. I'm going over to the Hotel Utah Building and escort the President and his counselors to their seats."

Grant knew that the President and the First and Second Counselors entered the Tabernacle from the tunnels connecting the buildings. Unknown to most of the security personnel and even to the Apostles, Mahoney had requested that they remain sequestered on the private church floor of the Hotel Utah Building until conference was about to begin. Mahoney and Grant both felt that the President was safe until conference was underway. They believed that the killer would not try anything before the President was seated in front of the faithful. He undoubtedly wanted an audience. Still, there was no use taking chances.

Pushing the elevator button, the door slid soundlessly open and Mahoney stepped into the small cubicle and pushed the down button. He felt himself descending the short distance to the floor below.

As the elevator door opened, both Lance and the bald man took a step forward. Mahoney held up his hand and said, "It's okay, men. I'm Mahoney with the Salt Lake Police Department. We're going to bring the President over now, stay on your toes."

Mahoney looked at Lance and his security badge, and then at the bald man and his badge. He looked only briefly at the men and then nodded and moved down the long hallway toward the two men standing at the other end. A small doubt crept into Mahoney's consciousness, but he couldn't place why. Maybe it would come to him. Still, he was sure things were under control. As he got to the other end of the corridor, he introduced himself, again, to Charlie and his partner, a night patrolman he knew by sight. That made him feel better. Entering the elevator at the Hotel Utah Building's end of the corridor, he inserted a key, given to him by church security, into the elevator's locking button, and ascended to the church floor of the hotel. As he stepped into the lobby two men confronted him and checked his ID. Good, Mahoney thought. They finally let him pass, and at the same time picked up a dedicated telephone to announce him to the President.

There were no formalities, and the three men, being led by Mahoney, immediately left the President's apartment and headed back to the elevator. The President, Prophet, Seer, and Revelator, was holding a black briefcase in his hand as if he were about to attend a business meeting of routine importance. They entered the elevator, returning the nods of the two men standing guard, and Mahoney inserted his key once again and they descended to the lower floor and the tunnel.

Nodding again to old Charlie and the night patrolman the four men walked past them and down the long corridor toward the elevator to the Tabernacle. As they reached the end of the hallway, again there were nearly imperceptible nods as the four passed the two guards, Lance and the bald man, making little, if any, eye contact, and entered the elevator. They pressed the button and the door slid shut and the elevator began its ascent.

The bald man grinned fleetingly, thinking that human nature was so blessedly predictable. He and his new found friend, Lance, were underlings. They were hardly worthy of a glance from the great leaders of the church. The bald man had expected this, but Lance seemed crushed that the President of the Church hadn't spoken to him.

Mahoney seated the President and the Counselors in their appointed spots. Usually the President sat in the center seat, but on this occasion he was seated nearer the elevator door, and there was a perceptible rumbling among the faithful when they realized that their Prophet hadn't taken his usual seat. Mahoney retreated and joined Grant near the elevator door. The two of them stood motionless, scanning the crowd like Secret Service agents guarding the President of the United States. Mahoney was oddly uneasy, and he hated that he didn't know why. Something was nagging at him in the back recesses of his mind.

Preliminary speeches were made and then the President, Prophet, Seer, and Revelator was introduced. He stepped to the podium and spoke briefly about the mission and calling of the church and its importance in the world of today. His message was shorter than usual, and nothing was said about the turmoil everyone in attendance had been reading about in the daily newspapers. After all, conference was conference. The President took his seat once again. The black case, by prior agreement with Mahoney, remained by the side of the chair. It was a small violation of David's admonition, and Mahoney watched it intently during the President's address. No one else, other than Grant, took notice of it.

* * *

One floor below the bald man stood motionless eyeing the two men at the other end of the corridor. He reached into his jacket pocket and felt for the remote control device. He calmly pushed the button. Nothing happened. The bald man instantly realized the signal from the remote control was too far away from the device to be effective from this position. At that same moment he moved to his right toward the door of the stairway that was just out of sight of the two men at the other end of the corridor.

Lance watched him move, and said, "What are ya doing?"

Leaning over and peering at the door handle, the bald man said, "Take a look at this, Lance. Does it look odd to you? Something's not right here."

Always curious, Lance moved toward the door and leaned down to inspect the door handle. The bald man brought his hand down sharply on the back of the man's neck and Lance Davidson fell to the ground like a buffalo shot in the head. The bald man removed his Ek-Warrior from its sheath and plunged it into the back of the man's neck and checked his pulse, keeping the knife in place until the movement of the artery stopped.

Holding the knife by its handle with the blade up and behind his wrist, the bald man began walking rapidly down the corridor toward the other two men. They took no notice of him until he was over half-way to them.

Reaching into his left pocket the man pulled out a folded slip of paper and waved it in the air. The motion bought him another fifteen-seconds or so until old Charlie called out, "Is everything all right?"

"Yeah," the bald man said, "Lance just wanted me to give this to you . . . new instructions from Mahoney."

The bald man was almost on them when the night patrolman sensed something was wrong and started to reach into his jacket for his gun. The bald man lunged forward and plunged the knife into his heart while old Charlie stood frozen watching what his mind told him couldn't be happening. As the patrolman gasped and began crumpling to the floor, the bald man doubled his left fist and threw the back of it against Charlie's jaw. The old guard recoiled into the side of the elevator door and began fumbling for his gun. But it was too late. Pulling the knife from the patrolman, the bald man's left hand pressed against Charlie's hand pinning it to his side, and at the same time he plunged the knife into Charlie's stomach. Charlie began to scream, but the scream quickly died as the bald man churned the knife inside Charlie's belly. Charlie's eyes widened and he fell back again and slid to the floor. The man pulled the knife out and plunged it into the heart of old Charlie. This time Charlie didn't move. Rechecking the pulse of both men, he was satisfied they were dead. He was now considerably closer to the circuit box than he had been at the other end of the corridor. He reached into his jacket and pushed the button and this time heard a muffled explosion and watched as all the lights in the corridor dimmed and then went out. Seconds later emergency lights, battery powered to turn on during a power outage, came to life and dimly lit the hallway at each end.

The bald man grinned momentarily and then bolted down the hallway toward his original post. This is where they would bring the President for safety. To the tunnels.

On the floor above a mild panic set in as the lights failed. Battery pack emergency lights placed throughout the Tabernacle turned on almost immediately, bathing it in a warm glow, and the faithful mumbled, but to their credit, remained reverently in their seats. One of the Apostles had been speaking and urged calm. Mahoney and Grant were making their way toward the President. The Prophet and Mahoney made eye contact and there was fear on his face and his eyes seemed glazed. Mahoney motioned that he should join them. The President rose and began to move. Mahoney pointed to the briefcase, and the President reached back and picked it up.

As Mahoney, Grant, and the President entered the elevator and pushed the button, Mahoney could see the First and Second Counselor moving toward them. The elevator door slid closed in their faces and began to move. At that moment Mahoney visualized what he would see below, and as he did an image instantly formed of the guards and what would undoubted be a dimly lit corridor.

"Jesus Christ, the ear! It wasn't pierced!"

Grant and the President of the Church thought for a

moment that Mahoney had gone nuts.

"The ear! The bald man . . . he's the killer!"

The door to the elevator was sliding open and Mahoney yelled at Grant to take out the bald man, and at the same time shoved his body back and against the President of the Church forcing him into the corner of the small cubicle.

As Mahoney yelled his warning to Grant, Grant had no time to react. He reached for his gun and had it halfway out as a 9mm slug ripped high into his shoulder and the gun fell to the floor. The door was open now, and Mahoney, who had pulled his gun and held it directly in front of him, squeezed off two shots directly into the hallway, but the hall seemed empty in the dim light. As the loud report of the two gunshots boomed in the confined quarters of the elevator, Mahoney was groping for the button to close the door. Just as he reached out Mahoney saw the body of a man holding a gun roll into view on the floor in front of the elevator. He knew the gun was pointed at him, but before he could react the man on the floor fired two more shots into the cubicle.

The first round grazed the side of Mahoney's head and knocked him unconscious, while the second shot buried itself in the back of the elevator an inch to the right of Mahoney's neck. As Mahoney slumped to the ground, the bald man leapt to his feet and entered the elevator. He struck the President of the Church on the side of the face with the automatic to contain him while he kicked and pulled Mahoney from the elevator into the hallway. He reentered the elevator and shoved the automatic against the throat of the President and pushed the up-button. Grant, on the floor, had not moved. The door slid shut and the elevator moved up to the Tabernacle's main floor.

As the elevator door opened on the main floor the bald man spotted a security guard standing outside the entrance and shot him squarely in the forehead. He dropped immediately. Grabbing the President from behind and placing the gun at his temple, he pushed his way out to the main seating area for the Apostles and the First Presidency. Some of the audience had panicked and were running for the exits, others lunged beneath seats and behind strangers, but the majority, sensing they were an audience for an extraordinary event, remained eerily motionless, transfixed, as if in shock.

They seemed to be holding their collective breath.

The man pushed forward and those on the speaker's stand moved to the sides as if they were glued together, cowering slightly as the man turned and moved to guard his flanks and back. When the bald man and the President stood before the podium, no one was behind them. The members of the choir were cowering to the sides along with the Apostles and other dignitaries.

Abruptly, a security agent on the left side of the hall took aim at the bald man, hesitating because of the gun placed at the temple of his President. The bald man saw this and roughly maneuvered the President's head between his and the agent's. Just as quickly the bald man raised the gun over the President's shoulder and placed a well aimed slug into the chest of the guard. He swung to the right and fired two slugs into the chest of a policeman edging near the front of the main seating section. One of the bullets penetrated the policeman's body and lodged into the shoulder of a woman sitting directly behind him. Just as quickly the bald man replaced the muzzle of the gun at the temple of the President.

Panic was now palpable in the main hall. People were sliding from their seats onto the floor. Those in the balcony were already on the floor, and those around the slain guard were prone and praying. The rest of the guards in the hall had their guns pointed directly at the bald man, but he doubted they were good enough shots to risk firing at someone so near to their Prophet. The bald man yelled into the microphone, "Lower your guns, NOW, or your Prophet is dead!" Slowly, haltingly, the guards began to lower their weapons.

"That's better." His voice now seemed friendly. Bizarre, but friendly.

What the man hadn't noticed was that the elevator door had silently shut behind him.

Mahoney awakened from the graze to his head with the pain of a hundred migraines. He could hardly concentrate. He fought to stay conscious. The elevator door was closed and the dim light made his world on the floor of the hallway seem hazy and claustrophobic. He knew David was in the Tabernacle hall. How he knew he wasn't sure. He just knew. He needed help. He dragged himself to his feet and pushed the elevator button. After seconds had passed the elevator door silently opened and he found himself pointing his gun above Grant who was out cold on the elevator floor. Looking closely at Grant he realized that the bullet had completely shattered his collar bone. Grant had passed out from the pain. He slapped Grant's face. His entire shoulder was covered with blood, Grant moaned and began to regain consciousness.

"Wake up you son-of-a-bitch, I need help. He slapped him again. He hit his shoulder. The pain might awaken him faster. Grant screamed himself into consciousness and shuddered as the movement brought searing pain from his shoulder.

"You'll live, goddamn it, get to your feet!"

Grant, summoning up something from his gut, crawled to his feet and leaned into the corner of the elevator to keep from collapsing.

"Here's your gun! Cover me when I go out! Do it now!" Mahoney yelled.

With effort Mahoney ejected the clip from his own gun, and rammed home a new one. Mahoney fought off the ringing pain in his head and pushed the up elevator button.

"Grant, goddamn it! Don't let go! Cover me when this fucker opens or we're all dead!"

The elevator rose and the door began to glide open.

Standing in front of the podium, the bald man had his gun pressed against the temple of the President, Prophet, Seer, and Revelator. There was still an audience — bent, supplicant, prone, wailing, and transfixed. But it was still an audience. Those who watched, and those cowering at the sides, on the floor, and under seats, were either afraid to move or couldn't bring themselves to miss the drama unfolding in front of them. Fumbling at his back with his left hand, the bald man pulled out his knife and brought it around and under the chin of the President, pressing it firmly against his neck. He pressed it so hard that a trickle of blood ran down the Prophet's neck as he drew the knife slightly to the left.

There was a collective gasp from the audience.

The bald man leaned slightly forward and spoke over the President's shoulder into the microphone arching from the podium.

"I am an avenging angel of the Lord, and I have come here today to set you free from the burdens of this man and his unholy church. In a moment we will be leaving here, and I will keep this knife pressed against your Prophet's neck, and this gun pressed to his temple. If anyone attempts to shoot me I will kill this man before I fall from the impact of a bullet. I will pull the trigger in response to a single gunshot; with my left hand I will cut open the throat of this man and spill his blood on the Tabernacle floor. I will do it! You have my promise. We are now going to move toward the elevator to the left and behind us. If anyone tries to stop me you will be personally responsible for the death of your Prophet and President. Do not move. Stay where you are for ten minutes or I will kill this man as surely as I stand here now!"

The bald man whispered into the ear of the President and told him to bend at the knees and pick up the black bag as they passed it. He told him to carry it with him, and not to drop it, or he would die instantly. "Now move," the man said.

The two men began inching back toward the seat where the bag rested. The bald man kept the knife at the President's throat, and the gun at his temple. David had not yet looked at the elevator.

When the elevator door silently opened several people saw the figure of Mahoney leaning against the far wall. Another man, behind Mahoney, pointed his gun toward the killer as well. But he looked weak and unsteady.

Mahoney was aiming his pistol at the head of the bald man. No one said anything. No one moved. There wasn't even a murmur. Mahoney had heard David's admonition against anyone shooting, and the grim consequences if anyone did. Mahoney kept his gun leveled at the man's bald head, the side of the elevator door now steadying his hand from the shaking caused by the pounding inside his skull. Blood ran down the side of Mahoney's face, and he looked for all the world like a standing dead man.

As David and the President inched back toward the bag, Mahoney knew that it was now or never. David hadn't seen Mahoney or Grant, since he had not taken his eyes from the President or the possible threat of guards and policemen to his front. As the two men stopped at the bag, and began bending their knees, Mahoney momentarily stopped breathing, resighted, and fired one shot into the shiny bald head of John Douglas Davies.

A woman, somewhere, screamed "No!" as blood sprayed out in an arc and crimson drops landed on those still hunkered down in their front row seats. The privileged few.

The faithful began to wail and scream.

The moment the slug slammed into the front left quarter of the bald man's head, the automatic he was holding kicked up and to the right and he fired it a millisecond later. The bullet plowed into the upper tier of the Tabernacle and buried itself in the hand of a woman who had been peering over the railing. The knife at the Prophet's throat slid to one side and cut deeply into old flesh.

The bleeding was stemmed with Murphy's wadded up tie, as the President was rushed to a waiting ambulance, a grim precaution at all sessions of the General Conference. He was rushed to the nearest hospital, given a tracheotomy on route, and over twenty stitches after he arrived. He remained in critical condition for three days and was released a week later.

John Douglas Davies had died in the Tabernacle, his body splayed on the black briefcase that had rested at the feet of the President. He was unceremoniously removed. A few hangers-on applauded when the black body bag was zipped and he was hauled off like so much cordwood in a sling.

Sunday: Day Twenty-Eight, Mid-Morning

The annual conference of the Church of Jesus Christ of Latter-day Saints concluded without further incident. The First Counselor of the church conducted the ceremonies, and no further mention, other than brief updates and a prayer for the speedy recovery of the President, Prophet, Seer, and Revelator, was made of the ugly incident in the historical Tabernacle.

The faithful had been vindicated, an official said. The church was intact despite its enemies. Conference ended following the Sunday afternoon session as it had begun, with a prayer for salvation.

Monday, Day Twenty-Nine, Morning

Mahoney and Grant sat in the Chief's office along with members of the department's Internal Affair's force who were conducting an investigation into the shooting of Davies. It was concluded that Mahoney had acted in a reckless and unprofessional manner, placing the life of the President of the Church and others of the faithful, within the Tabernacle, at grievous risk of their lives.

It was decided that Mahoney would be demoted in rank and suspended for 120 days, without pay, as penalty for his unprofessional conduct. It was suggested he might consider retirement.

Tuesday: Day Thirty, Afternoon

The newspaper's morning headlines, in their special editions, screamed in large-point type that the President of the Church had survived a particularly savage attempt on his life. Editorials took sides, alternatively praising Mahoney and condemning him for his actions. Mahoney was quoted only once, but all newspapers in the area carried his brief statement:

"I did what needed to be done. Had Davies been allowed to take the President of the Church into the tunnels beneath the Tabernacle, he would have killed the Prophet. I am sure of that. Anyone who isn't, doesn't know this kind of killer. Not only that, had Davies escaped, he would have continued to kill the leaders of the church, and particularly those in direct succession to the Presidency. If I had it to do over again, I would do the same thing. My only regret is that so many were killed and injured before Davies was stopped."

The afternoon papers carried the following story released from the public relations office of the church:

"Today, from his bed in LDS Hospital, the President, Prophet, Seer, and Revelator of the Church, remarked on the outstanding police work done by the entire Salt Lake City police department in cooperation with the excellent performance of the Security Office of the Church. Heading up the search for the killer, Detective Thomas Mahoney is to be commended for his actions in not letting the killer continue his reign of terror on the Church and its leaders.

"It is my wish that all charges be dropped against Detective Mahoney, and that he be reinstated immediately with a promotion for his dedication and willingness to put his life and professional reputation in jeopardy in the line of duty. I am confident that without his intervention in the Tabernacle, I would now be dead at the hands of a maniac. The killing would have continued. Detective Heber Mark Grant, also wounded in the line of duty, deserves our gratitude as a credit to Salt Lake City and our police department."

The church statement went on to eulogize the policemen and security guards killed in the line of duty in the Tabernacle. Although three died beneath the Tabernacle, no mention was made of the existence of any tunnel.

The *Deseret News* ran the release verbatim. No mention of a tunnel was made in the many sidebars that complimented the main story. The *Salt Lake Tribune*'s main story contained statements from the official church press release, but quoted reliable sources who stated that three men had been killed in a tunnel beneath the Tabernacle that connected it with the Temple and the Hotel Utah Building. The primary story ended with the statement:

"When asked to verify the deaths that occurred beneath the Tabernacle, Mormon church officials declined comment."

Detective Mahoney was reinstated immediately on publication of the statement by the President of the Mormon church. He was promoted two grades and placed in charge of a special task force to combat civil terrorism. Detective Grant also received a commendation and his wife and family were safely returned to their home.

Detective Mahoney, when asked for a statement by television crews covering his reinstatement, set a powdered sugar donut on his desk, wiped his mouth, and said, "No comment."

He ignored the reporters' pleadings and went back to his coffee and donuts. As the reporters finally moved away and sought out more productive interviews, Mahoney brushed some powdered sugar from a page of the book in front of him, and once again, ignoring the mounting stacks of paperwork, began browsing through *The Art of Catching Rainbow Trout*.

Through-the-Year: Book I: 365 Days of Prosperity,
Telesco $5.95
This creative book provides 365 ways of drawing prosperity your way
- a great take-along read!

Dance on the Water, Leffers $12.95
Fiction/Native American Mysticism
After a personal assault by a few young hoodlums, Belle MacKay decides
to take back control of her life and moves to an island she's inherited from
a grandfather she'd never met. But once on the island, Belle confronts
more than she'd bargained for, including midnight chantings over the
water.

A Question of Time, Bryce $6.99
A quiet Rocky Mountain clearing at twilight . . . and a UFO abduction
make this a compelling read for fans of science fiction and the paranormal.

Cataclysms?? A <u>New</u> Look at World Changes
Hickox $12.95
In the '80s, predictions of worldwide destruction once again surfaced and
some are now indicating this destruction will arrive along with the new
millennium. But are we really approaching the "end times" - or the
"beginning times?"

The Ascent: Doorway to Eternity, Cross $6.95
A new look at the life and times of Jesus as it was originally supposed to
be written. This channeled book is truly enlightening!

The Knowing, Bates $15.95
A fictionalized story of the discovery of a UFO, the pilot who flew it,
government cover-ups, Dreamland, and what it has to do with the future of
this country! A MUST read!

The Antilles Incident, Todd $6.99
A face-to-face confrontation at sea with a submerged UFO. A fictional
account of a factual incident!

Apache Tears, Mustain & Livingston $15.95
A chance meeting between two combat veterans, the attack of a 15-year-
old Apache girl, and the Spirit Quest of an Apache paramdeic combine to
lead the Apache to declare independence from the U.S. government. A
rivoting adventure!

More from Blue Star Productions

Brothers of the Pine, Simmons $15.95

During the Apache wars, two Chiricahua brothers were mystically bonded by sharing the same pine tree birthplace. Though their trails went in separate directions, their bond could not be broken.

And Coming Soon -

The Best Kept Secrets, Charles Wright
From the Hearts of Angels, Dezra*
Me 'N God in the Coffee Shop, Rene Donavon

Check with your local bookstore or use the below order form.

Submit title, check/money order for amount shown above, along with $3.00 s/h for first book, .50 for each additional book, to: Blue Star Productions, 9666 E Riggs Rd #194, Sun Lakes AZ 85248.

Name:_____

Address:_____

City: _____ State:_____

Zip:_____

Allow 4-6 weeks for delivery